CHRISTOPHER FLORY

Trust Betrayed

a Paul Dodge novel

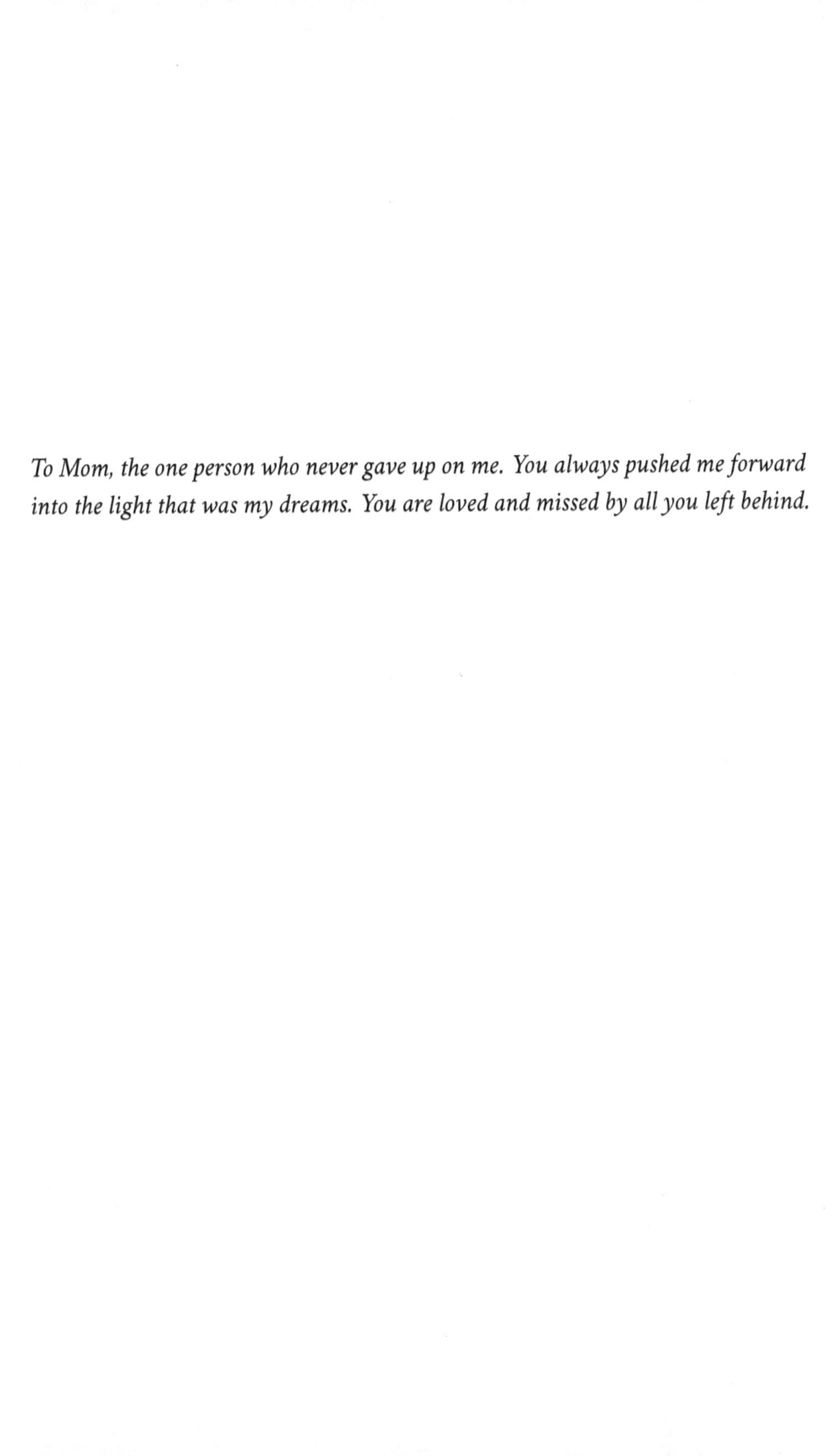

To Mom, the one person who never gave up on me. You always pushed me forward into the light that was my dreams. You are loved and missed by all you left behind.

Contents

Chapter 1

The sunlight glaring through the lenses of his 60x power binoculars nearly blinded him. He couldn't afford the best equipment. Not on an ex-marine's disability pay. The newer models had a special coating that dulled the reflection from the sunlight. Not his. His pair had made the family rounds, from his grandpa to his father and finally ending up in his hands as a deathbed gift. There were better models made in the past fifty years, but this pair had sentimental value. He had made his first kill using this set of eyes. A six-point buck in the mountains of West Virginia as a child. His family had owned a cabin tucked back in a holler twenty miles from the nearest town. Nothing but coal mines and toothless hillbillies, more concerned with growing weed and refining moonshine far as the eye could see. As he glassed his target, he thought about the equipment he had as a marine sniper. They engineered each set of field glasses to be comfortable, yet durable. Both are important when you're in the desert of Iraq, or the rocky, mountainous terrain of Afghanistan, peering through the lenses for hours on end. He certainly had better pairs. But this was his lucky pair. He wouldn't have chosen a thousand-dollar pair of Simmons over this tried and tested eyes. Not for this mission. This was too important to place in the hands of fate. Failure was not an option.

He blinked just as she came into sight. He had created the perfect shot. Precise timing placed her right where he wanted. Watching as his prey drifted from left to right through his cross hairs. His pulse increased. He blinked again. He had to remind himself to blink or his eyes would dry out, causing a blur in his vision. Then he briefly opened his non-dominate eye to capture the entire scene. There was only one entrance into the park for cars. And he knew what time she passed through the gates every day. It had taken weeks of watching, waiting, and observing her daily routine. He knew what time she ate. When she bought her groceries. When she left work. Hell, he even knew her bathroom habits. She was a creature of habit. Military trained. No surprises. Everything timed out perfectly. So, at this time of the day, he knew where to find her. She would take a walk along the lake shore, just as she had every day for the past month.

As he peered through the glass of his scope, the sun warming his body, he felt a slight pressure in his abdomen causing him to shift and readjust his position. It'd seem weird to anyone who has never served, but a career in the military trains your bladder. A soldier can hold the urge to urinate longer than anyone in the world. Just ask the guards at the Tomb of the Unknown Soldier. He once saw them at Arlington National Cemetery. He stared in amazement as the soldiers performed their task flawlessly while ignoring personal needs and the abuses from the elements. Those guys were heroes. That's what he wanted to be. A hero.

Unfortunately, his chance at being a hero was short-lived. After four years in the marines, health issues reared their ugly head. His recruiter had convinced him to lie to the processing doctors about his condition. It was all about the numbers during the surge. Get as many dumb-ass high school graduates as you can to enlist. Ineptitude wasn't a concern. If they have a pulse, get them to sign on the dotted line, raise their hand to God, and swear allegiance. Uncle Sam needed bodies for the meat grinder. Screw the consequences.

Had the recruiter turned him away on day one, he wouldn't be on this rooftop, staring at a woman who didn't ask to be in the position she was in. But that didn't happen. Now he was under orders, just from a different organization. Following orders had been the one thing in his short military career he was good at. Orders made him a weapon. A killer. Point him in a direction, give him a mission and it'll get done. Or he would die trying. The Corp didn't care which ending came to fruition, as long as the soldier followed orders. That was partially why he made Recon Squad as a Lance Corporal. The brass loved a soldier willing to overlook personal safety to complete a task. To the Pentagon, a recruit resembled a rough diamond buried deep in the soil turned over by a farmer's plow, then sold to the lowest bidder. Cut. Ground. Polished. Finally, shaped into a fine gem. Worth millions on the open market. That's how he saw himself. As a fine gem. All the rough edges shaved and polished to a high shine. One of a kind.

He watched as the car door opened. Her left shoulder led her through the crease into the open air. A black purse hanging from her left arm. The leather strap positioned exactly halfway between her shoulder and neck, hanging diagonally across her chest. Half of an X marks the spot. But it was enough for him. He lined up his vertical sight line to the purse strap, completing the X. The horizontal line was dead on center mass. He wiped the sweat from his brow with his brace hand. It was hotter than he had imagined it would be, lying on that rooftop. There had been plenty of recon work, but he failed to lie with his back up to the sun as part of his test run. He didn't want to take the chance of getting caught. He needed this rooftop. The risk wasn't worth losing his perch.

Waiting, lying in the sun for hours, was almost unbearable. He felt as if someone threw an electric blanket over him, then weighted it down with cinder blocks, pressing the heat into his skin. His mind wandered. He needed to concentrate on the target or the mission was going to fail.

The cold steel of the trigger felt good against the pad of his finger. He missed that. The rush of adrenaline. The second was guessing. Then acceptance. It wasn't a person. Just a circle on a paper target. One of a thousand he had riddled with lead. A controlled explosion moving at over one-thousand feet per second. No conscience. No remorse. Finality in its purist form.

The trigger mechanism clicked as his finger squeezed slightly. It was all about waiting for the right moment to complete the motion. The crosshairs lining up on center mass. One more step and it would be all over. He was excited, causing a slight jerk of the trigger. It wasn't how he had trained, but the motion wasn't enough to affect the outcome. The rifle's foregrip jerked up off the rest and his eyes instinctively closed at the sound of the exploding charge. He had never gotten used to that.

He reopened his eyes just in time to see her body collapse to the ground. He was out of practice and the trigger pull made the round hit higher than he wanted. The round impacted her head, just above her nose, cutting clean through the skull. The lead flattening on impact and bursting out the other side. Tearing into a man who had the unfortunate timing to be standing too close to the target. Despite the initial intent to avoid collateral damage, it was now inconsequential. Unchangeable. He disassembled and packed his rifle. Looking at his watch, he imagined the teardown would have beaten his best time, and he sighed. Once the container was closed and locked, he tucked the weatherproof plastic container away deep into a corner behind a couple of cooling units. People would have heard the shot and he would have looked suspicious carrying a rifle case around right after someone's head had just exploded. He picked this area to hide the weapon because the units appeared to be newer, reducing the risk of a mechanical failure, forcing some lowly maintenance worker to stumble upon his weapon before he could retrieve it. Originally, he thought about waiting until nightfall for his escape, but decided putting as much distance between him and the impending police presence was the best course of action. He briefly closed his eyes, thinking about the money he would soon have. Things would be different this time. This time, he would use it to better himself. There would be no splurging on strung out hookers and blow. He needed to get out, and the payoff from this job was his ticket.

****

Dodge sat in his corner office, watching the other agents sequestered to the cubicles lining the center of the room. Desks and chairs bounded on three sides by low partition walls. Each perfectly positioned in a manner that met the strict standards he developed to help ensure a productive but, most importantly, safe workplace. The idea for the new office design came about after attending a conference in Florida a few years back about violence in the workplace, with a special emphasis on law enforcement and social services settings. He attended, thinking the focal point would be on the risk workers face from disgruntled clients and family members. Something he experienced many times in his career. However, after the introductions of the panel members, it became clear the point of emphasis wasn't from outsiders. But they spoke at length about the growing number of workplace assaults and shootings by insiders. Mainly disgruntled employees and how people failed to recognize the warning signs. As Dodge listened to the presenter, his mind wandered to the many times he had noticed odd behavior from colleagues. Things he should have paid attention to. Changes in attitudes. Chronic absenteeism. A sudden lack of productive activity. A shudder ran down his spine. Years of training taught him to notice those exact behaviors, but in his parolees and criminal suspects. He never applied the same logic to his coworkers. A practice that was sure to begin as soon as he returned to work.

But there was one session amid all the psychological mumbo-jumbo Dodge found interesting. The presenter was a retired police detective who held a doctorate in psychology and Interior Design. And his expertise involved maximizing safety in an office environment by changing the layout and design to allow for easier exit routes and a better line of sight for responding emergency personnel. Dodge listened intently and took detailed notes. Later that night in his hotel room, on the back of the conference syllabus, he sketched out a detailed map of the parole office back in Virginia. He wanted clear sight lines. No high walls between cubicles. Every agent on the floor carried a weapon. If anyone tried to do harm, other agents would see the threat and be able to react quickly. More experienced agents lined the outside walls while he and Chief Johnson's offices faced the two entry points. When finished, he studied the layout, running scenarios in his mind, visualizing the chaos of an active shooter scene, and trying to predict likely outcomes. The whole thing made him sick to his stomach. While Dodge loved the design for its simplicity and practicality, he despised its necessity.

As he peered over the half empty room, he smiled, knowing this morning would be routine with business slower than normal. Holiday weekends had that effect on an office. Half the staff took a long weekend, planning to spend the extra day off with family at the beach or maybe a short flight to

Vegas or Atlantic City for some gambling and maybe dancing girls for some of the younger men in the office. Dodge had given up both gambling and strippers years ago. The return on investment was usually lower than he liked.

The other half of the staff worked because they had no family in the area or couldn't afford to get away. They came in to simply to avoid rattling around in an empty home on a three-day holiday weekend. If you must be in town and alone, might as well save the vacation time for a big payout when a better job comes knocking one day.

Dodge differed from the others in his office. He had no one of consequence who occupied space in his life, but that wasn't the reason he was sitting in his office watching the other agents drinking coffee and telling stories. It was simpler than that for him. His reason was ego. A belief the office couldn't function without his presence. It was a ship without a captain. Sure, the chief was there, but Dodge saw the chief's chair as more of an administrative position. The overseer. Head pencil pusher. It wasn't an insult to Chief Johnson. Dodge had a huge amount of respect for the man and, at one time, had been a stellar parole agent. But too many years of playing lackey to the powers that be in Richmond left him a little round in the waist and age made him slow on the draw. He saw himself as the captain on the ship's bridge, barking orders and keeping the vessel on course. The office needed him and he needed the office and all the people in it.

But at that moment, he wasn't supposed to be there. He was officially on medical leave. As a parole agent and an expert in dealing with sexual predators, Dodge is one piece of the local Sex Crimes Task Force. The task force focuses on murder cases containing sexual components, like if a murder victim showed signs of sexual assault. Ripped clothes and bruises around the thighs were just a few things that might lead to him being called to a homicide scene. Any death involving prostitutes garnered his attention as well.

A few months back, he and his task force partner, Detective Renquest, had been chasing down a serial killer targeting local prostitutes. The case became personal when the Savior, as the media dubiously named him, turned his focus on members of the task force, including Dodge himself. The case culminated in a showdown where the Savior slipped through the task force's fingers, but not before leaving Dodge clinging to life in a pool of his own blood, with two bullets lodged in his chest. He had been careless, and it almost cost him his life.

The wounds have healed on the outside. There are remnants of pain, but it lessens as each day passes. Emotional pain is a different beast entirely. The night sweats still hit hard, but the dreams happen less frequently and he doesn't obsess over the details of that night as much now. Even with all the physical therapy and counseling sessions, the department psychologist won't sign off and declare him fit for duty and the terms of his extended medical leave prohibit any contact with parolees or case related work. His presence in the office at all could place the chief and himself in front of a disciplinary committee. Dodge had completed all the required head shrinking appointments, but the final two. He dreaded those last ones. Not because he thought he wasn't ready to return to full duty, but because it wasn't up to him. He had no control over how the psychologist evaluated him. And the injuries sustained on duty, coupled with stab wounds from earlier in his career, the department could force him to take an early medical retirement. Medical retirement came with a full pension he could collect immediately. Retirement? At his age? He would probably drink his liver into submission within the first six months and be dead in a year. He needed to work. Work was all he had. Without the job, he wasn't sure who he was. Something he had no intention of sharing with the psychologist.

Dodge stared at the clock on the wall, which read two-thirty in the afternoon. The boredom of not being allowed to do anything, coupled with multiple cups of awful coffee, had taken a toll on his mood. He could hear the tick from the second hand as it circled the clock's face. The longer he sat in that office, the more the tick sounded like a hammer pounding a nail into a steel plate. His fingers dug deep into his temples, trying to massage away the growing tension. It was funny how you only notice the passage of time when there was little going on in the way of work. It was psychological torture. That infernal ticking made him think back to his senior high school literature class. The teacher had made them read an Edgar Allen Poe story about a beating heart buried beneath the floorboards driving the owner to madness. He remembered enjoying the tale, but liking a story and living it are far different things.

"I need a coffee," he said to no one.

Then he eased out from behind his desk, stepped through the office door, and into the bullpen area. With only a handful of agents working, the place had an eerie feeling, like a graveyard. Dodge glanced across the low partition walls at the chief's office. The blinds were up and Dodge noticed his boss sat behind the large wooden desk. A small laptop perched on the center of the desk forced him to hunch over and squint to see what was on the screen. Dodge chuckled to himself as he noticed the reading glasses resting high on top of his bald head. His desk faced the wall closest to the interior window, allowing him to glance over the top of his monitor for easier monitoring of the agents in the bullpen. Most of the agents felt the chief micromanaged their cases a bit too much with random pulls from their file cabinets and reviews of case notes but, as a senior parole agent, he understood the responsibility that went with having the "Chief" nameplate on a door, so he didn't mind a little cautious snooping. Besides, a little fear goes a long way in keeping order.

Dodge made his way around the outside aisle of the bullpen and poked his head through the chief's open door. "I'm going to get a coffee. You want anything?"

"You going to the cafeteria?"

Dodge shook his head. "I've had enough of that swill for one day. I'm going to hit up Pedro before he shuts down for the weekend."

"For God's sake, Dodge. Just go home. Hell, you can't do anything here, anyway. I never should've agreed to let you come into the office at all. If I'm being honest, you've been a pain in my ass since taking that bullet."

"Ahh, Chief. That hurts my feelings. I've been a pain in your ass long before I got shot." Dodge paused, his hand rubbing his shoulder "And it was bullets."

"What?"

"I took two rounds, not one. So, it's plural, bullets."

Chief Johnson smirked and nodded. Then his hand bristled against the whiskers on his chin. "He sure can brew a good cup of coffee."

"Pedro's the best," Dodge said.

"I'll take a Mochaccino," Chief Johnson said, rising from his seat and reaching into his front pocket, digging for some loose change to pay for the four-dollar cup of caffeine.

"Having trouble finding your wallet?"

"No. I got some spare change that's been rattling around in my pocket all day. It's been driving me crazy." His hand free of his pocket, he tossed a few pieces of lint, a paper receipt, and a few quarters onto his desk. "There, see. That's easily a couple of bucks."

Dodge shook his head. "I'll tell ya what, I'll get this one and you can get the next one."

"Are you sure?" he asked, as he fumbled to pick up the change from the smooth surface of the desk.

"Why don't you save that for the vending machine, big spender," Dodge said and let out a laugh.

Turning to walk toward the elevator, he heard Chief Johnson yell, "Make it a large!"

Without looking back, Dodge raised his right hand and gestured his index finger to the sky as the floor bell buzzed and the elevator doors opened.

The deep blue sky, devoid of any clouds, stretched out above the tops of the buildings. A warm breeze carried a gentle touch, the temperature hovering in the low eighties, as the afternoon sun beamed its radiant light, warming everything it touched. There was a hint of sea air as the wind whipped down the busy city streets. Pedro was busy meticulously sweeping away the scattered remnants of torn sugar packets, his movements precise and efficient, from the small metal shelf attached to the side of his truck that held napkins, coffee straws and extra sugar packets. The coffee truck owner was small in stature but carried a personality the size of a professional wrestler. His face donned a smirk that registered with Dodge as annoyance.

"Why do they always toss out the actual packet but leave the torn top and the plastic straws on the counter?" Dodged asked as he held out his hand.

The smirk vanished, replaced by a smile at the sight of one of his oldest customers. "People lazy. They figure Pedro will clean up after them."

"Throw it all away. Throw none of it away. For God's sake, decide, make a commitment."

Dodge noticed the lack of customers. "So, you're packing up early today?"

The short but stocky man replied, "The day, it's been very slow. No workers. No business."

"Yeah. These three-day weekends are rough on all the roach coaches. You should stay home and take the day off."

Pedro shook his head, his hands waving defiantly in front of his chest. "No time off. Daughter going to college. Very expensive."

Dodge smiled. A couple of years prior, he had helped Pedro with a minor problem concerning his daughter and a known street thug she got involved with. Pedro was grateful for the advice and free coffee was how he rewarded Dodge. Dodge always felt guilty about the free coffee, as he had done very little. At first, he even tried to pay, but the stubborn, yet grateful man refused to take his money. Dodge even tried slipping a couple of bills into the tip jar resting on the counter, once or twice, but Pedro caught on and would remove the jar when Dodge showed up. So now he only orders black coffee.

"You got enough time to make a Mochaccino and a black?" Dodge asked.

"Si," Pedro said, tossing the trash he had gathered into a small waste bin. He entered the truck through a door in the back and, within a few seconds, the air was awash with the whine of the coffee grinder motor as it whirled the fresh beans into a fine powder.

"Make the Mochaccino a small," Dodge said. His head bobbed as he chuckled to himself.

While Pedro prepared his order, Dodge leaned against one of the large circular cement pots separating the sidewalk from the small plaza, providing access to the building's entrance. He reached into his front pocket and slipped out a pack of cigarettes. After a few taps against the palm of his hand to pack the tobacco tighter against the filter, he tugged on one of the filtered ends and placed it between his lips. An orange flame jumped from the top of his Zippo and, with one deep drag, the end of the cigarette glowed red. He inhaled deeply, holding his breath for a moment before letting go of the warm smoke. Dodge loved that feeling. The rush of introducing something into the body. Like that first swallow from a glass of Blantons. The soothing warmness as the brown liquid passed over his tongue and washed down his throat. He could think of nothing he enjoyed more.

Maybe sex. But even sex had its initial moment of intimacy. Two sets of lips flushed with blood, moist, pulsating, pushing against one another. He always believed it was a blessing that he never experimented too heavily with drugs, as he knew he would have quickly succumbed to addiction. Doomed to a life chasing the dragon for the next big thrill. He pulled the smoke into his lungs again as he gazed up at the expansive blue sky. It was no use. It'd never be as enticing as the first time.

A harsh screech reverberated around the square, reflecting off the surrounding buildings, snapping Dodge from his thoughts of addiction and alcohol. His head dropped and his eyes followed the noise to the coffee truck where Pedro was leaning out the window, fingers in his mouth, ready to belt out another whistle. He took one last drag from the half-smoked cigarette, then snuffed it out on the sole of his shoe before discarding the butt in a nearby trash can.

Once at the truck's counter, he reached into his back pocket for his wallet, but before he could pull out any money, someone standing behind him reached around and placed a twenty-dollar bill on the counter next to him.

"This one is on me."

The voice was gruff and firm. He turned and saw a familiar face staring back at him. One he hadn't seen in over ten years. A gigantic man from a time long past towered over him.

Chapter 2

The behemoth standing before him reached six and a half feet into the air. A hulking frame Dodge imagined weighing over two hundred and fifty pounds cast a shadow that seemed to stretch on forever. His legs were bigger than most tree trunks lining the city streets. His arms were long, with biceps fighting through the cuffs of the short sleeves and testing the fabric's strength each time his arms flexed from movement. Hands that would have looked more at home dangling from the wrists of a gorilla, able to snap a man's neck like a twig. Sitting on top of a set of the broadest shoulders he had ever seen was a head the size of a watermelon, with the face of a battle-hardened soldier peering down at him. A scar stretched from under his left eye to his ear. The edges were rough and jagged with scar tissue wider than it should've been. Dodge knew a shrapnel wound when he saw one. Battlefield triage was not for the faint of heart. Nor was it a controlled environment with time to stitch someone up. The end product left a lot to be desired because, if someone is bleeding in combat and it's not critical, closing the wound with whatever you have to get soldiers back into the fight is the priority. Dodge knew many soldiers once back home would have cosmetic surgery to lessen the impact of the battle wounds in their civilian lives. But not the lifers. The ones who plan on dying on the battlefield wore their scars proudly.

The man stuck out his jumbo-sized hand. "Good afternoon, Captain Dodge."

Dodge reached out, his hand immediately smothered in rough skin, hair, and knuckles. "It's just Dodge now. I haven't been a captain for a long time."

The man eased his grip and gave a one pump shake before letting go. "Sorry, sir."

"No need to apologize, Airman Daughtry. Is it still Airman?"

The behemoth snapped to attention like a proud service member.

"Yes, sir," he said. "I wouldn't know how to live any other life."

Dodge nodded. "You get used to it. At ease, soldier."

The airman relaxed his posture, his eyes focused on the smaller man before him. "Sir, I have orders to retrieve you."

Dodge cracked a smile. "Son, I'm not in the Air Force anymore. Nobody retrieves me."

"I'm afraid those are my orders, sir."

"Who is your commanding officer, soldier? Who sent you?" Dodge asked.

"I'm not at liberty to say, sir."

Dodge's attention turned to the coffee in his hands. "My coffee's getting cold. And since I'm not obliged to take orders anymore, go back and tell whoever sent you they can find me here, or at my home, if they want to talk."

The muscular airman peered down at Dodge with a puzzled look on his face. Dodge guessed a man of his stature wasn't used to being told no.

"Sir, my orders are to bring you back with me. No excuses."

"Well, you and your boss are going to have to get used to disappointment," Dodge said. "And if you are thinking about getting rough, you might win, but I will put a round in your leg and it will be a long limp home for you. Understood?" His right hand moved to the butt of his Glock.

The hulky airman's eyes followed Dodge's hand. "Roger that, sir."

"Good. Now you can go back and tell your boss if he wants to have a serious talk with me, he can call or come to my place later tonight. Alone. Mention to him, or her, that I don't enjoy being fetched, nor do I like being jerked around."

Airman Daughtry stood silent. A look of bewilderment pasted on his face.

"What is it, son?" Dodge asked.

The man shrugged his broad shoulders, his feet shifting slightly. "Aren't you even going to ask what this is about?"

"Since you won't tell me who sent you, you either don't know why you're here, or are under orders not to divulge that information. Either way, it is a waste of my time."

Dodge tipped his head at the airman and began the short walk back toward the building's entrance. He heard a voice shout from behind him.

"Sir, I'm going to need an address where to find you,"

Without turning, Dodge said, "Your boss knows."

The elevator bell dinged as Dodge exited. He made his way across the bullpen, a coffee in each hand, saying hello to the few agents who remained before making his way to Chief Johnson's office.

"Jesus, Dodge. Where the hell have you been? I was about to send someone to look for you."

"Sorry, Chief. I got sidetracked."

"Was she at least pretty?" the Chief asked.

"No. She was a six-foot-five hairy gorilla."

"Sounds like your kinda woman." A bubble of spit formed in the corner of his mouth as Chief Johnson bellowed out a laugh.

The chief found himself hilarious. Most everyone else did not. Still, the rest of the staff would smile and try to cover their uncomfortableness with their best forced laugh. Dodge and the chief had been in the field together. Shot at together. There was a bond. One that gave the senior parole agent the confidence not to laugh at his boss's terrible jokes and feel okay not doing it.

The two men spoke for a few more minutes. Just as Dodge turned to leave, Chief Johnson's phone rang. The sound sent an eerie feeling through Dodge's body. Something was in the air and the woo-woo hairs on his neck stood at full attention.

"Yeah, this is Chief Johnson." He then nodded and simply replied, "Yes, sir," every few seconds until the person on the other end of the phone ended the call. The chief put the receiver back in the cradle and peered up at Dodge, a worried expression painted on his face.

Dodge asked, "Who was that?"

"It was the commandant of the Virginia National Guard. What the hell have you gotten yourself into?"

"What are you talking about?" Dodge asked.

"He wanted to know if I could get a message to you?"

Dodge sat back in the chair parked in front of the chief's desk. "Why would the head of the state guard be calling you about me?"

"Dodge," Chief Johnson said subtly. "Why were you gone so long to get coffee?"

The confused agent raised his hands, cupped his face, then ran them through his hair. "Shit."

"What is it?"

Dodge shook his head. "While waiting for Pedro to make your fancy milk drink, I was leaning up against a planter having a smoke. Someone I knew from my military days appeared out of nowhere. He flipped a twenty onto the counter for the coffee and said he had orders to take me somewhere."

"That's all very clandestine. Did he say who he wanted you to meet?" Chief Johnson asked.

"He wouldn't tell me but, whoever it was, they obviously knew me. And using an active-duty soldier to find a civilian means he has some pull and isn't worried about getting into trouble."

"What are you going to do?"

Dodge stood. "Nothing. If whoever it is wants me that bad, they will come and find me."

"You aren't the least bit curious what they might want?" the chief asked.

Dodge shook his head. "Nope."

"Well, whatever it is, keep it the hell away from my office. I answer to Richmond enough about the things you do while on duty. I don't want to have those conversations about your personal life."

"I wouldn't count on it," Dodge said.

Chief Johnson stood and said, "I think you should go home and find out who is pulling the strings on this."

Dodge shrugged.

"I'm serious. Get ahead of whatever this is," the old man said, shaking his finger in Dodge's direction. "Your almost cleared for duty, so don't go and do anything stupid."

"Chief. When Have I ever done anything stupid?"

"Get out."

Dodge turned to leave, stopping in the doorway, and glancing back. "It's still in my top desk drawer."

Dodge kept a business card for a lawyer's office out of Richmond in his desk drawer. The office oversaw managing his estate in the event something ever happened. If he wound up dead.

"You won't need that. Just find out what's going on and let me know," Chief Johnson said.

A quick nod and the veteran agent disappeared into the bullpen, making his way past the line of desks and toward the elevator. The lobby was quiet as he stepped off the elevator. Only one guard on duty stuck monitoring the X-ray machines. Most of his interactions that day were likely answering questions for visitors trying to meet last-minute deadlines before a long weekend. Mainly fathers with child support obligations and possibly some parolees making restitution payments after getting their weekly check. Normally, he would've stopped and chatted with the security guard on duty, but his mind was elsewhere. Back to a small base in the middle of Afghanistan, about a hundred clicks north of Kandahar. Backed by mountains on one side and a vast open desert bounding the other three. He hadn't thought about it in years. That place and that time were a distant memory now. Forgotten but not erased. Buried deep and locked in the box in his head. Airman Daughtry showing up outside Pedro's truck jogged his memory and pried the lid open wide enough for the long-forgotten memory to seep out.

Why this memory? He couldn't remember Daughtry being there with him in 2008. Truth was, he hadn't spoken to a single airman, marine or special forces soldier since leaving the desert for the last time over ten years ago. His first interaction with the massive wall of a man came on his last assignment, nowhere near Afghanistan.

A ray of sun glistened off a glass window across the street, catching the corner of his eye, snapping him from his thoughts of that far-away place. With a shake of his head and a few deep breaths, he hit the reset button in his brain. Air filled his lungs with each deep breath. Then a slow, controlled release. A deep breath in expanding the lungs to their capacity. Followed by a slow exhale. Rinse and repeat until an unobstructed path connects your gut to your brain. The place where the actual work happens. After a few minutes, the memories of brown sand, hot days and frosty nights faded. Squeezed back into the box in his head, with the lid firmly secured once again, he could finish his day. But a quick glance at the clock on his phone told him it was time for a drink. The time didn't really matter. He needed a drink.

It was his kind of place. A dive bar. Old and dim. Decades of cigarette smoke, drunken patrons sloshing mugs of beer and shots of whiskey on the floor as they threw darts and played pool, left a lingering musty odor in the air. The brown paneled walls gave the room a rustic feel. Like something out of a Cecil B. DeMille movie. Various beer themed mirrors surrounded the bar and walls, which reflected a world that looked almost upside down. Hazy. Distorted. Unclean. Yeah, it was his kind of bar. Not a place one would bring a date. Or anyone you were trying to impress, really. It was a place where the beer on tap is from St. Louis and Milwaukee, and the whisky all comes in the same shaped bottles. He wouldn't be getting a shot of Blantons here. The palettes in Smitty's Corner Pub were not sophisticated, just in need of alcohol to ease the pain of life. A simple drink to wash away the stench of the day.

Dodge pulled out a seat at the bar, eased in and laid a twenty on the faded and chipped wood top in front of him. The bartender was a thin older man. Maybe in his mid-fifties. What remained of the hair that once surely covered his head, tied back in a ponytail. More of a rat tail, if he was being honest with himself. A flannel shirt hung off his frail shoulders, like the coat of a golden retriever left out in the rain; the right pocket tore loose in one corner. Dodge counted four buttons missing down the front. Most men's shirts have six buttons from the neck to the waist, which left wardrobe batting about *two-hundred*. Not getting into the hall of fame with those numbers. But having been in this establishment for all of five minutes, Dodge guessed the man hadn't much use for all the buttons on a shirt. The dress code appeared to lean more towards wife-beater tank tops and biker leather.

As the out-of-place parole agent pulled his stool closer and placed a twenty-dollar bill in front of him, the bartender opened his mouth to speak, revealing a gap about the size of two teeth, dead center in the top row of his mouth.

"What can I get ya?" The gap in his teeth caused a slight whistle as he spoke.

"You got any bourbon?" Dodge asked.

The bartender looked over his shoulder at the line of half-empty bottles stretched across the shelf behind him. "You got eyes."

"And I have money. So, you can leave the cute shit at home and pour me a double of Big Bird."

The button challenged man looked back at the shelf again. "We ain't got Wild Turkey. Got some Black Bird if that'd suit ya?"

Old Crow. Dodge remembered finding a bottle of Old Crow once as a kid. A friend's house had caught fire and burned. A total loss. Nothing left except a blackened bottle of whiskey. Only the stamp on the metal cap revealing its contents. The two boys took it as a sign and drank the bottle back on a hill overlooking a small creek. It was the worst thing he had ever put in his mouth. Heat changes the chemistry of alcohol. Makes it taste like kerosene or fuel oil. But they drank it all, sitting on that creek embankment. They both were sick as dogs the next day. Oddly, that day was one of the fondest he could remember.

The bartender smacked the shot glass down right on top of the twenty-dollar bill. Some of the brown liquid splashed out onto the bar top.

"If you want me to pay for a double, make sure I get a double," Dodge said, downing its contents in one swallow.

The old man's ponytail flipped to one side as he turned around to put the bottle back on the shelf.

"Leave the bottle," Dodge said. A thud reverberated throughout the bar as he smacked the empty shot glass against the wooden bar top. The sudden noise caught the attention of a few of the regulars. He smiled. The parole agent wasn't just here for the bad booze and poor bartending skills. He was looking for something. Someone. The events earlier in the day put him in a mood, and the primal urge to blow off steam was gnawing at his subconscious. A place like this. No one is calling the cops. Some broken furniture and a little blood on the floor here would add to the ambiance. Not to mention, a part of him wanted to know how ready he was. The shooting had taken a toll on his body, but the self-doubt from the events of that day planted into his head was the damage that ate at him the most. He knew physically he could win a fight. But if things went south, would he have the mental fortitude to finish one? He was about to find out.

He reached across the bar and snatched the bottle from the old man's hands. It was like taking a sucker from a kid on the street. Bourbon splashed over the rim of the glass and onto his hand as he poured another shot.

The bartender looked at him and took a step back. A little ball of spit formed in the corner of his mouth as he shouted, "That's going to be a triple!"

Dodge lifted the glass, again swallowing the drink in one gulp, then he licked the over-spray from his hand. After slamming the glass against the bar again, he reached into his pocket, pulled out another twenty, and laid it next to the empty glass.

"That should more than cover a watered-down bottle of whiskey."

When he reached for the bottle to pour another drink, a hand reached out and gripped his right shoulder. It wasn't a friendly touch, but not enough pressure to keep him from rising out of his seat. He looked at the bartender, who was grinning from ear to ear as he snatched the two twenty-dollar bills from the bar and stepped away. Dodge glimpsed his own face in the mirror on the wall behind the bar before spinning to face his target.

Chapter 3

It was morning when Dodge finally opened his eyes. As he lay on the couch, one foot resting firmly on the floor to keep the room from spinning, a pounding behind his temples prevented him from sitting up too fast. Each attempt to right himself brought a sensation as if there was a beating drum submerged deep inside his skull. After failing several times to get upright, he decided the best course of action was to lay his head back and close his eyes for a while longer.

Nearly an hour passed as he lay regretting the previous night's choices, before the weary and aching agent heaved himself up into a sitting position. He leaned forward, cupping his head in his hands and brushing them through his short and slightly graying hair. Something wasn't right. A sudden stinging sensation on the left side of his face made him wince. He slid his hand over his left eye, carefully pushed around his cheek, moving up to the eye area, instantly flinching as the pain intensified from his touch.

"What the hell did I do last night?" he said to himself.

The constant pounding inside his head ebbed enough to allow him to stand up without wanting to empty the contents of his stomach on the living room floor. A pot of coffee and some painkillers was all he could think about. After filling the coffeemaker with water, he tossed the old coffee grinds into the trash and dumped four heaping scoops into the basket. He raised his hand to his eye again, pressing slightly on the fleshy area covering the lower rim of his swollen eye socket. Then he pressed the start button on the brew machine and leaned back, listening to the water as it gurgled and dripped into the carafe.

The bag of frozen peas he pulled from the freezer stung the side of his face. After 20 minutes, the swelling dissipated and numbness ruled the side of his face. The idea of cold objects on his skin never appealed to Dodge. Even when he was younger and played sports, he never enjoyed having injuries iced down. The pain from the sudden introduction of cold to his skin was so intense he contemplated giving up sports altogether to avoid it. But after graduating, he joined the Air force and never played organized sports again.

Once finished, Dodge tossed the bag of peas into the trash. As he passed through the kitchen, he glimpsed himself in one of the glass inserts of a cabinet door, jogging his memory and taking him back to the previous night. He remembered a mirror, but the scene was hazy. Alcohol dehydration made recall more difficult. Then he noticed a minor cut below his left eye. *Must have been a glancing blow*, he thought. He gently ran his finger across the afflicted area again, attempting to jar his memory, but details still eluded him.

As the man in the glass stared back at him, he said, "I hope the other guy looks worse than me."

Dodge realized he spent most of the morning talking to himself. It wasn't uncommon for him to verbalize a crime scene or read aloud from a case file, but this had an air of uncomfortableness to it he hadn't noticed before.

Feeling flushed, he grabbed a towel out of the linen closet next to the shower. With a grimace of pain, the battered and hungover agent turned the shower dial to the right, hoping the hot water would ease his soreness. He then stripped off his clothes, tossed his pants and shirt into a hamper, and stepped into the steaming water. His wounded eye stung as water trickled down his face. The healing powers of a hot shower lifted the weight from his shoulders; his body aches eased, and the pounding in his head lessened. The water cooled the longer he stood in its stream, and after fifteen minutes, the hot water supply was exhausted. Dodge finished rinsing the soap from his body and stepped out of the shower into the fog to dry off.

As he gently patted his skin with a towel, a loud banging reverberated through the house, breaking the stillness. A knock at the door? He held the towel still and listened. Then he heard it again, louder this time. Someone was beating on his front door. Salesmen usually only rang or knocked once. If no one answered, they would cut their losses and leave a flyer with the name and phone number. A third knock. *Thump, thump, thump.* The person was clearly not going away.

Water beads trickled down his back as he stepped into the bedroom, picked a clean pair of jeans from his dresser, which wasn't a dresser but an old chair he tossed clothes onto after doing laundry. After buttoning his jeans, he pulled a t-shirt over his head. Teeth dug into his bottom lip as the agony in his eye returned when the neck of his shirt scraped against the wound on his face while he struggled to pull the garment over his soaking shoulders.

Unable to recall exactly what had happened the night before, he grabbed his weapon from the kitchen table on his way to see why someone was at his house so early. He held the weapon in the small of his back and positioned himself to the left of the door handle.

In the morning, the sun shone directly on his front door, rendering the peephole useless. He gave a quick glance anyway but saw nothing but a sunburst staring back at him. Then he placed his right foot about six inches back from the bottom of the door, to prevent anyone on the outside from shoving the door open and bursting inside. During his career, Dodge had kicked hundreds of doors. Anyone on the other side received a face full of wood and metal as the door blasted open. Using a foot as a stopper might break a toe or two, but his nose wouldn't be a bloody mess.

The knob in his hand rotated slowly, and his muscles tightened. He drew the door toward himself, then halted. Once he realized he wouldn't get a face full of wood, he slid sideways into the opening. His eyes took a second to adjust to the sudden burst of sunlight and a giant torso filled his vision.

"Captain Dodge." The booming voice was unmistakable.

Dodge looked up at the man on his stoop, who was standing to the side of the door and, as he centered himself, blocked out the sun, bringing his face into focus. There was a cut on his lower lip. The sight of Daughtry, and the wound to his mouth, cleared the cloud hovering over the previous night. Details he couldn't recall before were suddenly swirling around in his mind. He immediately went to work putting the mental jigsaw puzzle together.

After a few seconds, the previous night's events tumbled like dominoes.

Now having a better idea of how he received the cut on his face, he stepped back and pulled the door fully open. "Did I give you that?" he said, pointing at the mark on Daughtry's lip.

The man's massive hand reached up to rub the wound. "You've got a good punch. For a little guy."

Dodge stared at his right hand, his fingers stroking his knuckles. "I'm surprised I didn't break it on that huge melon."

Daughtry said nothing. His eyes registered he had been the brunt of insults before, and Dodge immediately wished he could've pulled the words back into his mouth.

"Come on in, I guess. No need to get the nosey neighbors all riled up."

Dodge slid back against the wall as he opened the door fully. The thick chested airman turned sideways to slide past his host. It wasn't necessary. There was plenty of room for him to pass comfortably, so either he was used to his colossal frame getting in the way, or he was trying to make Dodge feel insignificant by facing off as he passed by. Once he cleared the entryway, he stopped.

"Go on in," Dodge said, waving Airman Daughtry into the living room.

The airman took three steps in and stopped. Still standing at half attention.

"You can relax. I'm not a captain anymore," Dodge said, stepping past and into the kitchen. "You want some coffee?"

"No thank you, sir."

"It's just Dodge."

Daughtry said nothing.

Dodge topped off his coffee mug and returned to the living room and sat on the couch. "Have a seat."

Airman Daughtry moved closer. The distance was about ten feet and the giant man covered the distance from the dining room to the sofa in what seemed like two steps. He reached into his shirt pocket and pulled out a folded piece of paper.

"Sir. My instructions were to give this to you personally."

His arms weren't only muscular, they were long. Dodge didn't have to move off the couch to take the piece of paper.

"What's this?"

"I don't know, sir."

"You must know something?" Dodge said.

Daughtry looked down at Dodge. "Not my job to ask questions, sir. I was told to keep an eye on you and place that in your hand this morning."

Dodge thought about his sore eye. "That's why you were at the bar last night? To keep watch over me."

The man nodded.

"Why did I hit you?" Dodge asked, pointing to the cut on his guest's lip.

The airman smiled for the first time. "That was my fault, sir. After following you to the bar last night. I stayed outside, choosing to monitor you through the window. After you had several drinks, you weren't being very polite to the bartender, so a few of the locals took an interest in you. I extracted you before they had a go at you."

"It was your hand on my shoulder?"

"Yes, sir. But I should've declared myself. I apologize for that."

"I hit you, and you apologize." Dodge laughed. "No need for an apology, son. If I gave you that, I deserved this," he said, tapping the cut on his left eye.

"I didn't give you that, sir."

"What?"

"After I got you out of the bar, I was trying to get you into my car. You weren't quite ready to go, and well…"

"I hit you," Dodge said.

"Yes, sir. Like I said, you got a nice punch for a little guy."

"But how did I get this shiner?"

For the first time, Daughtry relaxed his posture. "Sir, you took another swing and missed. Lost your balance and hit your face on the car door. Knocked you out cold. I picked you up, put you in the front seat and drove you home."

"That explains the lost time. But how did you know where I lived?" Dodge asked.

"Like you said yesterday, my boss knew."

"Well, thanks for keeping me out of trouble and getting me home safe."

"Just following orders, sir."

Dodge nearly forgot about the paper the airman had handed him. He looked at Daughtry, then back at the paper in his right hand. "You know what this is?"

"Above my pay grade, sir."

Dodge's fingers slipped into the space between the folds and manipulated the small square of paper into a full notebook sized sheet. Printed on the top of the letter, in bold letters, was a name. One he hadn't heard in years. He read on.

Colonel James "Jimmy" Patterson (Ret)

Dodge,

I hope this letter finds you well. I'm sorry for all the cloak and dagger surrounding the delivery of this letter. Please don't feel slighted by Airman Daughtry's approach to this request. You always told me when the situation was a nail, you needed the biggest hammer you had in your bag. He was the biggest hammer I had. I've only told him what he needs to know to complete his mission. The cloak and dagger routine was my decision alone, and I take full responsibility for how this has all played out. I'm sorry for not coming to you directly, but I wasn't sure who I could trust.

I find myself embroiled in a situation. One that I can't solve alone. I need someone I can trust will do the right thing, no matter how this all turns out. I need you, Paul Dodge. Please come with Airman Daughtry and I will explain everything. I will make it worth your while.

Your friend,

James Patterson

Dodge reread the letter, hoping he would catch something he missed the first time. Maybe a line or phrase that might give a clue to what his commanding officer might be involved in requiring him to seek help outside of the military machine in which he spent most of his life. But he saw nothing.

His head cocked to the right, the letter still clinched in his fingers as his hands fell to his lap.

"Are you ready, sir?"

Dodge stood. "Why are *you* here? I understand why Colonel Patterson didn't come himself, but it's just as easy to deliver this type of message over the phone or by email. Why did he send *you*?"

"I'm not sure what you mean, sir."

Dodge nodded. "That's how it's going to be?"

"My orders were to find you and bring you to Colonel Patterson. That's all."

Dodge picked up his phone off the coffee table and placed his duty weapon on his desk. "Guess I won't be needing that."

Daughtry watched his every move, finally speaking once Dodge appeared to have completed his pre-travel tasks. "If you're ready, sir."

Not sure of his ultimate destination, or what awaited him once they arrived, the parole agent and his personal escort piled into a tan chevy sedan. Daughtry pulled away from the curb and sped toward the highway.

Chapter 4

Neither man spoke much as the pair traveled west toward the man who Dodge credited for making him the man he was. Colonel Patterson taught him responsibility. What it meant to examine a case from all sides. How to place himself in the victim's shoes. But most importantly, his old boss pounded his brain with rules. Many of which he relied upon to this day. Some of which had saved his life more than once. Dodge mulled over the idea of asking Daughtry again about his old boss's intentions, but he suspected the airman would remain tight-lipped about his knowledge of the situation. Which Dodge felt was more than he was letting on. He also knew nothing short of waterboarding would get this soldier to disobey orders. So, he leaned into his seat and watched the trees roll past the window, resigning himself to waiting for answers. Which wouldn't be as long of a wait as he thought.

The car exited the interstate onto a state highway and, after two miles, veered left onto a county road. Potholes littered the road as it bent and turned, mirroring the path of a small creek which wound its way through the pastures and fields of Central Southern Virginia. The car rocked and Dodge could feel his insides bounce every time the tires fell into a pothole. The frequency with which the car's tires hit the blemishes in the roadway made him feel as if Daughtry was intentionally trying to hit them. A motorist's version of Whack-a-Mole. After a few miles, the road straightened out and the potholes all but disappeared. Ten minutes later, they made a right, followed by an immediate left on to the first access road. A classic white board fence, reminiscent of sprawling horse farms, contained the long straight lane flanked by towering trees on either side. The only thing missing was the horses. His eyes perused open pastures stretching for hundreds of yards in all directions. Not a single animal in sight.

After a few minutes, the silhouette of a modest home emerged from the distance. As they drew closer, he noticed the house was small compared to its surroundings. The long drive down the lane teased visitors with thoughts of an expansive mansion at the end of their journey. This was the home of a modest man. Someone who thought in terms of comfort, not extravagance. The house of a retired combat veteran. He smirked and laughed to himself. For even this was more house than he could ever afford as a state employee. Modest house. Hardly.

He stared out the passenger window; the house disappearing in the mirror. It wasn't long before the drive morphed into a path. Two tire ruts with a strip of grass growing between them. Daughtry followed the smaller, narrower drive, which wound around a few small, dilapidated outbuildings leading toward the rear of the property. As they rounded a sharp bend atop a small hill, a large wooden structure appeared below them. The barn loomed large and was much bigger than anything else Dodge had seen on the drive through the property. Natural siding covered the façade of the barn with no stain or paint. A red metal roof stretched from end to end, the only color he saw on the entire structure. Again, as in the pastures he saw bounding the primary drive, he saw no horses. No goats or pigs. No barking dogs. Nothing. Pure solitude.

The tires ground to a halt outside the main doors on the south side of the barn. A gap in the sliding doors was big enough for a person to slip through.

"He's in there, sir," Daughtry said, pointing toward the barn.

Dodge stared at the barn door. He wondered what awaited him inside. He wasn't sure what to make of this whole thing yet, but the woo-woo hairs on his neck stayed flat, for now. Dodge slid out of the passenger seat, closing the car door behind him. Then he turned for a quick glance back at Daughtry, who nodded in approval, before he made his way through the door and disappeared inside.

The change in brightness from outside to inside made it difficult to see.

Dodge closed his eyes for a few seconds to help them adjust to the dim environment. When he opened them again, he was stunned at the expansive interior before him. Water glistened on the freshly washed cement floor, which seemed to stretch out half a football field in front of him. Music fell softly from speakers mounted on thick wooden beams overhead. He struggled to make out the artist; it sounded like a blues piece unfamiliar to him. To his right and left, rows of empty stalls stretched along the walls. A coat of fresh stain covered the boards, making up the gates, and each hinge glistened under a fresh polish.

As he continued deeper into the interior of the barn, the scene remained the same. More empty stalls, the smell of fresh paint, and crisp steel hinges. Dodge stopped when a booming voice echoed from the far end of the building.

"Daughtry?"

He didn't answer.

"Airman, is that you?"

Dodge stood silent, choosing to wait for his host to show himself. A few seconds later, a head popped out through the gate of the last stall on the right. Dodge instantly recognized the horseshoe hair pattern and subtle facial features. The balding head belonged to his first commanding officer, Colonel James Patterson. A slew of emotions flooded his senses. First, he remembered a man he hated when he came under his command. Dodge was a mouthy Airman First Class who hadn't taken to the military yet. But Colonel Patterson saw something in Dodge. Something buried deep inside. Something no one else had noticed. It was loyalty. He took Dodge under his wing and taught him how to be strategic. Learn to play the long game and to stop worrying about what was happening in the moment. "It's about what happens next," he used to tell the stubborn airman. Under Patterson's tutelage, Dodge learned to stretch his thought processes out over weeks, months and even years into the future.

"Obedient soldiers always prepare for the future," Colonel Patterson used to tell his men. It didn't take long for his prize pupil to move up the ranks. By his sixth year, he held the rank of First Lieutenant and was given his first command. A security force unit, on a tiny airbase in the middle of the Afghan desert. He took the knowledge he had gleaned from his commanding officer, by then also a close friend, and led his team through several successful missions. There were commendations and medals. Handshakes and hugs. And a few funerals. By the time he left his first deployment, Dodge no longer needed the Colonel's help. He was well on his way to making his own future.

It had been a long time since he had seen his old boss. The colonel he admired long ago wasn't the man standing before Dodge that day. His command presence had all but disappeared. The hair that once topped his stately head had thinned and faded to gray. His face looked weathered, beaten by time and the demands of a career marred by war. Seeing soldiers die changes you. Sending them to die haunts you. It damages the body and spirit. Dodge knew the feeling well. His last tour in Kandahar had been one of the deadliest in the war. He wrote more letters to parents than he cared to remember. Though he remembered all of them. Every letter he mailed. His inability to move on from the inevitable death in war proved too much. It was one reason he opted to leave the service.

As he stared at the frail-looking man in front of him, he knew the choice he made was the right one. The idea of transitioning from a revered soldier to the broken-down shell of a man which stood before him is what kept him up at night.

"Colonel Patterson," Dodge said. Muscle memory forced his body to attention.

"Dodge. I'm afraid it's just Patterson these days." The frail man reached out a hand. "Good to see you, my boy. I wish different circumstances preceded our overdue reunion."

Dodge stood silent.

"At ease," Patterson said, the smile easing from his face. "I haven't been an officer for some time now."

Dodge relaxed and nodded, then took his mentor's outstretched hand. "What can I do for you, sir?"

The retired colonel pointed to a couple of hay bales propped up against the front of one stall. "Come over here and have a seat, Dodge."

Dodge tossed the bales into the middle of the aisle and flipped them longways. Turning them like two facing chairs in an office. There weren't a lot of differences in bailed hay. One was just as good as the other for resting. But he felt it was only proper to let the elder man have first choice. Patterson took the bale closest to the stall and Dodge sat across from him.

There were a few seconds of situating himself for comfort, then a sigh, before Patterson said, "I am sure you have a lot of questions."

"Yes, sir. I have a few."

"You're here, so I assume you received my letter?"

"Hand delivered by Airman Daughtry. He followed your orders perfectly."

His mentor's eyes glanced to the other end of the barn. The front of the car was still visible through the gap. "He's a good man," he said, returning his gaze back to Dodge.

"How long has he been with you?"

His right hand raised to his face. Long, narrow fingers rubbed his forehead. "About as long as we were together, I suppose."

"Well, you taught him well. He kept your secret and even got me out of a jam the other night." Dodge paused, allowing time for his mentor to answer. He said nothing, so Dodge continued, "Now, why don't you tell me what this is all about? What is so important that you couldn't just pick up the phone and call?"

"I'm sorry about that, Dodge. Looking back, I suppose I could've handled it better. But that's in the past now. So, I'll stop stalling and get down to brass tacks. For me to put this all together cost me a career's worth of favors. I only ask that you listen to the ramblings of a feeble old man and if, when I'm finished, you aren't interested, I'll have Daughtry transport you back home."

Patterson paused. His eyes focused on a thought or a faraway memory. It was the first time since he arrived Dodge had seen a sign of the once powerful man he proudly served under.

"I'm going to need an answer."

Dodge sat silent. He thought about the choice ahead and what it might entail. What might it cost him? After a moment, he decided he would hear the proposal. "I'll listen to what you have to say, but I can't make any promises, sir."

"Good then. I knew I could count on you. You always were my best soldier."

Dodge nodded. Leaned forward on the hay bale, perched his elbows on his knees and clasped his hands in front of him.

Patterson leaned back. His eyes fell to the ground, focusing on something that wasn't there. Maybe something from deep in his past. When he finally looked back at Dodge, his face carried a far-off expression. A tear ran down his cheek.

"Sir?" Dodge asked.

The old man straightened his back and perked up. "I'm fine. You would think as many times as I've told this story—I'd be used to it by now. Excuse me for a moment." He tilted to one side and pulled a paper napkin out of his front trouser pocket, wiped his eyes, and cleared his nose. Once done, he placed the napkin back in his pocket. A deep breath followed, then he leaned forward. At first his mouth opened and his lips moved, but no sound came out. He took a deep breath and started again.

"What I am about to tell has been told many times before. To Generals, Inspector's General, investigators, and anyone who'd listen. No one takes it seriously. No one takes me seriously. That is why I need you."

"Just take your time and start from the beginning," Dodge said.

"This all started when the US was still going strong in Afghanistan. We were working with the new government, trying to keep the Taliban from re-emerging. The Pentagon had spent billions in taxpayer money and thousands of lives to save some semblance of a self-governed, peaceful country. We knew what they were capable of, and what they would do if they took power again. So, it became US policy to back anyone who was anti-Taliban." He paused and shook his head. "But there were some senior officers and State Department officials who knew it was all going to be for nothing. The past fifteen years had been one disaster after another. Sure, we put the fear of God into the insurgency, but where you cut off one head, two grew in its place. Nothing we did in the couple of years before leaving town was going to make a damn bit of difference. The Taliban were going to take back the country, and we were powerless to stop it."

"I remember. You'd kill five and 10 would trek down from the mountain caves armed with rifles we provided to the Afghan Security Forces to defend their own country."

"We won battles, but unless we could guarantee a commitment of a hundred years, it was going to end up just like it did." Patterson paused and wiped a bead of sweat from his brow, then continued. "But that is a cautionary tale for another time. Anyway, we had sent a group of intelligence officers over to Bagram Air Base to keep track of the power players and dig up as much actionable intelligence as they could. Things we could use as leverage with the Taliban during negotiations for our inevitable exit."

"One last round of drone strikes to kill the key players before we leave. Maybe burn a poppy field or two to send a message?"

"Right out of the DoD playbook. Cause as much chaos as you can before turning tail and running," Patterson said.

"What were they looking for, specifically?" Dodge asked.

"The usual. Family members, known associates, addresses, anything they could find really. If we had some data, maybe we could make some connections. We would pass along anything unaddressed to the current government, leaving it up to them to decide how to handle it."

Dodge shook his head. "Are we talking about kill lists?"

"We didn't ask and frankly didn't care what they did with the information. Decisions like that are made far away in Washington," Patterson said.

"Got to love the bureaucracy."

"The tour was supposed to be for a couple of months but ended up lasting over six. The soldiers did their jobs, as expected, and gathered some good intel. Then, one night, after receiving their orders to return home, they had a party. Someone had snuck in some alcohol and the whole thing got out of control. There were civilian contractors and military personnel drinking and even reports of illegal drug use."

"It happens. Bagram is a big place, and we always knew there were drugs and alcohol on base. It was impossible to keep it out. People gonna be people."

"Yes, they will. But with that group of intelligence officers was a young army corporal on her first deployment. She was twenty-five years old and due to be promoted to sergeant."

"What happened?"

The old man's head fell again. A glint from an overhead light gleamed off his balding head. "That party happened."

Dodge waited and said nothing.

"Well, things got out of hand. Several contractors and an army sergeant drank too much and began making advances toward the corporal. She rebuffed them, deciding instead to leave and return to her bunk. She made it halfway to her hooch." A tear fell from his eye and he refused to wipe this one away. The water rolled down his cheek, finally dripping from his chin and ending as a small wet spot on his shirt.

"The men followed her out?" Dodge asked.

"Three of them. They caught up with her and pulled her into a small storage shed. Then held her down. Each took a turn with her. The attack went on for more than an hour, eventually too drunk or high to continue. They kicked her a few times and told her if she ever told anyone about what happened, they would kill her. Then they left her lying on the floor of that shed, like a pile of discarded trash. A contractor walking back from the showers found her and carried her to the infirmary. She refused to tell anyone about what had happened, so they patched her up and command put her on the next flight out."

"Did she come back stateside?"

"No. New orders placed her in Stuttgart, Germany. I think it was because the army didn't know what to do with her. But as the months dragged on, she couldn't hold it together. Started missing work. In and out of the hospital. Then one night, she told another female soldier she bunked with about the attack. This other soldier talked her into reporting the incident to her commanding officer, who created an official report."

Dodge nodded. "Army cops are usually good at their job. Did an investigation ensue?"

"They assigned the case to an officer in CID, a good soldier from what I could tell, but someone shut it all down before his investigation could gain any traction."

"Did you ever find out why?"

"Scuttlebutt has it, one of the contractors she accused of attacking her was the son of a congressman. From Texas, if I recall. It doesn't matter because he held a position on the House Oversight Panel on Appropriations. This allowed him to put pressure on the right people, effectively killing any chances for justice for the young corporal."

Dodge rubbed his chin, contemplating what he had just heard. "That's a compelling story. I certainly feel for the young soldier. But I have one question."

"Yes?"

"How did an Air Force Colonel get involved in a sexual assault case involving an Army soldier on a base ten thousand miles away?"

"The corporal was my niece." He buried his head in his hands and began sobbing.

Dodge sat quietly. He had nothing to say that would make a difference. A wave of sorrow flowed over him. His heart ached for his former mentor, but he wasn't sure what he could do. It was years old. Not even a cold case. A dead case, killed in a backroom deal in Washington. Not to mention the fact it involved two separate branches of the military and what was likely a large government contractor. He tried to hide the concern on his face, but the old man picked up on it.

"Her name was Shannon. Corporal Shannon Roberts and I know what you are thinking, Dodge. A cross jurisdictional investigation leading to the halls of Congress? It seems impossible, I know."

"The likelihood of anyone going to jail is remote, sir. You're handing me a stacked deck."

"I know, son. But I don't have anyone else. This wasn't a decision I came to lightly. And I know it puts you in a tough spot. Please understand, I had no other choice."

Dodge sat quietly, replaying everything he had just heard in his mind. The task laid out before him would not be an easy one. With endless wars and huge public failures over the last fifty years, the Department of Defense evolved into a massive cluster of bureaucracy wrapped in a million layers of red tape. Every layer protected the next one. It was almost impossible for an outsider to get any information from the Pentagon. Let alone something that happened on a classified mission in a war zone, with major political implications. But shying away from the good fight simply because it didn't seem winnable was not Dodge's style. His rule was, *always fight the good fight and never worry about the outcome.*

Dodge nodded at the broken man across from him. "I worked on a lot of investigations into sexual assaults during my time in uniform. It was always an uphill battle, and I hated the way the military tried to cover its ass when people got hurt. So, one more chance to stick it to the suits at the Pentagon? Count me in."

The old man smiled. A glint of hope in his eyes. "Thank you, son."

"Don't thank me just yet. This is going to be a fight and I'm likely to rattle some cages that don't take kindly to being shook. But first, I'm going to need to speak with your niece. Is she still in uniform or is she a civilian now?"

The smile disappeared from his mentor's face. The hope in his eyes wiped away as quickly as it had appeared.

"What are you not telling me?" Dodge asked.

The silence was deafening.

"Sir?" Dodge asked again.

"She died. Shot three days ago in Dallas. She was jogging in a park and someone just… shot her." He began weeping again.

"Do the local authorities have anyone in custody?"

"As far as I know, they have no leads. They've labeled it a random act of violence."

"Has anyone told them about the attack? I mean, what happened to her in Afghanistan?" Dodge asked.

"I haven't been able to get much information from the police. Since I'm no longer in the military, they won't provide any details. I'm simply a grieving family member to them."

"How long had Shannon been out of the service when this happened?"

"For a while. She had a good job set up with a government contractor as an intelligence analyst."

"Clearances?"

"Top Secret and higher."

"I assume the Pentagon is stonewalling local police efforts. Giving them the *national security* speech?"

"It's what they do. I'm waiting for them to come in and take over the whole thing. Then they can bury everything in a big hole and cover it up."

"So, you think there's a link between what happened in Afghanistan and her death a half a world away in Texas?"

Patterson nodded. "I do."

Dodge stood up and walked over to one of the closed stalls, his footsteps echoing throughout the empty room. As he leaned on the gate, he imagined the sound of hooves and the smell of hay that once filled the now-empty stable. He wondered if one day he would be sent away and put out to pasture. Relegated to an old farm in the middle of nowhere. Helpless and defeated. Waiting for the sweet sound of death's footsteps. After a few minutes, he shook off the thoughts of his own mortality and turned to his old friend. "Where should I start?"

Patterson stood and walked back into a stall. When he returned, his hands held two files.

"This should give you a starting point."

Chapter 5

Deafening silence filled the car's interior on the drive home. Almost as if the air was thick. Too heavy to carry sound. Daughtry stared through the windshield, his eyes rarely moving from the road as it passed beneath them. In the passenger seat, the files Patterson gave Dodge were open, the contents spread across his lap. The first contained copies of reports regarding Shannon Roberts' assault in Afghanistan. The file was slender, holding only the initial complaint and one interview. A one-page statement by her friend and confidant, Sergeant Lilly Tremble. The file's creator stapled two small sheets of paper to the inside of each side. One being the orders assigning Major Elijah Waters to the case, and the other being the order to close the investigation. No case notes. No pictures. No list of suspects. Nothing to run with. Patterson had been right when he said the whole thing had been shut down and swept under the rug. Powerful people had a way of getting what they wanted and, all too often, it was at the behest of some DC insider wanting to keep his misdeeds secret. If Dodge wanted to find out what happened to Shannon Roberts, he would have to start from the very beginning.

As the car pulled up to the curb in front of his brownstone, a lady walking her dog, carrying a small green plastic bag in her left hand passed by. He stared out the window as the tiny dog did his business and the woman used the baggy to pick up the waste. The simple act triggered something in his memory, to the woman who previously lived across the street. His head turned to the still vacant home opposite his own. He hadn't known her more than to say a simple *hello* as she walked her small white poodle around the block. Neither of them knew a serial killer, bent on revenge, would turn her quiet home into a gruesome murder scene, gutting her dog and a guy who found himself at the wrong place at the wrong time. Dodge winced as a bolt of pain shot down his arm. A gift that kept on giving from the same psychopath. Two bullet wounds. And a heavy psychological burden as a side dish. Unintentionally, his hand rose and touched his shoulder. A sour feeling filled his gut. By the time he turned back toward the woman and her dog, she was walking away. A leash in one hand and a small bag of dog shit in the other.

"You alright, sir?"

He turned to Daughtry. "What do you think about this whole thing? And please stop calling me sir. Dodge is fine."

"It's above my pay grade."

"I asked you what you thought, not the enlisted man's equivalent of *no comment*. I'm going to need you with me on this. I'm going to be digging up things someone would prefer to stay buried. Your status as a military man may help smooth over some of the rough spots."

"And my size?"

Dodge grinned. "That'll help when the uniform doesn't."

The airman maneuvered his bulky frame and turned slightly in the cramped quarters. "I think the whole thing stinks. Colonel Patterson is one of the finest men I have ever served with and for people to just blow him off this way, it pisses me off."

Dodge asked, "Do you think there is a parallel between the attack and Shannon Robert's murder?"

"Doesn't matter. Colonel Patterson does. And that's good enough for me."

Dodge sat quietly, watching, reading the airman's face. After a minute, he asked, "How is it you are helping a retired colonel and still on active duty? Why aren't you assigned to a unit or deployed?"

"The colonel's expert knowledge of the Middle East is of value to the Pentagon. He doesn't get paid for his work, but his research for DoD is mission essential and they provide him with access to classified materials. I am assigned to make sure he gets what he needs and maintain security over any sensitive information passed between him and the Pentagon."

Dodge nodded. "Got any plans for the next few days?"

"The Colonel stated I was to assist you in anything you needed. So, I go where you go."

"Good." Dodge opened the sedan's door and stepped out onto the sidewalk. He bent down and peered back through the open door. "Be here first thing in the morning."

"Roger that."

"And bring coffee."

Dodge closed the car door, and the sedan sped off, its taillights fading in the distance.

As he turned to make the short walk to his stoop, the woman and her dog passed by again. The poop bag no longer dangling from her off-hand. As the pair passed, the dog casually brushed against his pants, leaving a tuft of hair behind. His eyes followed the dog and its owner as they crossed the street. She climbed the steps and entered a home three doors down from the vacant house. He wondered why he had never noticed a dog living directly across the street. Seems like a detail he would've remembered. Another moment passed before he bent over and brushed the hair from his pant leg, then made his way up the stoop and through the front door.

Tink. Tink. The ice bounced off the bottom and sides of the glass as he dropped two cubes into a rocks glass. A crackle followed as the warm liquid doused the ice, filling the glass just short of the rim. A heavy pour. But they all seemed to be heavy lately. A trend that hadn't gone unnoticed. What started off as a way to help him relax and ease the pain from his wounds had morphed into something more permanent. A double shot had become more of a necessity and less of an indulgence. A situation that could turn into a real problem. He raised the glass to his lips and let the brown liquid wash over his tongue and down his throat. A problem to worry about another day.

The file containing Major Waters' investigation lacked anything about Roberts' attack in Afghanistan. No phone logs of calls made or received. No maps of the base showing where the party had taken place or the location of the attack. At a minimum, there should have been a list of those the victim served with and the names of anyone at the party. Everyone at the event had been a witness to something. Gathering witness names and describing the area would've been the first thing Dodge did as lead investigator. And according to Colonel Patterson, Major Waters was an honest man and a superb investigator. Dodge fingered through the file. He saw the opening date of the case. Then he looked at the orders, closing the case. Almost a month. A short lifespan for an investigation for sure, but plenty of time to gather the basics. It was almost as if Major Waters knew his investigation was going to be shut down. Why put the effort into a case that is going nowhere? It just didn't sit right with him. A capable investigator would have started from the beginning. In Afghanistan.

As evening transitioned into night, Dodge diligently read through the files, jotting down questions in the margins, and making notes on areas that required further investigation. Once the margins were full, he flipped the pages, using the back of the sheets to write out the rest of his thoughts and concerns. By the time he was on his third glass, the amount of writing in the reports had more than doubled. A result having both an upside and, similarly, a downside. By creating more lines of inquiry, he also made more leads needing to be tracked down. That meant more interviews and more travel.

With a timeline now roughed out, he leaned back and drank the last swig of bourbon. The task in front of him was daunting. First, he needed to find the names of every soldier in Robert's unit somehow. There were records for sure but, as a civilian, how would he get his hands on them? He also needed the names of contractors assigned to the base during that time as well. That he would never get from the Pentagon or the contracting firms who provided the labor. That information was likely classified Top Secret and above. Not to mention contractors often left a company for a new contract once the old contract ended. There was no telling where any of them were now. Up to this point, Dodge hadn't even considered the travel. People scattered all over the globe. He knew nothing about Colonel Patterson's financial situation, but plane tickets and hotel rooms weren't cheap. It would only take a couple of flights overseas to inflate a bill into the tens of thousands.

As he sat there, his optimism faded as quickly as the brown liquid in his glass had. The roadblocks seemed insurmountable. The colonel used a lifetime of favors already, but it sounded as if that well was now empty. Not to mention there was no way he could ever visit the attack site. The military dismantled the base before leaving and Afghanistan was off limits to everyone, since the Taliban had taken back over. Except for State Department Officials and maybe some spooks from the CIA.

Dodge handled the kink in the plan the way he always handled disappointment. With a drink. Then he leaned back onto the couch and closed his eyes. The warm brown liquid soothed his nerves as he ran scenarios until he faded off to sleep.

***

The soft rays of sunlight filtered through the blinds, creating a playful dance of light on his face and gently stirring him from his deep slumber. Sleep crust filled his eyes, only releasing its grip as he rubbed them with the backs of his hands. Corrective eye surgery assured daily use of eye drops to counteract the dryness effect caused by the procedure. A few drops in each eye and he was ready for the day.

The cracking in his joints as he pulled himself upright on the couch reminded him of popcorn popping in the microwave. He stretched his arms above his head and let out a loud yawn. On the coffee table beside him, there was a glass with one last swallow of bourbon and a pack of cigarettes. A Zippo lighter sat perched near the edge of the table.

He rubbed his face and ran his hands through his short, partially graying hair. He had over-indulged the brown goddess the previous night, falling prey to her siren song, as had become his routine over the past several months. There was no reason for his increased alcohol intake, other than having been shot and now not allowed to do the one thing he was good at. No one had died. Despite being alone, he felt no lonelier than he did on any other day. There were women. There were always women. A random smattering of female cops, a couple of bartenders from around town, and a few one-night stands. But nothing serious. The ever-wise Detective Renquest, his partner on the task force, had told him for months to put himself out there. Find a girl and go on a proper date. So, he tried it. Turns out, he sucked at dating. *Put yourself out there. What a crock of shit*, he thought.

He glanced at the clock on his phone and realized he had thirty minutes until Daughtry arrived to pick him up. Still needing a shower and a shave, he picked the glass of bourbon off the table, poured its contents into the kitchen sink, and prepared a fresh pot of coffee. Only the machine didn't turn on. Dodge pushed the brew button again. Nothing. With one hand, he checked the outlet. He wiggled the plug. Still nothing.

"Well, shit," he mumbled. "I hope Daughtry remembers the coffee."

By the time Dodge finished showering and dressed, Airman Daughtry was waiting on the stoop outside his front door. The car double parked with its engine still running. Dodge opened the passenger door and slid into the seat.

"Sir," the airman said as he climbed behind the wheel.

A quick glance at Daughtry and Dodge thought he might have gotten even bigger overnight. Or maybe he was wearing a tighter shirt. His muscles bulged as the cuffs tried to choke his biceps. The man was a monster. Dodge placed the two files at his feet. "Morning, Daughtry."

"Where to first, sir?"

They needed information about Shannon Roberts' unit. And he knew where they might find it. "Where's the local army recruiting station?"

"All the branches, and those coast guard twinks, all share one big office now. They call it the Armed Forces Recruiting Station, and it's across town, inside the mall." Daughtry shot Dodge a puzzled look. "Why do you want to go there? I'm not sure how much help a recruiting sergeant can be to us. Those guys are a special kind of dumb," Daughtry said.

"Don't think about his rank or position. He is an enlisted soldier and must obey his superiors. Like say, a captain with his trusty sergeant. We just need a list of names. He should be able to locate that easily enough. If we're lucky, some of her old unit members will still be active duty or reserve. They should have assignments on file as well."

"The list of names alone could number into the thousands," Daughtry said. "Not to mention military retention rates are at an all-time low. Many of the men who served with her likely dropped out and disappeared into the civilian work force."

"True, but it's all we have for now. We can start by eliminating anyone under the rank of corporal. It's been a couple of years and anyone who served with her in a war zone worth their weight would be a corporal by now. Most of them are likely sergeants and higher, but we will start at the lower rank and work our way up."

The airman put the sedan in drive and inched away from the curb. Careening his head to look for traffic coming from behind. After he was sure it was safe to pull out, he pressed the accelerator and pushed out into the street, and the pair headed toward the opposite side of town.

Dodge predicted the drive would take no longer than twenty minutes, given the current time. Traffic was lighter than normal. A three-day weekend had a way of making some of the more annoying things about living in the city disappear. Even if only for a short while. Most residents relished the thought of holidays, if only for the ease of congestion.

A small white sign attached to the wall of the building read:

Reserved for Veterans. The Mid-Town Mall thanks you for your service.

Daughtry eased the nose of the sedan into the parking spot, stopping inches from the sign. The parking lot was empty except for the spots furthest from the building. The ones mall employees used so customers could have spots closer to the building.

Dodge checked the clock on his phone. It read 07:45. As he reached for the door handle, Airman Daughtry tossed something into his lap. He picked up the black bi-fold wallet, opening it and raised it to his eyes.

"I thought you might need those. They look authentic enough to get you past any civilian agency. But don't flash them at any official DoD facility. You'll have a real bad day."

The wallet held a military identification card. Complete with photo, be it an old one, name, rank and service branch. Wanting a better look, Dodge slid the ID from its case. A small piece of paper inserted behind the identification card fell into his lap. Lifting the slip of paper from his lap, he felt the rigid edges and slick texture between his fingers. It was a photograph. He flipped it over and the face in the picture stared up at him with haunting eyes.

"The Colonel also wanted you to know who you were doing this for," Daughtry said.

The woman in the photo held his gaze. Shannon Roberts was an attractive girl. Something about her appearance made her seem tall in the picture, even though the shot was only from the chest and head. Her shoulder-length brown hair pulled into a ponytail. A smile adorned her face. The photo pre-dated her attack. Dodge was sure of that. What happened to her changes a person. A casual smile is often the first thing to go. In his experience in dealing with victims of sexual assault, photos for months, and even years after the attacks, looked fake and the smiles forced. He understood why, and it was one thing that drove him in his search for justice.

He pushed the picture and identification card back into the slot they had come from in the wallet and shoved the whole thing into his pocket. He looked up at the entrance to the building.

"We will need to wait until 08:00 for the doors to be unlocked for the mall walkers."

Daughtry nodded. The two sat in silence until the clock on the car's radio signaled it was time.

"Are you sure there will be anyone here at this early hour?"

"The sergeant in charge of the office will be here. I had to interview him a couple of years ago concerning an ex-parolee who wanted to join the army. During the interview, he complained about being the only people in the building that early, except for morning walkers. He said sometimes they would work with new recruits on physical training and drill to get them ready for boot camp."

"I wouldn't imagine he is still here. Recruiting duty is usually a temporary gig. Maybe a couple of years."

"I'd say zero chances. But he made it seem like the policy was more of an order and less of a guideline. So, I expect we will find someone in the office."

The two men entered the mall through the front entrance, after waiting for the small line of elderly men and women attempting to ward off death by walking laps around the mall's interior to clear. Once inside, the pair headed toward the food court. The food being a central hub for the thrones of shoppers combing the aisles for clothes, jewelry, and other over-priced wares at various name brand stores. A prime location for the recruiting station.

The smell of fresh brewed coffee from the only kiosk open filled the air. The aroma from the grinding of the beans stirred a desire for more caffeine in Dodge, but the pair continued past to the Recruiting Center just on the other side.

Interior light from the fluorescent bulbs filtered out into the halls. A soldier in camouflage fatigues sat at a desk, sipping coffee and staring at a television on the wall. The screen featured an advertisement for the Navy and the Army soldier sat smiling, almost laughing, at the commercial. Airman Daughtry opened the door and Dodge pushed past and into the room.

The soldier's attention turned to the two men, and he stood to greet his visitors.

"What can I do for you gentlemen?" he asked. His lips curled up, a forced smile. To make it seem like being in the army was an auspicious time.

Dodge reached out his hand and the young soldier took it and shook.

"My name is Paul Dodge."

A booming voice from behind him said, "Captain Paul Dodge."

The sergeant looked at the man in front of him and quickly pulled his hand back. Snapping to attention and throwing up a formal salute.

A quick glance over his soldier revealed a grinning Daughtry. His impromptu bark just made clear who was going to be the good cop and who was to be the bad cop.

"Relax son. No need for all of that," Dodge said. He was a little uncomfortable with the remark about his rank. But he ignored it and moved forward.

"What can I help you with, sir?" the sergeant asked, motioning to a set of chairs in front of the desk.

Dodge sat. The advertisement on the television stole his attention for a moment. The sergeant noticed, then grabbed the remote and muted the sound.

"Squibs," he said. A smirk on his face.

Everyone but sailors hated sailors.

"I need some information on an army unit that was deployed to Afghanistan two years ago."

The sergeant scratched his head, leaned forward, inserted an access card into a little slot on the laptop's side, and his fingers stroked the keyboard. It took the computer less than twenty seconds to spit out results from the search. Those little boxes had their useful moments. The sergeant poked one more key, then a printer on the other side of the office roared to life. The machine shook, buzzed, and hummed. Once the noise died down, several sheets of paper slid out onto a side mounted tray. The sergeant didn't even get out of his chair. Choosing instead to push off the desk with his legs, vaulting himself and the chair toward the printer and returning the same way.

"Here you are, sir," he said.

Dodge took the pages, still warm from the printer. The first sheet was the obligatory Department of Defense cover sheet. A green piece of paper with the word "UNCLASSIFIED" emboldened on it. That word disclosed the information in the preceding pages posed no risk to national security. The second page summarized a brief history of Roberts' unit, the 201st Battlefield Surveillance Brigade. Headquartered at Joint Base Lewis-McChord, in Washington State.

Dodge skimmed the pages to look at the command staff's achievements. All seemed to be serious, professional soldiers. He skipped to the rear of the stack of papers, locating what he was searching for on the next-to-last page. A list of names of the unit's soldiers deployed to Afghanistan during the same period as Corporal Roberts. The list was shorter than he expected, twenty-five names at most. As he thought back, he remembered news outlets reporting Pentagon sources had begun the last reduction of force during the time her attack took place. The rumors being something like, one soldier deployed for every ten it had previously sent to the sandbox. Contractors comprised the bulk of remaining intelligence analysts deployed. The move saved the government millions in legacy costs. Most of the contractors were ex-military, allowing for the retention of capable analysts with field experience. Just someone else paid their salary, insurance, and travel expenses. A win-win for the government.

Dodge handed the sheet containing the names to Daughtry and tossed the rest in the bin marked for shredding at the corner of the sergeant's desk.

"Anything else I can help you with?"

Dodge had no other questions, so he thanked the sergeant, who threw up a half-hearted salute from his chair. The move infuriated Daughtry, who made a move toward the overly relaxed soldier, but Dodge shook off the play and tipped his head toward the door. The lowly sergeant didn't know how close he had come to being ground into powder. Besides, Dodge wasn't really an officer. The two men exited the same way they came in, retracing their steps back past the coffee kiosk, through the food court and out the doors to the parking lot.

The pair had gotten what they wanted. But the issue was going to be with the brass in Washington, DC. He knew they'd shut him down as soon as he started asking the right questions. If he was a betting man, the smart money would be in a week. Two at most. He would receive an early morning visit from a couple of military police officers with an idle threat to stand down. They would seize any files or papers he had gathered. They might even rough him up a little. Just to send a message. The military would do what it always did when it saw trouble brewing. Use force and cover it up.

"What's next?" Daughtry asked as the pair sat in the car. He started the engine so the air conditioner could fight the onset of the heat of the day. Eighty degrees at nine in the morning. It was going to be a hot one.

"Can I ask you something, Daughtry?"

"Yes, sir."

"What do you make of all this?"

"Not sure I follow you, sir?" Daughtry asked.

As he thought about Daughtry's question, Dodge wasn't even sure what he wanted. He had a feeling deep in the pit of his stomach that something wasn't right. That he was attacking from the wrong flank. The interaction in the recruiter's office had been too easy. The recruiting sergeant, too accommodating. It was as if he already knew they were coming. Bookmarked and indexed so he could get them out of the office as quickly as possible. Most people won't question motives for quickly filled requests. It's time that stirs the inquisitive mind.

"You feel like that was too easy?"

Daughtry nodded.

"You wanna go back in there?" Dodge asked.

The muscular airman smiled.

"I'll wait here," Dodge said as Daughtry exited the car and headed toward the mall's entrance.

Dodge reached into his pocket and pulled out a cigarette. The lighter lid made a familiar *click* as he flipped it open, and the flame danced as he took a deep drag; the end of the cigarette glowing a bright red. Not wanting to fill the car's interior with smoke, he was leaning against the front fender when Daughtry pushed through the front doors. His face was all business. As he approached the car, peered back over his shoulder toward the mall's entrance.

"So, what'd you find out?" Dodge asked.

"The whole thing was a setup."

"He knew we were coming?"

"That's an affirmative," Daughtry said.

"He got a call from some officer in Washington and was told to provide me with a list of names?" Dodge said, taking another drag from his cigarette. "But only certain names?"

"That would be correct," Daughtry said.

"So, we are missing at minimum one, but likely more names?"

"According to the sergeant, that would be correct."

Dodge took one last drag from his smoke, dropping the butt on the ground, smashing it under the sole of his shoe. The CYA, or cover your ass, maneuvering started sooner than he had expected. Someone knew Patterson had asked him for help and set him on the right path. He would need to know who that person was in the future so he could pay them a visit. But that was a fight for another time. His plan to get information from the army was now dead. By now, the Pentagon had surely flagged any name associated with the case. Any federal agency with access to Department of Defense records would be useless to him now. He needed to come at this investigation from a different angle. One that didn't involve the Feds.

Chapter 6

The sound of the tires rolling across the pavement hummed throughout the car's interior. Dodge stared at the list of names the recruiting sergeant provided him. All nice and neat. In alphabetical order. Ranks from private to lieutenant. None of them of any use. It was the names left off that he needed. And he had no way of getting those names now. If he wanted to find the person responsible for killing Shannon Roberts—he needed to focus on the end. The place where Roberts spent her last months. Texas. The army would have no sway over a large metropolitan police department. He could gather information about her shooting, then work backwards. If a link existed between her murder and the incident in Afghanistan, finding her killer would be the first step. He pulled his phone from his pocket and began searching the internet for any news related to the shooting in Dallas.

Dodge completed a cursory search for news articles from the Dallas area on his phone and turned up nothing, aside from the original story of the shooting. There had been no follow-up articles or press releases by the police since her murder. The local authorities were playing their cards close to their vests. Which also meant they had made very little progress. If there had been a break in the case, the police would have made a statement. His own task force had employed the same strategy on stalled cases. If he wanted to know what the police knew, he needed to speak to the detective in charge of the case. A charge ran through him. He had a plan.

Daughtry dropped Dodge off at his house, with strict instructions not to tell anyone where they were going. Keeping their trip to Dallas secret gained him valuable time. He imagined the list of names bought him a few days. Whomever was keeping tabs on his inquiries would monitor every federal facility within a two-hundred-mile radius of DC. Photos of him hanging in the records offices. Notes typed across the bottom, instructing staff to call if he showed up requesting information. But he wouldn't be making any requests. Not anywhere near the Pentagon, that is.

After a few days of radio silence, they would make one of two assumptions. The first being, when things got hard, Dodge gave up, tucked his tail, and ran. Concluding the favor he had promised his old friend was an impossible task. One he was ill-equipped to succeed at, so he simply gave up. The second, and more likely outcome, would involve net widening. Expanding the search. Throwing a larger net out and trolling to see what information they can collect and piece together. Scour all the federal databases looking for him. TSA could provide a passenger manifest for any flight. Airport security cameras would show him renting a car or even what taxi he slipped into. There was not much he could do about all of that. Big brother was everywhere, watching everything. He just needed a few days without having to look over his shoulder. Either way, they needed to get to Dallas as soon as possible.

Dodge stuffed an extra pair of pants, two shirts, some socks, and three pairs of underwear into a backpack. He folded the list of names the recruiter had given him and shoved it into a pocket on the front of the bag. Out of habit, he grabbed his task force identification and state parole badge, tucked them in his backpack on the off chance the Dallas police may be more likely to cooperate with a fellow officer. Professional courtesy, they called it. As he looked around the room for anything he might have forgotten, he decided not to pack his duty weapon. Passengers must follow TSA's rules and place their weapons in a locked, durable case in the cargo area. Dodge didn't have a hard case with a lock. Nor did he have the time to find a sporting goods store to purchase one. He would also need to fill out a federal form listing his state issued weapon on a manifest. The idea of a paper trail with his name linked to a weapon while traveling halfway across the country made him uncomfortable. Texas was a constitutional carry state and people were free to carry a handgun in the open or concealed without a permit. He could easily purchase a firearm at any pawn shop in Dallas, if he needed one.

After checking his wallet to make sure he had ample cash and his highest limit credit card; he called the airline and purchased an open-ended ticket from Richmond to Dallas. He could have had a non-stop flight if he flew out of DC, but the traffic on I-95 could be murder at this time of day. Richmond was a smaller airport and, while there would be a layover in Atlanta, the number of people flying out was significantly less than Regan National or Dulles. Eight hundred dollars later, he had a seat booked and had checked in online.

The next call was to a rental car company. He chose a full-size SUV. The cost was a little more, but in the land of big trucks and bigger egos, fitting in was more important than fuel economy. The lady on the other end of the line took his phone number. Then his address and payment information. Dodge declined the insurance, as he always did. He had never needed it before and just couldn't bring himself to pay for an event that may never happen. With the rental car reserved and plane ticket purchased, he only had one more thing to do.

The sun shone brightly, and the afternoon sun blazed down on his stoop. He sat on the top step—his carry-on bag resting between his legs, one step below him. Sweat beads formed on his forehead, racing each over his brow before dripping over his eyes. Daughtry was running late. The flight to Dallas left at seven-thirty and the drive to Richmond would take about an hour. A holiday weekend meant lines would be longer. The idea of being late caused an uptick in his anxiety. Even though he served for over ten years in the Air Force, he still wasn't particularly fond of flying. It wasn't a fear of heights. Or a fear of crashing. The fear came from why he was in the aircraft. Deployments and flag-draped coffins are what he remembers when boarding a plane. Memories he'd prefer to keep locked away.

The tires moaned as they scraped the curb. The passenger window rolled down and Daughtry waved his hand in a *hurry-up* motion, adding to his already festering frustration. Dodge tossed his bag in the backseat and slipped into the passenger seat. Once in the car, Daughtry pushed his foot on the accelerator. The tires chirped, pushing the car forward before making a right at the first intersection.

Traffic was steady, but still lighter than normal. Neither man spoke much the entire trip. Dodge found himself lost in his thoughts, finalizing his plans for the day's activities once on the ground in Dallas. Daughtry pulled into the parking garage, securing a spot on the third level. Dodge checked the time on his phone. The trip was quicker than expected, leaving the pair more than an hour before boarding. A rumble in his stomach reminded him he hadn't eaten since lunch and he needed sustenance.

The lines at security were heavy but moved efficiently. The pair passed through TSA security without incident. After slipping into his shoes and fetching his wallet from his bag once past the checkpoint, Dodge located their flight on the departures board. Their flight was on schedule with no delays. It appeared to be a good weather day for flying.

Daughtry grabbed a couple of sandwiches and two diet sodas from an airport magazine store they had passed on the way to the gate. Dodge scarfed down his meal, swallowing the last swig of his drink, as the attendant announced the flight was about to board. Daughtry stuffed half of his sandwich in his mouth, washed it down with a gulp of soda, then tossed the remaining bit into the trash. For a military lifer, waste was a part of the job. He knew there would always be more food supplied to him by his employer. Three squares a day, guaranteed.

Once on the plane, Dodge laid his head back and closed his eyes. He opened them twice during the trip. Once for the flight change in Atlanta and the other when the plane touched down in Dallas. Once the Boeing 737 came to rest and the flight attendants opened the cabin door, Dodge stood and pulled his backpack from the overhead compartment. He waited while the other passengers stretched and moaned. Older passengers waited for younger ones to help retrieve their bags. The whole de-boarding process was an exercise in patience. On his way out, Dodge nodded to the pilot.

"Thanks for Flying United," the young woman in a dark blue uniform said.

Dodge smiled, noticing the USAF lapel pin on her right collar. A sense of pride washed through him. Daughtry noticed and took it a step further, choosing to salute the woman who happily returned the gesture.

The pair made a quick stop at the restroom before boarding the rail train for the short ride to the main terminal. Ten minutes later, the two men headed for Downtown Dallas in the black SUV rental. Once off airport property, Dodge typed an address into the navigation system and, after a slight pause, a computerized voice broke from the speakers, saying the drive downtown would take thirty minutes.

"What's the plan once we get to the hotel?" Daughtry asked as he merged into the bustling interstate traffic.

"Get some dinner and a drink, followed by a good night's sleep so we can start fresh in the morning."

"I don't drink, sir."

"Bully for you," Dodge said with a smirk. "It's a good thing I drink enough for the both of us."

They made the rest of the drive to the hotel in relative silence. Dodge wanted to trust his new wingman, but something rubbed him the wrong way. Daughtry never had an idea or a suggestion. It was always *what's next*. A lot of servicemen were like that. A lifetime of taking orders instead of giving them. Or maybe his new partner wasn't the sharpest tack in the drawer. The military wasn't like a Fortune 500 company recruiting the best and brightest. They did that, but to be an effective fighting force, you need people to run into fire without hesitation. Brave people. An effective military also needs slow-witted folks to do the grunt work. Maybe that's the category Daughtry fell into. Point him in a direction and bark an order. He'll follow it loyally. Until Dodge could determine which category the airman fell into, he'd continue to play his cards close to his vest.

Once at the hotel, Dodge pulled his bag from the back seat and pushed through the rotating glass doors into the lobby. The floor was an intricate design made from enormous diamond shaped tiles laid end to end. All pointing to a center piece noting the hotel's name and brand. Paintings of cityscapes from around the world hung on the walls. Some of them Dodge recognized, and some he didn't. After taking in the luxurious surroundings, he spotted the front desk and made his way to the counter. As he finished checking in, Daughtry sidled up next to him at the counter after finding a parking spot in a garage just down the street. Once the airman completed the same check-in routine, the two men dropped their bags in their connected rooms, washed up, and made their way back to the lobby.

Not only was the hotel elegant in design but, according to a sign next to the concierge desk, its restaurant maintained a reputation for serving the best filets in Dallas. Dodge didn't have a frame of reference, as he had never been to Dallas, but he had eaten plenty of good steaks. As far as this one was concerned, it was better than most, but not the best piece of meat he had ever had. He finished his second Blantons and said goodnight to Daughtry, who said he wanted to catch the end of the Reds game on TV.

Dodge took the elevator up to his room on the fourth floor of the Weston Downtown. The hotel had a keyless entry system, meaning he could use the hotel chain's mobile application to unlock the door to his room. He wasn't a fan of the technology, but he also wouldn't lose his key. Technology would continue its march into the dystopian future despite his personal opinions on the matter. His cell phone hovered over the pad above the door handle and soon he heard a click and a tiny red light changed from red to green. He opened the door, stripped off his clothes and climbed into the king-sized bed. He pulled the thick down bedspread up to his chest, only to overheat, kicking it to the foot of the bed. The hotel had the thermostat set to sixty-eight degrees, but the oppressive summer-like heat pushed the unit hard for every breath of cold air.

As he lay in bed, fighting off night sweats, the glow from the television created a ghostly effect in the room. The volume turned down low enough to be white noise, but not loud enough to keep him from falling asleep. Rolling to his side, he stared at the clock face. Its red numbers burned the time into his retinas. He rolled back over. Took several deep breaths and closed his eyes. He felt himself drifting off. Peaceful. Then a loud knock on the door wrestled him from his slumber.

Chapter 7

The morning sun shone through the gap in the curtain, piercing his eyelids. He stumbled, throwing his legs over the edge of the bed, trying to gain his balance. Then he hastily searched the floor for the pants he shed the night before, only to trip over them. Falling headfirst onto the bedside table.

"God damn it!" he said as he lay between the bed and the wall. His hand gently feeling his head for any signs of blood. "Hold your fucking horses. I'm coming already."

Once untangled from his pants, he slipped them up over his waist and zipped them up. He glanced around the room for something to throw over his bare chest. Spotting a t-shirt draped over the back of a chair, he slid it over his head before making his way to the door. Normally steeped in cautiousness, he didn't use the peephole because he had told no one where he was. His left hand flipped the safety latch and his right hand pushed down on the handle, pulling the door open. He let out a sigh. It was Daughtry.

"What in God's name are you doing beating on my door?"

"It's zero seven hundred, sir."

"So..."

"We need to get breakfast and rendezvous at police headquarters. The record department opens at zero eight hundred."

As Dodge shut the door, he said, "I'm going to take a shower and if you knock on that door again, we'll finish what we started in the bar the other night. And I'm not drunk this time."

After a hot shower and a shave, Dodge dressed in a pair of brown khakis and a button-down shirt, hung in the bathroom to let the steam release any packing wrinkles. A quick exhale into a cupped hand reminded him to brush his teeth again. Tossing the wet toothbrush on the vanity, he stopped in the bedroom to put on his boots. Then he opened the door to find Daughtry standing in the same position as ten minutes earlier. There was a look of annoyance painted on his face. But each hand gripped a cup of steaming hot coffee. Dodge reached out and took one, then closed the door behind him.

The elevator hummed. Lights blinked across a row of descending numbers above the door as the two men descended to the lobby. A burst of air filled with the scents of bacon and maple syrup rushed into the elevator as the doors opened. Dodge's stomach rumbled in protest. He exited the elevator and headed for the street. Daughtry followed closely behind. When they stepped through the doors and into the open air, it felt as if they had walked into a sauna. It was like being punched in the chest. The humidity and heat were almost unbearable, even at eight in the morning. Sweat beads instantly formed on his back, causing his shirt to cling to his skin.

"Sir, where are we going to eat?"

A quick glance in both directions and he soon saw what he was looking for. He pointed to a food truck a block east on the opposite side of the street. The men double timed it across the street during a brief opening in the morning traffic. As they approached the truck, and the small line of people already waiting to place an order, the aroma of Mexican spices wafted around them. The line moved quickly and before long; it was their turn to order.

"A breakfast burrito, no tomatoes, please. And a black coffee."

"Same," Daughtry harped from behind Dodge.

Within a few minutes, the man inside the truck placed a tray on the ledge and waved his hand at the two men. Daughtry grabbed the tray, carrying it over to a nearby bench. Each man ate his burrito and sipped coffee, not taking time to speak.

Dodge swallowed the last bite of his burrito, then crumpled the wrapper before tossing it in a trashcan nearby. Then he took one last gulp of coffee before pitching it next to the burrito wrapper. Daughtry did the same.

Dodge brushed some food crumbs from his chest before asking Daughtry, "Did you find the address to the police department?"

The airman dug into his front pocket and pulled out his phone. His fingers swiped the screen a few times, then he flipped the phone in his hand so the screen was facing Dodge.

"It's on the corner of Cockrell Avenue and Bellview Street," he said. "Less than a mile away."

Dodge looked around. He wondered if it would be worth it to retrieve the rental car from the garage or if hailing a taxi might be easier. The taxi would certainly be quicker. He saw several pulling into the portico of the hotel in the short time they had been standing outside. Walking a mile in the Dallas sun, even that early in the morning, was out of the question. The two men would resemble drowned rats by the time they arrived. Daughtry must have read his mind, because he stepped off the curb and shoved his hand out into the air just as a yellow sedan approached.

The driver hit the brakes hard, causing the nose of the car to dip toward the pavement as he pointed the tires toward the curb. Daughtry had to leap back up on the curb to keep the car's front bumper from plowing into his legs. The car came to rest and Daughtry opened the door. The pair slid into the back seat.

"Fourteen hundred Botham Jean Boulevard," Daughtry shouted over the Middle-Eastern music pulsating from the car's speakers.

With a push of a red button, the fare meter reset to three dollars and began its upward journey. The driver pulled out into traffic without a single glance over his shoulder, almost clipping another car, then made a left on South Griffin Street. They traveled through a tunnel under the Dallas Convention center and past Interstate 30. Next was a right on Wall Street, followed by a quick left on Bellview. Dodge noticed a man on the curb flailing his outstretched arm, trying to gain the driver's attention. The car lurched toward the curb and stopped directly in front of the waiting fare. Dodge slipped the driver a ten, then exited onto the sidewalk. He barely had time to close the door before the car jerked out into traffic, disappearing as it turned at the next intersection.

Police Headquarters resembled most city government buildings built in the late twentieth century. A brick façade and lots of windows to let in natural light. High summer temperatures caused many western states to issue rolling brownouts. He had always wondered if it was more important to pay for lights or endure the brownouts. He pushed the thoughts of eco-friendly architecture aside and waved his hand for Daughtry to follow him.

Security personnel stood ready to greet the two men as they pushed through the revolving door. The first guard waved the men over and pointed to a pedestal sign, which instructed visitors, in English and Spanish, to remove all objects from their pockets and place them in a bin on the table. The two men followed the sign's prompts, emptied their pocket contents into a plastic bin. Then, one by one, stepped through the arch of the metal detector. An alarm buzzed as Dodge passed through the magnetometer and he had to be wanded by hand because of a metal pin in his leg from a parachuting accident. Satisfied with his explanation after lifting his pants leg to reveal a jagged scar running down the side of his knee, the second guard waved them past. A large electronic board provided the floor and room number for each department. Homicide was on the second floor. Room 200.

An escalator took the pair to the second floor and a large sign with an arrow directed them to a small waiting room. An officer sitting at a desk behind a plexiglass barrier was talking on the phone as the two men approached.

After hanging up the phone, the lean young man with a military style buzz cut looked up. "Can I help you?"

Dodge nodded to Daughtry, who stepped up to the glass and pressed his identification against the glass. The glass clanked as the metal badge touched the window. The officer's eyes widened as he focused on the bulky man standing before him. After giving the identification a thorough examination, he put down his pen and leaned back in his chair.

"What can I do for the military police today?"

Dodge leaned closer to the round speaker inserted in the center of the pane. "We need to speak to the detective assigned to the case concerning the murder of Corporal Shannon Roberts."

The officer perked up. "The sniper victim," he said. "That would be Detective Alder. I'll let him know you are here. He's been trying to reach someone from the military but keeps getting the runaround."

"Well, I suppose he'll want to talk to us then," Dodge said.

"Let me see if he is busy."

The officer spun to face the computer monitor and began typing. He then stared at the screen—his fingers tapping a beat from inside his head. He pushed a few more keys, then looked back up.

"I've told Detective Alder you are here and he will be with you shortly. He asked that I have you wait in the conference room."

The officer felt under the desk, then a buzz and click came from the door to the men's left. Dodge pushed through, and the officer led them down a short hallway to a large conference room on the right.

"Have a seat and Detective Alder will be here shortly. Can I get you anything to drink?"

Both men shook their heads.

"Alright then, just step out and holler if you need anything. My name is Officer Conrad."

Dodge said, "Thanks," and pulled out the middle chair from the wooden table and settled in for a wait. Daughtry remained standing.

Dodge rested his elbows on the table's edge. His fingers caressing the morning stubble covering his chin. After a moment, he turned to Daughtry. "When we were standing in the lobby, the desk officer told us the detective in overseeing of Robert's case had been trying to contact anyone from the military for help."

"He did," Daughtry said.

"Which implies he hasn't spoken to anyone from the Pentagon regarding Roberts' murder."

"We don't know what, Detective… what was his name?"

"Alder," Dodge said.

Daughtry nodded. "We don't know what Detective Alder has or hasn't done. But it appears he may have had trouble getting through the switchboard red tape in DC."

Dodge leaned back, shaking his head. "That's not what he said. He said the detective had been trying to reach *someone* from the military. As if he had spoken to a particular person and couldn't reach them again." Dodge paused so what he said could sink in before continuing. "And didn't Patterson say he called and spoke to whoever the lead detective down here was? And if he reached out, I'll bet my left nut he dropped his rank into the conversation."

Daughtry stood silent as a tree.

Dodge felt a tingle on the back of his neck. He knew if Patterson had made any inquiries to the police, the airman would've known. Hell, it was likely Daughtry would have dialed the number. Patterson would've leveraged anything he could to get answers. Colonel would've been the first word out of his mouth. Dodge knew because he'd done it too many times to count himself.

Daughtry's continued silence on the matter spoke volumes and annoyed Dodge. He didn't like being kept out of the loop. And he hated being lied to.

"Well, did Patterson place a call to the Dallas Police Department and speak to a detective? Did he speak to anyone?"

"It's Colonel Patterson," the large airman snipped.

"He's not in the Air Force anymore, which means I can call him anything I damn well please. I've earned that right. I gave over ten years of my life to that place. Two tours in Iraq and one in Afghanistan, and I have the scars to prove it. So, you can shove that shit right up yours and his ass."

Before Daughtry could get any words out, a voice spoke up from behind them.

"I hope I'm not interrupting anything."

Both men turned to see a tall, portly man standing in the doorway. He looked to be about six foot two. He wore a dark blue suit, which was too small for his frame. His brown hair had a spattering of gray, as did the stubble on his face. Dodge guessed the man to be in his early forties and considered him a handsome man. There was an air of confidence surrounding him. He stepped into the room with an outstretched hand.

"I'm Detective Alder, Dallas Homicide."

Dodge took his hand. "I'm Paul Dodge. And this is Airman Daughtry," he said, tipping his head toward the burly man beside him.

"Sir," the airman said.

"Now that we all know each other, let's get this show on the road." The Detective gestured toward the table. "I've got to tell you—I felt I would never get to speak to anyone with the Army about this. Every call I made, I ended up transferred to someone else or referred to Army CID, who kept saying this was a civilian matter."

CID was the Army's criminal investigations division. Dodge had partnered with some CID agents on cross jurisdictional cases while in the Air Force. Most he knew were capable investigators, but jurisdiction confined staff to army matters only. CID would not assign their investigators to the case unless Roberts' death had any connection to her service, national security, or army personnel. Dodge understood the detective's frustrations and had questions of his own but knew, to get cooperation, it was best to let Alder take the lead. He felt bad about pretending it was he who was there to assist. It was deceptive, but if he could get a look at the file, it would help a ton.

"Anything we can do to help," Dodge said.

The detective circled the table, pulled out a chair, and sat opposite the pair. Reaching into his pocket, he pulled out a small notebook. Dodge recognized it instantly. Standard equipment at any police academy. One of two required items a recruit is to always have on their person during training. A metal ball-point pen and a pocket sized non-spiral notebook.

Alder opened the notepad, flipped through several pages, stopping when he reached a blank sheet and wrote something at the top. Then he looked up at Dodge.

"Paul Dodge, was it? What is your role in all of this?"

"Dodge is fine."

Alder scribbled in his notepad. "What can you tell me about Shannon Roberts?"

Dodge peered over at Daughtry, who appeared ultra focused on their host. He dipped his head in an approving manner.

"Shannon Roberts was a corporal in the US Army until a few years ago. After her separation, she moved to Dallas, finding work as a contractor on a

DoD special project. Someone shot and killed her a week ago. That's what we know."

"What can you tell me about her work here in Dallas?"

"I'm afraid I can't tell you much. However, she worked as an Intelligence Analyst for a private contractor."

"Can you tell me anything about her employer?"

"That's classified," Daughtry said.

Detective Alder tossed his pad and pen on the desk. Leaned back into his chair. His hands tossed up in disgust. "You Pentagon people are unbelievable. I have a dead woman here. No clues on why she is dead. Less on who might have shot her. When I ask for help, it's classified this and classified that. Throw me a damn bone here, would ya?"

Dodge and Daughtry shared a glance. They needed to be careful, constrained by laws governing the release of classified information. They could find themselves in serious legal trouble for saying too much, even if it could help solve a murder.

Dodge leaned forward, cupping his hands before laying them on the desk. "Roberts was no longer in the military. She was a private contractor working on a Department of Defense project concerning national security. I can't get into specifics about her duties but, I can tell you, her murder and employment appear unrelated."

"While I appreciate your professional opinion, I would prefer to determine that for myself." The detective's tone revealed his agitation.

Dodge let out a long breath. "I can pass along your concerns to see where it leads, but I wouldn't hold my breath."

Detective Alder shook his head again and stood from his chair.

"Well, I suppose this meeting is over."

Dodge stood, followed by Daughtry. It wasn't the best time to ask, but he wasn't sure if it ever would be. "I have a few questions. About the murder, if you have a few more minutes."

Detective Alder's eyes gleamed with annoyance. Dodge knew the look well. He needed to change tactics.

"Look. I'm a badge back home. Same as you. I was called by a friend and asked to look into the death of his niece. I'm not here to step on your toes and I won't get in your way. We are just looking for some answers. DOD can be a tight-lipped organization but, officially, I don't work for them. I'm here of my volition. I promise to share anything that may help you catch her killer."

The detective said nothing, trying to get a read on Dodge. Finally, he pulled the chair out and nestled up next to the table.

"Well, shit. Ask your questions."

"Thank you," Dodge said, returning to his chair. "Let's start at the beginning."

"Okay."

"Where did the shooting take place?"

"A walker stumbled upon her body along the edge of a trail at White Rock Lake."

"Any idea of why she was there?"

"It's a park with a walking trail that circles the entire lake. A pretty popular place with the locals. Though the west side of the lake where they found her is a little less popular. Joggers mainly use that side of the park, and there are some homeless folks who've claimed a few of the benches as their personal property. The eastern shore is home to the arboretum, medical offices, and a hospital."

"You mentioned some homeless people sleep in the park. Anyone come forward claiming to have heard the shot?"

"No one to this point. I've assigned some units to cruise through in the evenings to get some names, but those folks get a little skittish. They usually bolt at the sight of a black and white pulling into the parking lot."

"Makes sense," Dodge said.

"But there was another victim."

Dodge turned to see Daughtry's eyes dart away. "So, there were two people shot that day?"

"Yes," Adler said.

The veteran agent's eyes narrowed before turning his attention back to the detective. "If there were two vics, what makes you think Roberts was the intended target?"

The detective's face carried a blank expression. Then he said matter-of-factly, "Because she's the dead one."

The answer astonished Dodge. Based on what he knew of Roberts' attack in the sandbox, it never occurred to him someone else could have been the target. A second victim meant there was a possibility her murder was collateral damage. Just someone in the wrong place at the wrong time. He would need to see the coroner's reports along with any evidence the Dallas Police Department had gathered from the scene. He needed to see the spot where the shooting took place for himself. Walking the scene in person, even days or weeks after the murder, could still provide a better understanding of what happened. Pictures are a great tool for jogging a memory, but nothing takes the place of being at the crime scene. Walking in the footsteps of the deceased. Breathing the same air. He would've preferred to go around the same time the incident took place. But time was a factor.

"Is there anything you can tell us that may provide a better understanding of what happened that night?"

"I can give you a summary of what I've pieced together so far. But the actual reports are off limits until I get some cooperation from y'all."

Dodge knew the offer was the best deal he was going to get. At least for now. He stood and shook the detective's hand.

"Thank you," Dodge said. "I'll forward your request to the powers that be. Airman Daughtry will keep you in the loop. Anything we know, you will know."

He had little to offer and hoped his words would buy a little goodwill. He maintained eye contact as the veteran detective stared back at him, his eyes filled with skepticism. Finally, a nod.

"I'll get the case file," Alder said.

Dodge watched his Dallas counterpart exit the room then turned to Daughtry, who was still standing in silence, and shook his head in disbelief. The hesitancy to trust new people was something he understood well. It's built through years of working in a career where everyone, even those you work with have secrets, and covering your own ass is a way of life.

"I didn't know if that would work," Dodge said.

"What will you do when we have information we can't share with civilians?" Daughtry asked.

"That's a future Dodge problem. Right now, I need to get as much information as I can. And if not being completely truthful gets me what I need, then so be it."

Daughtry shook his head. "You should have stayed in the air force. You'd fit right in with the other officers."

Before Dodge could respond, Alder returned, a file folder cradled in his left hand. As he sat, he removed a piece of paper and slid it across the table in Dodge's direction. Dodge pulled the paper toward him, then carefully scanned its contents. The details were vague. A brief description of the location the shooting took place and a list of evidence gathered from the crime scene and surrounding area. The detective then slid another piece of paper across the desk. A summary of the coroner's report. It contained very little information. Listing the cause of death as a gunshot wound to the head. Not much to build an investigation on, but it was about all the sharing the Dallas PD was going to do for the time being.

Dodge thanked Alder, then he and Daughtry exited down the same hall they entered through an hour earlier. Once the two men pushed through the front doors and were out of earshot of a couple of employees smoking and talking by the building's entrance, Dodge turned to Daughtry.

"We need to go to that park and see the scene for ourselves."

"A lot of time has passed since the shooting. Not much of a chance we find anything, sir," the airman said.

"I'm not looking for shell casings or discarded cigarette butts."

"Then why go?"

"I need to see the scene, to stand where she stood. I want to see what she saw in the last moments of her life. It will help us get a better idea of where the shot came from. I'd like to know how far away the shooter set up."

"How will that help us figure out who the shooter was?" Daughtry asked.

"The report, if that's what you could call it, said the weapon was likely a rifle. Making this a professional hit. Muggers use pistols and knives, not high-powered rifles. And they do their work up close, not from fifty yards away. The fact the killer used a rifle means the shooter was a professional."

"This is Texas, sir," Daughtry said, almost laughing. "There are more guns here than people. I bet there are a thousand people who could make that shot in Dallas alone."

"Maybe," Dodge said, scratching his head. "But only one of them had a reason to be at that park, on that day, with a rifle pointed at Roberts."

"Or the other victim."

Dodge nodded. He looked at the piece of paper Detective Alder had given him. The only mention of the other victim was his name and address. He had survived and Dodge needed to speak with him.

Chapter 8

After leaving Police Headquarters, the two men split up. Daughtry said he needed to return to the hotel so he could report what they had learned to Patterson. The idea of daily progress briefings never appealed to Dodge. He preferred to brief when he discovered something of importance, or needed muscle only the brass could provide to help move the investigation forward. But he understood Daughtry's situation and stuffed it in his pocket to be dealt with later. It wasn't like they discovered some unknown secret. The only extra detail learned involved the second victim. Information, he assumed, Patterson already knew. Instead, he wanted to pay a visit to the crime scene. With temperatures still rising, and sure to be in the nineties by afternoon, now was as good as a time as any.

The park the shooting took place in was a thirty-minute drive North-East from downtown. According to Google, it was called The White Rock Lake Recreation area. After hailing a cab, the taxi driver took the I-30 Expressway to Garland Road. Garland was a four-lane thoroughfare that cut diagonally across the city and was littered with stoplights. After twenty minutes of stop-and-go traffic, the driver turned into the entrance of the park. Dodge slipped out of the back seat and handed the man thirty dollars.

"Keep the change," he said, before shutting the door and watching the car disappear into the mass of vehicles heading back downtown.

Dodge studied his surroundings. He saw only one entrance, at least from where he stood. The Parking lot looked to have the capacity for fifty to seventy-five vehicles. Near the edge of the parking area a small building stood, its paint chipped and weathered. A faded sign hung over the door, inviting visitors to use the facilities and purchase snacks and refreshments before venturing deeper into the park's interior. A piece of paper in the window read, FREE MAPS INSIDE. Cold air hit his face as he opened the door. Perched on a stool behind a cash register, just inside the front door, was an old man. Dodge grabbed a free pamphlet from a rack on the counter next to where the old man sat. He nodded and stepped back outside. Unfolding the map, he located the area where the shooting took place according to the report Alder gave him. Then stuffed the map in his back pocket. Then he made his way to the trailhead, which followed the edge of the lake north to an area named **T and P Hill**.

The trail hugged the shoreline of White Rock Lake for half a mile, then zigged back inland past another parking area and a small outbuilding that rented kayaks and paddle boards, fifteen dollars for an hour. Dodge imagined, even in his out of shape state, he could have paddled across the entire lake in about ten minutes. Figure in twelve to thirteen minutes for the return trip, because of fatigue, and the whole adventure would take less than half an hour. He wondered if most people would turn in the equipment once back from the other side, allowing the rental office to have a quick turnaround on the rental. Though it didn't seem like a shortage of rental equipment was an issue, at least not that morning.

Dodge was a little shocked to notice a lack of people, even on a weekday morning. In Virginia, people stuffed every open grassy space with yoga mats and soccer balls as soon as the sun came up. Back home, the paved paths, complete with a yellow dividing line, filled up every morning with walkers, joggers and cyclists. His assumption that the same rules would apply in Dallas was wrong. The one factor he hadn't figured in was the oppressive summer heat blanketing the park, even in the morning. He pulled the phone from his pocket and glanced at the numbers on the screen. It read 10:30 am, and his shirt, wet from sweat, was already stuck in the small of his back. He wiped the moisture forming on his brow and continued to follow the path until the road forked. One path continuing along the lake shore and a second winding back into the center of the park.

According to the map he lifted from the visitor's center, the trail he needed to take veered to the right, crossing over a wooden bridge before reaching the area where another visitor found Roberts' body. As he reached the other side of the tattered wooden bridge, he noticed a hill. A notation on the map billed it as the highest point in the park, but it wasn't much of a hill. It was more of a mound bounded by the trail, which snaked its way along the shoreline at the base of the slope. First he made the short walk up the back side of the hill, which, as advertised, provided a complete view of the surrounding area. The only obstruction came from a small, oblong white building that housed a set of restrooms and a drinking fountain.

Reaching into his front pocket, Dodge pulled out the sheet of paper Detective Alder had provided him with earlier that morning containing details of the murder and scene. There was no map of the crime scene, but in the section that outlined the steps taken in recovering the body, two numbers, 32.826644, -96.728923, showed. GPS coordinates. With a few taps on his cell phone screen, a point showed on a map. He looked twenty yards to his northeast, at a point on the edge of the lake. He studied the area for a moment, then trekked down the hill, his attention focused on his phone until the numbers on the screen closely matched the ones in Detective Alder's report.

As he stood on the spot and gazed across the lake, he couldn't help but notice the location lacked anything special. It appeared to be no different from a dozen spots he passed along the lake's edge since leaving the entrance to the park. He wasn't sure what he expected to find, but hardly anything struck him as strange or significant about the ground beneath his feet or the area surrounding him. The obvious lone exception being a woman lay dead a few weeks ago where he currently stood.

He wondered how many of the walkers, joggers and picnickers who passed the spot every day even knew what happened there. Did they stop and stare? Did some of them pass by with a side eye glance, moving quicker until far enough away to quell the uneasy feeling associated with a place someone had died? He could feel a slight tingle rise through his spine and the woo-woo hairs on the back of his neck twitched as he stared at the patch of grass where Roberts fell. He could imagine her body, limp, blood oozing from a gunshot wound to the head. It was a strange feeling. The same uncomfortableness when one stood on a grave. He took a step to the side.

He spun to look back at the hill behind him and then turned back to face the lake. The one-page report in his hand didn't contain many details about the gunshot wound, other than it was a 7.62 mm round which entered the victim's skull above the bridge of the nose, exiting in the back and severing the brainstem. Lights out. Shannon Roberts' head was in *good* condition for having a piece of lead slam into it, traveling at over two-thousand feet per second. It was a long shot and didn't come from behind him. The hill was too close. A rifle round at that close would have disintegrated her head.

Turning to his south, he could see the parking lot and the white buildings making up the boathouse. The buildings could provide cover for a shooter, but the trajectory of the bullet through the victim's skull meant the shot came from a higher point than where he stood. The boathouse was a short, one-story building with a flat roof. Not over ten feet off the ground. From that distance, a shot would have been almost straight on. And the adjacent parking lot meant cars and people. Detective Alder said they received no reports from the public concerning gunfire. Even with a silencer or a suppressor, anyone within fifty yards would hear the shot. He quickly ruled out the park as the shot's origin.

He faced north. The park narrowed to a small strip of land bordered by the lake and a housing addition. A thick growth of trees separated the housing edition from the park. He could see the chimneys and roofs of the massive homes darting out above the treetops. All lined up one after another. Not over six or seven feet between each house. A terrible spot for a shooter to fire from and remain unnoticed. He ruled out the surrounding housing additions.

He then turned and gazed across the lake. The shot could have only been fired from one direction. The killer was on an elevated surface on the other side of the lake. As he gazed across the water in front of him, he could make out shapes on the other side. Some looked like small buildings. Others glinted from the sunshine reflecting off the surfaces. *Cars in a parking lot,* he thought.

Scanning the opposite shore from right to left, he saw office buildings and what looked like a park or garden area. It must have been the botanical area Alder spoke about. The trees were all small. Shrubs from what he could tell from that distance. He pulled his phone out. Clicked the camera icon, then zoomed in to the maximum setting. It wasn't as effective as a scope, but he could see people walking. What he didn't see was anything big enough to conceal a shooter with a long rifle, providing enough elevation to allow for the angle of the shot that killed Roberts. Doubt crept in about the theory he had just developed. Looking north of the arboretum, he noticed a building. It was taller than everything surrounding it. Dodge swung the phone and let the camera focus on the structure. He counted the windows from top to bottom. One. Two. Three. Four. Five. Five stories tall. It was easily a half-mile away from where he stood to the opposite shore. The gravel crunched under his feet as he turned and looked back at the hill behind him. Then at the ground beneath his shoes. Hell of a shot, but he knew over a dozen men, including himself, capable of making it.

The walk around the shoreline took about half an hour. A mile in total. It had warmed several degrees, so he took long strides and tried to keep to a pace that wouldn't have him looking like a drowned rat by the time he reached the opposite shore. When he arrived, he looked up at the tan building before him. There were six indoor floors in all. He couldn't see the main floor from his position across the lake. He increased the count by one, as the building had a roof. And all roofs have access points for maintenance of heating and cooling systems mounted on top of the building. That put the roof at nearly seventy feet from street level. Plenty high enough for a shooting perch. He had only one problem. A sign, emboldened with large red letters hung from the roofline read, ***Dallas Regional Hospital.***

Not a place he would have chosen. A public hospital for a kill shot? It seemed like such a high risk. Hospitals buzzed with people at all hours of the night and day. And how do you get a weapon in without being noticed? A weapon broken down into three parts, the buttstock, the receiver and a barrel, would still require a large case inconspicuous enough to not draw the attention of security. Something, say, like a guitar case. That might work.

He had read articles about people playing music for sick children and elderly patients to raise morale. No reason to not think the same thing wouldn't be prevalent at a normal hospital. There was likely a children's wing and an Alzheimer's, or dementia, wing as well.

He dialed Daughtry.

"What are you doing right now?"

The airman sounded as if he had recently awakened from a nap. His voice, graveled and strained. "Waiting for you to get back."

"You finish the call with Patterson?" Dodge asked.

"Over an hour ago, sir."

"Good. I need you to bring the rental over to Dallas Regional Hospital. It's off Garland Road and North Ruckner Boulevard."

"Are you ok?"

"I'm fine. I just went for a little walk," Dodge said, then rang off.

The trip to the hospital from the hotel would take Daughtry half an hour, minimum. Dodge used the time to walk the perimeter of the hospital, starting at the main entrance. He peered through the large sliding entrance doors. No security station. No metal detectors. Only a woman, most likely a senior citizen volunteer, manning a desk just inside and to the right of the doors. Her job was to greet visitors and provide directions to the elevators and patients' rooms. He imagined a normal-looking person, without a rifle, would easily blend in and gain access to the interior. But getting inside the building was just the beginning. They would still need to locate the stairwell with roof access, then navigate to the top unnoticed. He had seen no signs of a roof helipad, which meant the access door might have an alarm to keep wandering patients from gaining access and falling or jumping off the roofs. The idea of walking through the front door seemed too risky, and he was souring on the theory.

Walking counterclockwise from the main entrance, he noticed three large bay doors set back into the side of the building's exterior. Service bays that provided access to all the different vendors needed to maintain a hospital's functionality. Food trucks supplying fresh produce for the cafeteria and box trucks carrying laundered uniforms for the staff and hauling away dirty linens. Two dumpsters occupied a space the size of two large pickup trucks parked bumper to bumper. An operation this size must produce a ton of trash daily. He imagined it would take multiple trucks, picking up and dropping off new trash bins daily, just to keep up with the mountains of waste. City trash works on a schedule. One or two service days a week. The hospital would most certainly have to contract a private company that provided service daily. The dumpsters sat next to a concrete wall, maybe eight-foot high. However, a gap existed between the trash bins and the wall to allow the trucks to load the full containers and deliver empty ones. The space was plenty big enough for someone to squeeze into, away from prying eyes. Trash has a pungent odor and people shy away from things that smell bad. A bad guy could wait until night and sneak in through the loading dock, posing as one of the multitude of laborers needed to keep the hospital supplied and operating efficiently.

After taking a few mental notes of the service bays, Dodge continued his recon of the building's perimeter. A side entrance for employees, requiring a badge or ID scanner to unlock the door. Not impossible to beat but, tailgating, following an employee through after they scanned their badge, was a risky move. Having anything on their person deviating from the usual items nurses or doctors carry, like a guitar case, could stand out in someone's memory. Not something a murderer would want. He quickly ruled out anyone trying to use the employee's entrance to gain access to the roof.

The north side, which was also the last side, comprised a hodgepodge of short walls, service sheds, and a few more electronic doors. The front of one door had a sign that read, COMMUNICATIONS ROOM. Another had the words, FIRE SERVICE PANEL, painted in red across its white face. He scanned the rest of the wall, then he saw it. A ladder bolted to the side of the building, extending to the roof. The bottom of the ladder was about six feet off the ground, but he could make out a rope tied to the last rung. A firm tug of the rope released a latch and an extension would slide down, its legs stopping inches short of the ground. A quick ascension up the rungs unseen and the shooter would have an unobstructed view of the park's shoreline.

A vibration in his pocket broke his concentration. Daughtry was waiting by the front entrance. Dodge took one last look at the ladder and the surrounding area. He needed to get up to the roof to be sure that was where the shot came from. Given his belief the shooter was a professional, he had little hope of discovering any spent shell casings. He would return when the hospital was less busy to test his theory.

Chapter 9

Energized by the progress made in a short period, Dodge filled Daughtry in on the drive back to the hotel.

"To have an advantage, a skilled sniper would choose to position themselves on an elevated shooting platform," explained the airman. Then, with the afternoon rush hour gradually easing in, he turned his attention back to maneuvering the large SUV through the busy streets.

"It's what I would have done," Dodge said.

"So, what's next?"

Dodge stared out the window at the other cars. Their occupants locked into their own little worlds. A protective bubble of glass, plastic and steel separating them from the outside world. Some talked on the phone. Others sang along with the radio. One driver, a middle-aged man, was slamming the palms of his hands against the steering wheel of his sedan. The corners of his mouth turned down, forcing what Dodge imagined was a permanent frown. Their eyes met for a moment. He could see the rage burning in his eyes. His anger tattooed across his face. That look. It reminded him not everyone needed a reason to kill. Sometimes the daily chaos of life is enough to push someone over the edge. The world has changed a lot over the past fifty years. But murder, that never changed. Money, greed, power and revenge were the fuel that stoked a killer's fire.

Daughtry's question was a good one. What was he going to do next? He had every intention of honoring his word to Detective Alder. However, before he said anything, he needed to make sure his theory wasn't just that— a theory. There was no sense in leading everyone down a rabbit hole unless he was sure the shooter fired the fatal round from atop the hospital. Once the police were sure, a quick scouring of employee records for anyone on duty the day of Roberts' murder might turn up someone who saw or heard something unusual. They could dig through surveillance footage to see if anyone was lurking around the outside of the hospital. Especially the loading dock area where the ladder leads to the roof. It was a long shot, but it was more than they had right now.

"I'm going to go back to the hospital tomorrow. I want to get up on the roof to see if our shooter left anything behind that would definitely place him on that roof the day of Roberts' murder."

As the car eased under the portico of the Westin Hotel, Daughtry asked, "What do you need me to do?"

Dodge opened the door, climbed out and stretched his stiff and aching back. The muscles still ached sometimes. The gunshot wound had healed, but his body was still working on repairing all the damage. Sadly, he thought most of the pain he endured was illusory, existing only in his mind. A psychological reaction to trauma he hoped would disappear soon. He hadn't been able to stuff the events of that night into the box in his head yet. Something was preventing him from moving past it. He just didn't know what that was. But he would. Soon.

"See if you can dig up an address for the contractor Roberts worked for. The name of her supervisor wouldn't hurt, as well."

A young man moved out from behind a small podium positioned to the side of the main entrance to the hotel. He walked around the rear of the SUV and tapped on the passenger window.

"Keys?"

Daughtry stared at the man for a moment, then opened the door and placed the keys in the valet's outstretched hand.

"Thank you, sir," the valet said, before hopping up into the black SUV and driving it away.

Dodge needed to take a shower and change into a clean set of clothes. The oppressive heat and humidity at the lake and hospital made him sweat profusely, like a marathon runner nearing the finish line, leaving a sticky residue on his face and arms that made him incredibly uncomfortable. He stood in the elaborate walk-in shower, feeling the cool stream of water pouring from the rain shower head mounted on the ceiling after he stripped off his damp clothes. The water rinsed away the grime of the day, refreshing his mind and spirit. When finished, he dried and slipped into clean jeans, then pulled a t-shirt on. He stood staring at himself in the mirror. He felt the day had been productive. They knew more today than yesterday. And with any luck, more information would reveal itself, once they found the contractor's office and he scoped out the roof of the hospital. His stomach growled. He looked at the alarm clock in the room and realized he hadn't eaten lunch yet. He wanted a cheeseburger and fries.

Daughtry showed up to the room shortly after Dodge finished dressing. He left the door propped open after he finished showering and the airman let himself in. Dodge sat on the edge of the bed thinking about how much he should fill the detective in once he had confirmation in his mind the roof was the origin of the fatal shot.

"Where to now, sir?" the airman asked as he stepped into the box shaped room.

"We need to take a drive to the contractor facility where Roberts worked."

"I thought you said you didn't believe her death had anything to do with her current position?"

"I don't."

A hint of confusion painted on his face as the bulky airman asked, "So, why are we going there?"

Dodge rose from the bed, stamped his feet to get his leg cuffs to drop and ran his hand through his short gray dusted hair.

"It's a rule."

"A rule, sir?"

Dodge nodded.

Daughtry stood still. Silent. Waiting for an answer.

Dodge grabbed his wallet off the desk as he slipped past. He turned out into the hall, then looked back at Daughtry, who had stopped to make sure the door closed behind him, and said, "An old friend used to tell me, everything's ruled in, until it's ruled out."

The pair rode the elevator in silence to the lobby where, to their surprise, Detective Alder waited at the front desk. He appeared to be having a heated discussion with the manager. Dodge stopped and watched as the frustrated cop's hands flailed and his voice became louder. The manager stood stoically, taking the detective's verbal abuse in stride. A true professional. When Dodge was tired of watching the two men argue, he shouted the detective's name from across the lobby.

"Alder!"

Alder spun on his heels. His eyes scanned the lobby and, upon seeing the two men, locked eyes with Dodge. Then the detective made his way across the lobby, his dress shoes clacking with each step on the shiny floor.

"Detective, what brings you to my hotel?" Dodge asked.

He put out a hand and Alder shook it.

"I wanted to let you know I received a call from the State Medical Examiner after you left. He has amended his report after obtaining the forensics on bullet fragments recovered from the victim's head."

Dodge said nothing, wanting to make sure the detective had finished.

"The fragments were small, shavings at best. The coroner believes the shot came from a long distance. Maybe as far as half a mile." He paused and stared across the lobby, as if he was trying to visualize the distance. After a moment, his eyes returned to Dodge. "Who shoots that far?"

Before Dodge could answer, the look on Alder's face folded over to one of anger.

"Military people. Soldiers."

The detective's reaction caught Dodge off balance. His guess was exactly what Dodge was thinking. He glanced over his shoulder at Daughtry and tipped his head toward the bar area.

"Why don't you go get us a cup of coffee?"

The bulky airman's gaze moved to the detective. "Now?"

"I need to speak to the detective for a moment. In private."

Dodge watched as the agitated soldier turned on his heels and made his way to the cafeteria. Once out of sight, Dodge looked back at Adler, who had a serious and determined expression on his face.

"After leaving your office, I visited the park where Roberts got shot."

"What did you find?"

"After examining the area and accounting for the angle of entry, I determined one location provided the proper sight lines, distance, and cover."

"The hospital roof across the lake," the detective said matter-of-factly.

Dodge nodded. He was more than a little surprised. This guy was pretty good.

"Yes. But how did you know?"

"I spent some time at that hospital a few years back."

"Take a bullet on the job?"

Alder shook his head. "Cancer," the detective said. "I had to go through several months of chemo. I couldn't stand sitting in that chair for hours. The machines beeping. Everyone looking like they had given up. So, I started roaming the halls. Pushing that damn metal IV tree in front of me everywhere I went. And it made me feel better. One day, I overheard a nurse talking about going up to the roof to smoke, so the next day, I followed her. When she returned, I slipped up the stairs and got some much-needed fresh air and sunshine. It was the highest point in the area, providing an unobstructed view across the lake. I would just stand and watch the paddle boarders make their way back and forth from shoreline to shoreline. That time on the roof, it made the whole experience a little more palatable."

Dodge paused, remembering seeing the hospital and its roofline from the shores of the lake. "Have you been on the roof yet? I mean to search for evidence?"

"I was going to head out there after I talked to you," the detective said. "You are welcome to tag along, if you like."

The offer intrigued Dodge. It was an olive branch. A show of trust by the veteran detective. Dodge knew a mountain of evidence existed he hadn't seen yet. He also knew if he stayed close to Alder, he stood a better chance of getting access to that information.

"I think I'll take you up on that."

Daughtry returned right as the two men finished talking. He had two cups of coffee, one in each hand and pushed one out at Dodge.

"Thanks."

"We should probably get going," Daughtry said, shooting a glance at Alder.

"You go ahead. I'm going to go for a ride with the detective," Dodge said. "You know what to do but be back here by dinner. We have a lot to plan out for tomorrow."

The expression on Daughtry's face revealed his displeasure with the split and Dodge felt tension in the air. But it wasn't his job to make the airman happy. The directive from Colonel Patterson was to find out who murdered his niece and bring them to justice. The decisions made on how to do that were strictly his. As for Alder, he was a cop. A cop will always choose a badge over a non-badge. Cutting Daughtry out of the rooftop search just made things easier.

"Look, you run to the company and see what shakes out. Then we'll meet back here and put it together with anything we find."

The two law enforcement veterans watched the airman exit the hotel. His frame was so large he had trouble maneuvering through the rotating doors and, at one point, Dodge thought there was a chance the airman might get stuck and jam up the whole system. But it didn't happen and Daughtry pushed his way through, turning left and disappearing down the sidewalk, bypassing the valet.

He must have found a spot to park down the street, knowing they would be leaving quickly and not wanting to tip a valet for ten minutes of parking time. Military personnel were frugal. Cheap is the correct word but, in their defense, they learn to survive on a salary which in the case for enlisted men and women is usually at or below the poverty line. Frugality is a good trait to have when you have limited means.

Alder glanced over at me motioning with his hand to follow him. We went through the same revolving doors Daughtry had and I couldn't help but notice how much room there was in between the glass panels making up the space hotel guests used to exit. You could have put two of me in one slot. *That guy is a fucking giant,* he thought.

Once outside, the police cruiser sat waiting. Alder left it blocking one lane through the portico, much to the disdain of the valets trying to whisk away guest's cars as quickly as possible. A line had formed behind the unmarked cruiser and the young valets were rushing, trying to keep the backup from wandering too far into the street.

As Alder slid into the driver's seat, Dodge looked back at the line of cars. A lot of unhappy faces peered back at him. He couldn't tell for sure but thought one of the drivers was using the New York greeting—an extended middle finger. Dodge smiled and waved before opening the passenger door and hopping inside. With a twist of the ignition, the engine roared to life. Alder popped the shifter into D, then pressed the accelerator The rear tires squawked as the car lept forward and the sound reverberated off the roof and the windows in the enclosed area. The valet's necks all bent to watch them leave. Dodge was sure he saw a slight grin on Alder's face.

The twenty-minute ride to the hospital was quiet. Alder didn't speak much, so Dodge decided to let the silence be. It was easy to work around questions he didn't want to answer if they weren't being asked. We would have to deal with all the questions at some point but, for now, he was happy to let it go. Besides, it was hard to concentrate on anything the way Alder was driving. Every turn was g-force inducingly sharp. Each acceleration from a stop pressed his head back into the seat like a shuttle astronaut during lift off. And the stops? There will certainly be red marks from the seatbelt locking each time he touched the brakes.

As the car swerved into the hospital parking lot, Dodge braced himself one last time and placed his off hand over the lid of his coffee tucked between his legs. The car careened to a stop just inside the lot, and even with his hand over the lid, brown liquid splashed out, landing on Dodge's jeans, making a small wet spot in his groin. He shook his head and then glared at Alder, who was already halfway out of the car.

After downing the remaining coffee, Dodge crunched the cup in his hand as he exited the vehicle, then followed the detective toward the hospital's entrance. Alder stopped short of the pass-through.

"I'm going to go inside and talk to security to gain access to the roof from inside. See if you can get up there from out here. I won't tell them you are out here, because I want to see how difficult it is for someone to access the roof. Use the maintenance ladder over by the bay doors. I'm guessing it won't be too hard."

Dodge grinned. The two men had been on the same page. "See you at the top."

Dodge lingered around the parking lot, watching, waiting. He wanted to get a sense of how people came and went. Were there deliveries at that hour? Did the staff park in the farthest spots away from the building, saving the closest spots for visitors? He remembered the local mall back home in Virginia made the employees leave their vehicles in the parking spots at the edge of the lot and furthest from the mall. But he saw only a few people, mostly non-staff, going to and from their vehicles. No one seemed to notice he was even there. Everyone being more focused on their own problems than what was happening around them. Certainly, no one would come to a hospital simply to hang out and kill time. Everyone assumed if you were at the hospital, you *needed* to be there.

Originally, he imagined trying to sell the ruse by pretending he was searching for his vehicle. Keys in hand and pushing the button on the remote, then looking around in frustration. He needed no ruse. No distractions. He took one last look around and made his way over to the wall surrounding the loading dock bay. A quick peek around the corner verified no one was on the loading dock and he slid into the space between the dumpster and the wall, where he waited a few more minutes, just to make sure no delivery trucks might pull up and interrupt his ascent to the roof.

As he leaned against the wall, peering around the corner of the dumpster, he noticed a spattering of cigarette butts on the ground. He thought, *this must be where employees come to smoke.* It's out of view and separated enough from the parking lot so visitors won't complain about the smell of smoke. He stepped out from behind the dumpster and stepped back outside the wall into the parking area. Looking around, he noticed a little "gas and go" across the street. A large neon sign in the window read, CHEAPEST SMOKES IN DALLAS.

A few minutes later, he jogged back across the busy street, through the parking lot, and snuck back into the smokers' cubby behind the dumpster. A pack of Marlboros and a cheap plastic lighter in hand. He leaned against the wall and placed a cigarette from the freshly opened pack between his lips. The flame danced as the tip of the cigarette turned bright red. He took in a deep drag. Feeling the rush of smoke into his lungs brought a smile to his face. He exhaled and took another pull. This time, he held the smoke in a few seconds longer. His lungs burned, and it felt good. It was something only smokers could understand. Or an addict. Completely letting go of the habit would never happen. It was something he knew in his soul. He needed it as much as he needed the rush from his job, or the burn from the first sip of bourbon. He would always be a slave to his addictions.

It only took three more drags for the red ember to reach the filter. A quick glance around to make sure no one was watching, then he tossed the smoldering butt onto the ground and snuffed it out with the sole of his shoe. Then he took in a deep breath and stepped out from behind the dumpster and found himself face to face with a man in a white shirt. The word SECURITY emboldened in red above the right breast pocket.

Chapter 10

Expensive furniture filled the small but comfortable waiting room. Two suede leather chairs sat nestled against the wall, separated by a narrow bookshelf. Weathered bindings, stacked neatly on each shelf, arranged not alphabetically, but by color. Each neatly pulled to the edge to maintain a linear appearance. Daughtry sank into the suede couch, the oversized cushions enveloping him and causing his knees to rise higher than his waist. The whole thing was uncomfortable, and he wondered if he could climb out of the furniture without a helping hand. He gripped the armrest and slid forward, shifting most of his weight to the front edge. The wooden frame creaked under his massive weight, causing the secretary to give a concerning glance that told him she was concerned about the furniture's ability to stand up to the stress.

After fifteen minutes of staring at the bookshelves trying to determine if the books were real or simply decoration, a door opened to his right. A well-dressed man stepped into the room and looked at the secretary, who nodded in Daughtry's direction. The airman had worn a uniform for most of his life and knew little about the cost of clothes, but he imagined the suit the man now staring at him wore cost over three months of an Airforce sergeant's salary. He looked like a seasoned power player, with the same confident stride and commanding presence as those he had seen come and go from military installations over his career. Impeccably dressed, always sporting a forced smile. A smile that said, *I want something from you and I have the money and connections to get it.*

Daughtry pushed himself up to greet the man.

"You must be Sergeant Daughtry," the man said, his teeth practically glowing through his spread lips. "My name is Blake Williamson. I own this little operation."

Daughtry reached out and took the man's hand in his, squeezing a little tighter than normal as he shook. An opportunity to let the man know he wasn't one of the military brass he was used to dealing with. Williamson didn't flinch, nor did his smile waiver. Just like a politician. After Daughtry released his grip, Williamson returned his hand to his side and used his other arm to wave the large airman into the interior of his office. Then he pointed to a seat as he closed the door behind him. Williamson then moved around a large wooden desk and slid into a high-back leather chair, which perfectly matched the furniture in the waiting room.

"What can I help you with today?" Williamson said, as he leaned back into his chair, clasping his hands in front of his chest.

Daughtry sat straight. His back forming a perfect ninety-degree angle to the floor. "As I told your secretary, I would like to discuss the matter of Corporal Shannon Roberts' death."

Williamson leaned forward. His hands now resting on the edge of the desk. "Ah, yes. A tragic accident. My understanding is the Dallas Police are overseeing the investigation. When did Special Investigations get involved?"

"I'm not with Special Investigations."

"Army CID?"

Daughtry was in the Air Force, but was well aware of the Army's Criminal Investigations Division. He also knew it would be CID who would look into the death of a prior army sergeant turned contractor, if the Pentagon wished such an investigation to take place.

"I am not with the Army either."

The look on Williamson's face changed. The smile disappeared. Replaced by a concerned scowl. "I'm sorry. But if you are not with the Army or Special Investigations, why are you here?"

Daughtry paused, immediately recognizing his mistake. Government contractors were a suspicious group, held to government standards involving the retention and release of classified material. All the while, trying to keep and gain new contracts worth hundreds of millions in a cutthroat business inhabited by modern-day pirates.

"What I meant to say is, I am here at the request of Colonel Patterson. He has a personal interest in this case. You may or may not know Shannon Roberts was his niece."

The man cut him off. "I'm sorry. I'm afraid I can't talk to you about personnel matters." Williamson tipped his head slightly, then rose from his desk. "I'm very sorry for what happened to Ms. Roberts. And I truly hope the police can figure out who killed her and bring them to justice. While I consider Colonel Patterson a friend, I'm afraid I can't say anything else." Williamson paused for a moment before continuing. "I know also that our friend is recently retired and I would warn him to tread lightly on this matter. The Pentagon doesn't take kindly to people poking around in their business. And anyone brought into it, through loyalty or coercion, could also find themselves in a heap of trouble and on the wrong end of a court-martial."

The man straightened his jacket and tugged his shirt cuffs past his wrists, then strode to the door and opened it. Daughtry took the gesture as meaning the meeting was over. Stepping through the doorway, the airman came to a sudden halt, his gaze fixed on Williamson. He noticed the businessman now carried a look of concern on his face.

"Thank you for your time," Daughtry said.

The moment he was in the waiting room, two security personnel caught his attention. Each one taking a stance on either side of the door he had just exited. Both were smaller than him and they knew it. Which is what drew Daughtry's attention to the bulges at their waistlines partially hidden under their matching blue sport coats.

"These two gentlemen will escort you out. If you have any more questions, I suggest you contact the Pentagon." Williamson stepped back into his office, the door slamming behind him.

Daughtry knew if he really wanted information, it wouldn't be too difficult to dispose of the two guards, kick the door in, and beat the information out of Williamson. However, unless he broke Williamson's jaw, or pounded him into unconsciousness, the police would likely be at the facility before he could get out of the parking lot. His arrest would put his boss in a terrible spot. Not to mention a certain court-martial which would lead to a dishonorable discharge and losing his pension. The only option was to leave quietly and meet back up with Dodge.

He nodded at the two guards and pushed between them on his way out. He thought he noticed a sign of relief on their faces as he passed.

***

Dodge stood face to face with a large bellied man in a white shirt. A badge hung on the left pocket side and a Glock 9mm sat on his right hip. The two men stared at each other for a moment. Both appeared to be surprised to see the other.

The security guard spoke first. "You got another one of those?" he said, pointing to the square outline in Dodge's front pants pocket.

"Sure," Dodge said, reaching into his pocket and fumbling the pack of cigarettes before handing them over. "Take the whole pack. I'm trying to quit."

The man smiled and took the cigarettes. Then he disappeared around the corner of the wall. Dodge felt relieved and drew in a deep breath before making his way to the ladder that led to the roof. He looked over his shoulder one more time to make sure the guard was still out of sight. When he didn't see any hint of a white shirt, he pulled the rope, releasing the last section of ladder, careful to catch it before it clanked into the ground. One more look around, then he quickly scaled the metal rungs of the ladder.

The climb of about fifty feet took him just short of three minutes. Once at the top, he threw his leg over the ledge and stepped onto the roof. He had a clear view of the entire area. The land was flat as farmland in the Midwest. He could see for miles, if it weren't for the permanent haze caused by exhaust emissions that hung over the downtown area. He spun in all directions to get his bearings straight, then proceeded towards the other side of the roof. He had to maneuver around a protrusion that housed the stairs leading up from the floors below. As he crossed over to the other side, the sparkling water of the lake came into clear view. He also now saw Alder standing at the roof's edge, looking in the same direction.

Alder turned when he heard Dodge's footsteps crunching on the rooftops cracked surface behind him. He looked at his watch.

"It's about time. I was beginning to wonder if you were nabbed by the White Shirts."

Dodge strode up next to his new partner and continued looking across the lake. "Had to stop for a smoke."

"Those things will kill you."

"It's been my experience a bullet is more likely to do me in."

"Still, you don't want to end up standing up here with an IV in your arm and a drip of poison flowing into your veins hunting cancer."

Instinctively, Dodge rubbed the recent gunshot wound on his chest and decided to change the subject.

"What did you find out from security about the day Roberts was killed?"

"Not much. The guard on duty wasn't working that day, but he looked in the log book and didn't notice any notations by staff concerning any unusual activity that day."

"What about the security cameras?" Dodge asked.

"Erased every week," Alder said shaking his head.

Dodge bit down on his lower lip. "Usually, those type of records are kept for at least ninety days."

"That's been my experience as well."

"So, what's the difference here?"

"This hospital is not a state or county run facility. It is privately run and controlled by a board of directors. They have found through many years of litigation, it is better for them to not have to turn over evidence, especially video evidence, in a civil trial. You can't give what you don't have."

"And that's legal?"

"In Texas, corporations and money are king. And the king can afford whatever he wants."

"Are things different where you're from in Virginia?"

"I like to think they are but, in reality, probably not. We have to subpoena almost everything we want and sometimes they fight us and sometimes they don't."

Alder turned to Dodge. "See."

Dodge looked back at him—his eyes squinting in a look of confusion.

Alder returned his gaze to the lake. "It's cheaper to not have what they want."

Dodge nodded, even as the thought of not keeping potential evidence to avoid a lawsuit pissed him off.

The two men stood quiet for a moment. Then Dodge decided it was time to see what kind of an investigator Alder was.

"This is where you think the shooter waited and took the kill shot from?"

"It's the only place that makes sense. He…"

"Or she," Dodge interjected.

"Right. The shooter would need a clear view of the park across the lake. The parking lot here butts right up close to the water."

"So, nowhere to hide while holding and pointing a rifle at someone across the lake."

"Exactly. There are a few places a person could tuck down and hide in the Arboretum," Alder pointed to their left toward a green space with perfectly manicured trees and shrubs and walking paths. "The angle isn't right. No, the shot came from up here."

"Did you bring out the reconstruction team?"

Most larger police agencies had a group of evidence technicians who specialized in the reconstruction of accident and crime scenes. In a case like the Robert's shooting, the team would be equipped with lasers that could be set up to pinpoint where a shot came from based on the impact wound and position of the victim. But Dodge knew there would be a problem with the technique in this case. As did Alder.

"The issue is that, at this distance, we can only get a general area of where the shot came from. As the distance between the impact position and the suspected shooting perch increases, the wider the possibilities become. At ten feet, the laser will point almost directly at the position of the shooter. At a quarter mile, a slight error in the trajectory of the laser could throw it off by thirty feet. Of course, that is thirty feet in both directions. And you don't know where the mid-point is, so, you expand thirty more feet in each direction to cover all your bases. It is just a guessing game and instinct from there." Alder took a deep breath like he was planning on continuing to talk, but he fell silent.

Dodge knew all of what the detective said to be true. The man knew what he was talking about and clearly had experience in shootings before.

"For what it's worth, I think you are right. The top of this building makes the most sense," Dodge said.

"That's what I thought. But what makes you so sure?"

"It's where I would have been." As he answered, he caught the side eye from Alder and noticed that smirk again. He was beginning to believe the awkward facial expression was a tell. He smirked when he approved of or was happy with an outcome. Either way, Dodge was growing to like his new temporary partner.

"What's the next step?" the detective asked.

Dodge continued to look across the lake. He knew Shannon Roberts made a habit of taking walks through the park. It would have been easy enough for a professional to follow her and keep track of where she went and who she talked to. Then the shooter could have parked himself up on this roof and waited. Waited until the right moment to fire a round across the water, killing Roberts. But that is where this whole thing kinda started going off the rails for Dodge. The shooter picked this building then made a solitary trip up here and got the perfect shot on the first try? The luck involved in that had to put the odds at a million to one. Snipers will choose the perfect spot after multiple hard intelligence reports and hours of recon work. Then they will sit, not moving for days sometimes, waiting for the perfect shot. Sometimes that shot never comes. But this guy did it on the first try? *Not likely*, he thought.

"What's eating at ya?" Alder asked him.

"I don't know, exactly. It all just seems too easy."

"Ok, I'll bite."

Dodge explained to Alder his concerns. The timing. The surveillance. The shooting. "And he only came up here once? I mean I almost got caught on my way up. No way he made multiple trips up here and no one remembers some strange guy carrying a case big enough to hold a rifle, even a disassembled one, around the loading dock area. On several occasions? I'm not buying it."

"So, you think he could have taken the shot from somewhere else now?"

No," Dodge said, as he turned away from the lake. "He definitely took the shot from here."

"Well, if this roof is where he pulled the trigger, then the question becomes, how did he get up here more than once without being noticed."

"Exactly. Maybe…" Dodge paused. It had been staring him in the face the entire time. This whole thing wasn't a random encounter. It was set up. Roberts was where she was because that is where the shooter wanted her to be. "He only had to make the climb up here once, because Corporal Roberts was where the shooter wanted her to be standing exactly when he wanted her to be there."

The Dallas detective pointed across the lake at the area where Roberts was gunned down. "You mean she was planning on meeting someone?"

Dodge nodded. "And where better to meet someone you don't know or trust than a public place where she would feel comfortable."

"Son of a bitch," Alder muttered. "I can't believe I missed that."

"I missed it too. The important thing is we now have a lead."

The two men faced each other.

Alder asked, "It's a theory. A thin one at that."

"True, but it's a starting point. Did you run the vic's phone logs?"

"Yeah. Standard operating procedure after a homicide. But we didn't find anything unusual. In fact, she barely used her phone."

Dodge rubbed his chin. "Did you check her work phone?"

The detective's eyes rolled white. "No. We didn't even check to see if she had one. The only phone she had on her when she was killed was her personal cell."

"I think I should call Daughtry and see if he has had any luck with her employer," Dodge said.

"And ask about the work cell," Alder responded.

Dodge held his finger up as an acknowledgement as he pushed the phone up to his ear. The phone rang, but Alder heard it, too, because he turned his attention to the small protrusion on the roof where the door that leads back into the building sits. Dodge pulled the phone away and they both heard the ringing of a cell phone. Just then the door opened and Daughtry stepped onto the roof and into the sunlight.

Dodge disconnected and watched as the muscular airman made his way across the roof to the two men still standing at the edge. The large man's massive stride covered the twenty feet of distance in just under seven paces.

"Jesus, he seems even bigger in the sunlight," Alder said under his breath just as Daughtry reached them near the roof's edge.

"What did you find out at Robert's employer?" Dodge asked.

"Nothing. Said he couldn't talk about personnel matters."

"That's what I thought he might say," Dodge said.

"If you knew he was not going to cooperate, why did you send me down there?" Daughtry appeared agitated.

"We needed to talk to him. Feel him out and see what he knows. It was going to have to be done sooner or later. I chose for you to do it sooner," Dodge said. "That being said, do you think he knew more than he told you?"

"Sir, he told me nothing. I'm sure he knows something, but I couldn't say what or how much."

Dodge nodded. "I agree. We may have to take another run at him later if we come across anything that needs to be cleaned up concerning her employment."

Alder looked down at his watch. Even though the cell phone everyone carries with them everywhere provides the time at the touch of a screen, a lot of the old heads in police departments still wore wrist watches. Dodge did as well. It was a comfort thing. Plus, it was easier than reaching into your pants pockets to pull out your phone every time you needed to check the time. It was also easier to conceal a glance at your watch, than staring at a cell phone in your hand when trying to escape an uncomfortable situation.

"Well, boys, I gotta get back to the station. I'm working three other homicides besides this one." He looked at Dodge. "Your man give you a lift back?"

"Yeah. We're good," Dodge answered.

The detective waved over his shoulder as he passed through the roof access door, disappearing into the darkened stairwell.

"Let's get out of here as well," Dodge said to Daughtry.

"Where to now, sir?"

"We need to find the other person Shannon Roberts talked to about the incident in Afghanistan. Lily Tremble."

"How do we do that, sir?"

"We call in a favor," Dodge said, as the two men entered the darkened rooftop stairwell.

Chapter 11

After Dodge and Daughtry returned to the hotel, it took a couple of hours of reaching out to people who owed him favors and another hour of searching names and addresses on the internet, but he was able to locate a last known address for Lily Tremble. The Veterans Administration keeps meticulous records and, thanks to the military's policy on burning everything from trash, human waste and even dead bodies, most of the people who served in either Iraq or Afghanistan from 2001 to present day, had made a claim for disability and received a monthly check for exposure to dangerous toxins from Uncle Sam. Lilly Tremble was on that list.

The two men ate dinner in their rooms and packed for the trip to Mississippi to see if Tremble would be willing to talk to them about the incident involving Roberts in Afghanistan. Dodge made one last call before laying down to rest.

"We will be leaving tomorrow. Heading to Mississippi to follow a lead on one of her friends," Dodge said.

"Well, I'll keep you informed of anything I find on this end," Detective Alder said. "Good luck."

Dodge said, "Thanks," and rang off. He then laid back, glancing at the clock on the bedside table. The red numbers flashed, *10:00 pm*. The flight to Jackson, Mississippi, left tomorrow at nine in the morning. Which meant he would have to be up and showered by five-thirty. He laid back and closed his eyes. A myriad of thoughts flooded his head. Most of which he didn't have answers to yet. Other than discovering the shooting site had likely been a set up to get Roberts to where the shooter wanted her to be, he had learned very little else on their trip to Texas.

He hoped his new detective friend would find something, as he said he planned to make a trip to Roberts' employer himself and have a conversation with the owner, Blake Williamson. The detective was confident he could get a judge to sign off on a subpoena for Roberts' personnel file. Dodge felt the whole thing was a fool's errand and knew Alder was searching for something buried in its pages that would point to who killed her and why. Dodge wasn't as sure. He knew Blake's company, Advanced Systems Technology, or AST as it was listed on the business card Daughtry returned with, worked on classified projects and any request for records would likely be challenged in court due to national security concerns. There was also little chance if the personnel file contained any incriminating information, it would still be there. The first thing Blake Williamson would have done after Roberts' death would have been to review her file and make sure anything that could point back to AST, or him, would have been scrubbed. He wouldn't take the chance of losing millions in government money. However, Dodge decided to keep that thought to himself and let Alder do his job.

Dodge was jolted awake as the plane's wheels touched down on the runway at Jackson-Medgar Wiley Evers International Airport. While in the Air Force he had spent so much time on airplanes, many of them nothing more than a flying trash can with little to no creature comforts, sleeping as a way to pass the time became second nature to him. Nowadays he was usually asleep before the flight attendant finished the safety instructions. And rest was never a bad thing.

The two men gathered their luggage and made their way to the car rental counter. All the usual suspects were represented and while Dodge didn't have a favorite, he knew the major players were the shot at getting a large SUV. The smaller rental companies tended to have much lower prices and therefore cheaper and smaller vehicles. While he thought it would be funny to see Daughtry smashed into a compact, he knew after a few minutes his own body would begin to ache, from the wounds he was still recovering from, and he didn't need that kind of pain and distraction. They took the last full sized pick-up truck the rental company had in stock.

The airport lay about four miles to the east of Jackson, well out of the city limits and smack in the middle of a rundown industrial area spotted with gasoline storage facilities and metal scrap yards. Only one hotel lay on the airport grounds and it was a little fancy for the area, but Dodge didn't know how long they would be staying in Jackson and figured the closer they stayed to the airport, the more convenient for them when it came time to leave. There was also an added layer of security near an airport. Homeland Security had teams of agents who drove the area and surveilled the surrounding parking lots and building rooftops for suspicious activities. With the presence of so many fuel storage containers in close proximity to the airport, he assumed the presence would be double that of an airport its size anywhere else. An explosion of a fuel tank this close would cause large amounts of damage and snarl air traffic over the area for weeks. The cost for a few extra pairs of eyes was well worth the taxpayer investment.

After checking in at the hotel, the two men headed to the last known address for Lilly tremble. Records showed she got her veteran's correspondence at an address in a small town about ten miles south of Jackson called Florence. Her checks are auto-deposited into a bank account, as are all payments for federal employees and any disability and pension checks. A rule that went into effect a decade ago to help the government save money on paper and mailing costs. However, with the funds being deposited, the receiver could list any address and never change it, even when they move. Most people didn't care about the junk mail and other needless correspondence that comes in the daily mail, as long as they got their draw.

Daughtry turned west on I-20, the main US interstate traversing east to west through Jackson. They exited the freeway on to Highway Forty-one south just before reaching the downtown area. Traffic was light. Dodge couldn't imagine a time when traffic would be heavy. Jackson was a fairly small city, as far as state capitols go, with a population a tad shy of one hundred and fifty thousand residents. Having never traveled to Mississippi, he didn't know a lot about the state, so he had done some quick research before leaving Dallas. The state ranked last or nearly last in every category in which you wouldn't want your home state to be bringing up the rear. Last in health care. Last in workforce participation rank. Lowest per capita income. In fact, the only thing the state ranked first in was adult obesity rate.

Dodge wondered why a service member who had traveled the world would choose to return to such a depressing place. Her time in the military as an Intel Analyst would have bagged her any number of jobs in the contracting world. Add on her veteran preference points for serving in a war zone, and she would have been bumped to the top of the list for almost any federal job she applied for. According to internet, the state lost some twenty thousand residents between the 2010 and 2020 census. Something had to make her come back to a place like this.

Florence was a southern town. A southern one stop light town. The kind you read about in a Harper Lee novel. Restaurants, both fast food chains and locally owned, dotted the real estate bordering the main drag. The land was flat with the few trees giving way to church steeples on what seemed like every corner. Front porches were littered with rocking chairs—old men smoking pipes and spitting chewing tobacco occupying most. Grass was sparse and, where it did manage to take root, the decades of drought had turned it brown, giving the lawns more of a desert appearance than that of a suburban neighborhood. Dodge could feel his mood slowly change. It was all so depressing.

The truck veered west onto Highway 469 South and then made a right on College Street. As they passed the police department, Dodge made a mental note of the address and how many patrol cars sat out front. There were three. Which meant there could be more, but there were at least three patrol units. Good information to know if they needed to play in the gray area while in town. The road continued and Daughtry saw the address they were looking for. It was an apartment complex at the end of a dead end street. Not a cul-de-sac. The road simply stopped existing. A pair of orange cones were placed at the edge to warn unfamiliar drivers of impending tire damage if they didn't stop.

"Looks like this is it, sir," Daughtry said, pointing to a U-shaped building off to the right. The complex and the grounds surrounding stood in contrast to what the two men had witnessed on their drive into town. The grass was green. Flowers lined the sidewalks and well-manicured bushes welcomed residents as they passed through the main entrance to the building. The building itself was in excellent shape, with brightly colored trim adorning each window. Dodge thought the whole thing looked out of place. It would have fit in in Key West or a dozen other Caribbean islands he had been to, but not in Florence, Mississippi.

"Must be the nicest apartments in town," Dodge answered.

Daughtry said nothing and turned into the parking lot, finding a spot near the front entrance. A green sign planted in the sidewalk strip, the grassy strip between the sidewalk and the curb, read, "WELCOME GUESTS."

The two men exited the car. Dodge stopped in the portico of the main entrance, pulling the piece of paper containing Lilly Tremble's address. He stared at the paper for a long moment.

"What's wrong, sir?"

"There is no apartment number," Dodge said as he peered up at the three floors of apartments. "There must be forty or fifty apartments here."

"We can go to the office and see if they will give us Sergeant Tremble's apartment number," Daughtry said.

Dodges head swiveled from side to side as he stepped out of the sun and into the breezeway. Then he saw what he was looking for. Mailboxes. An entire wall dedicated to the US Postal Service. He stepped up, studying the aluminum-colored doors all lined up perfectly. Six across and seven deep.

"Forty-two," Dodge said.

Daughtry looked confused by the comment, but Dodge decided not to explain the simple math. It was unimportant.

"Look for her name," Dodge said as he moved to the far side of the panel and crouched down. "I'll start at this end. You start at the top corner of that end and we will meet in the middle."

The two men moved slowly, reading the names on each box. Some of the labels were old and worn—the names hard to make out. Dodge assumed if the label was that old and faded, Tremble's name would not be on it. She had separated from the Army less than a year ago and if she moved in recently, the label should be in fairly new condition. So, if he couldn't read the name, he skipped it and moved to the next box in line.

After a few minutes of bending and standing, Daughtry and Dodge met in the middle of the panel.

"Nothing," Dodge said.

"Maybe she doesn't live here? It's possible she failed to update her address with the VA and no one has caught it yet," Daughtry chimed in.

Dodge stared at unfamiliar names pasted on the boxes in front of him. He moved back to his left and gave a quick look at the faded names he had skipped over before. Nothing. The name Tremble was not there. Next, he stepped back, his finger scratching his temple as he contemplated the possibilities. Then his finger stopped moving. He made a grunting noise from his chest.

"What is it, sir?"

"Do you have the folder with the all the names from the unit in it?" Dodge asked.

"It's in the truck."

"Go get it."

Daughtry turned on his heels and double-timed it to the rental and returned a few minutes later with the dark brown folder in hand. He passed it to Dodge, who opened it and slid out the face sheet for Sergeant Lilly Tremble. He ran his finger down the page and when he saw what he was looking for, he flicked the spot with his finger.

"Bingo," he said.

Daughtry leaned over and glanced at the piece of paper. He saw the name Dodge was referring to. Both men returned to the corners they began their earlier search from and quickly began searching the names again. Dodge was two rows over and three boxes from the top when he saw it.

"Masterson," he said. His voice cracked, showing his excitement at finding the prize.

His large partner leaned in over his shoulder and stared at the name on the box. "How did you know she would be here?"

As Dodge stood, he let out a slow groan. His body was still aching from his wounds, but he shrugged off Daughtry's assistance. He didn't want to appear *not up to the job.*

"I didn't, if you want to know the truth."

The airman stared blankly at him.

Dodge continued, "The face sheet we had on her listed her as not married. Yet her VA benefits show she has family added to her Tri-Care insurance package."

Stoically, Daughtry said, "She has a child."

"That would make sense. So, a woman with limited means, a child and no job prospects when released from active duty, returns to her economically depressed hometown. Why?"

"Because her parents are here."

Dodge raised an eyebrow, then smiled and nodded. "Some things never change. When in trouble, go home to Mom."

The two men climbed the zig-zagging staircase up three floors and stepped into the open hallway. The apartment was located on the end, right outside the stairwell. Dodge knocked. They heard nothing. No footsteps. No crying children. No television. Nothing. He rapped his knuckles on the metal door, harder this time and leaned closer. Placing his ear within inches of the door, he listened for any signs of people stirring on the other side. It was quiet. As he started to pull back, he noticed a creaking coming from inside the apartment. It was faint, but had a rhythm to it. Soft at first then louder. The noise repeated. And then again. It grew more distinct each time. It was someone inside. Walking softly toward the door.

Instinctively, he quickly moved away from the door, sliding to one side putting him out of the path of any objects that might burst though and injure him. It was an old habit. Engrained deep inside his brain. The survival part, fight or flight. Purely second nature to him now. A reflex.

He glanced over and watched as Daughtry mimicked his movement. Sliding his large frame against the opposite wall. Dodge listened as the noise subsided. He fought the urge to continue hiding from the person inside, like a cop waiting for a criminal to attack. Finally, he relaxed his body and slid over in front of the door, so whomever was on the other side could see him through the peephole. Daughtry remained in his spot, tucked up tight against the wall. A good place for him, Dodge thought. His size alone could scare the shit out of someone. He watched as the pinpoint of light detectable through the small glass peephole, faded out. Someone was staring back at him.

The seasoned investigator took a half-step back. Partially to allow the person inside to get a better look at him. To see he wasn't a threat. Also, it allowed him a slight bit more freedom of movement. You could never be too careful.

His eyes darted to the massive human being waiting patiently next to the door. Then he looked back and introduced himself.

"Excuse me, my name is Paul Dodge. I'm looking for Lilly Tremble, Sergeant Lilly Tremble." He waited for a response. Nothing. "I'm here on behalf of Corporal Shannon Roberts." He waited again. This time the light reappeared in the viewing port. He heard a noise on the other side and the door knob turned. A three-inch crack appeared as the hinges creaked and the door slowly opened. A young black woman peered at him from the other side.

"Can I help you?" she asked.

Dodge noticed more than a hint of skepticism in her voice. He relaxed his posture even more.

"My name is Paul Dodge. I'm here about Shannon Roberts. Do you know Ms. Roberts?"

"We served together," the woman said both proud and nervously.

It was a common reaction to those soldiers who have been in a combat zone or had jobs requiring high security clearances. Dodge's years as an Air Force Security Specialist and Investigator ensured he was familiar with the suspicion soldiers and former soldiers viewed outsiders.

"Are you Sergeant Tremble?"

"It's just Tremble now. You can call me Lilly."

"Well, Lilly, I would like to talk to you a little about Shannon, if you have the time." Dodge motioned for Daughtry to step into view. "This is my partner, Airman Daughtry."

The bulky man stepped out from the wall, into full view. Dodge saw the fear in Tremble's eyes. A sheer look of terror fell over her face. At first, he thought the mere sight of such a gargantuan human caused the reaction he was seeing. Hell, even he was a little intimidated by his temporary partner. It was only natural. Then his logical brain took over. Tremble had served in the Army. She had been deployed to a war zone. There were men like Daughtry everywhere in the military. She would have had daily contact with alpha males who pumped iron all day when not on patrols or missions. They were a dime a dozen in Afghanistan. So, why was she so scared this time?

Dodge figured he had better tell Daughtry to wait outside, hoping that might set her at ease. But he never got the chance. The pain in the back of his neck was sharp. The blow sent shockwaves down his spine to the ends of every finger and toe. The light faded and he collapsed into a heap on the floor just outside the door.

Chapter 12

When Dodge came to, his head throbbed like someone was dribbling a basketball inside his skull. His vision was blurry and his knees were weak. His limbs felt as if someone was pricking them with needles and the sensation only intensified as he attempted to stand. After a few minutes, the aching investigator managed to get his feet under him and used the door jamb to pull himself upright. He stood in the threshold rubbing the back of his head. He could feel the knot. It was about the size of a golf ball. Whatever had hit him was hard and had been swung with massive force.

He checked his hand and it was void of any blood. That was a good sign. His neck cracked as he rolled his shoulders in an attempt to ease some of the pain from the blow to the head. Then he froze. On the ground, just inside the doorway, lay Tremble. Bruises covered her neck from ear to ear. Every vein in her eyes jumped out bright red. Both were a telltale sign of strangulation. And he couldn't help but notice his partner was no longer at his side. How could he have been so stupid?

The one nice thing about doing an investigation in a depressed area is, there are still pay phones dotted across the neighborhoods. The trick is finding one that works, which Dodge did after slinking down the back stairway out of the apartment complex. He had to hide and wait once while a woman on the floor below retrieved a food order from a delivery driver. But he was able to escape the scene without being noticed. He had closed the door to Lilly Tremble's apartment before leaving. He saw no need in frightening any poor soul who happened upon the dead body of a neighbor or possibly a friend.

He dialed 911 and told the dispatcher he heard screaming and breaking glass coming from inside Tremble's apartment. Then he hung up, wiping the handset with his shirt before resetting the receiver back on the cradle. There was nothing he could do for the woman now. Except, catch the large son-of-a-bitch who choked the life out of her.

After stopping at a convenience store for a bottle of water and a cup of coffee, he waited near the entrance from the road until a semi-truck appeared, moving in the direction of Jackson. A quick wave of his hands above his head got the drivers attention and the big rig slowed and stopped right next to where he stood.

A short haired woman in a baseball cap poked her head out the driver's side window. "You all right, mister?"

Dodge reached into his back pocket and pulled out his identification, flashing it at the driver he said, "Thanks for stopping."

"You didn't leave me much choice. You're standing in the middle of the road."

Dodge looked down at his feet and saw the white line showing the edge of the road lay two feet behind him. He was so caught up in his own head, he hadn't noticed he had shuffled out into the traffic lanes while flagging down the truck. "Huh. I guess I am." He turned his eyes back to the woman behind the wheel, who looked to be growing impatient. "Do you happen to be headed toward Jackson? If so, I could really use a lift."

"What branch you serve under?" the woman asked while scoping out his badge and ID.

"Air Force. Special Investigations," he shouted back over the idling diesel engine. "You serve?"

"Marines," the woman said, rotating her arm revealing a tattoo of a globe with an anchor through it. An eagle rested on top if it all. She smiled and waved Dodge around to the passenger side. He climbed up and slid inside, closing the door behind him.

"The name's Dodge. And thanks again."

"Lucy," she said. "Always willing to help out a veteran, even if you are *Chair*

Force." Chair Force was a derogatory term, though mostly used playfully by other branches of service, to describe what they considered lazy air force personnel.

The truck lunged forward as Lucy shifted into gear and let off the clutch. The cab hopped and shook as she cycled through the first three gears, but eventually the ride smoothed out as the rig gained momentum and speed. They'd be in Jackson in less than half an hour. Lucy's route had her passing by the airport and she offered to drop him off. He thanked her and the two talked for the next forty-five minutes about the military, their deployments and what life had been like since they transitioned back to the world.

As it turned out, the pair had a lot in common. She, like him had a rough time after separating from service. The horrors she experienced in theatre haunted her dreams. The marines did very little to prepare their soldiers for what would happen when they transitioned back to civilian life and it showed. Lucy knocked around from job to job for a couple of years. Got married, then divorced. Got married again. Had a miscarriage which led to a massive bout of depression and another divorce. Finally, she ended up finding a job as a truck driver. She said it fit as she drove fuel tankers in the military and she liked the time alone. The long days on the road gave her time for much needed introspection. She seemed happy.

Dodge thanked her again as he climbed out of the cab and hopped down onto the airport access road. She tipped her cap at him as she pulled away and he started walking. Luckily, it was a short walk because the heat of the day was starting to work on him. He was tired and pissed off. His only witness to what happened to Shannon Roberts lay dead on the floor of her apartment one town over. Killed by his partner. Now he had two missions. Find out who killed Roberts and Tremble and make them pay.

As he sat next to the window, watching the land below him fade into the clouds, he couldn't help but hate himself a little. Rarely had he let someone get over on him. His instincts were usually right when it came to people. Yet, Daughtry had slid one past him. He had seen all the signs, but he chose to ignore them. Dodge allowed his loyalty to an old friend, someone he trusted without question, to cloud his judgement. That was over now. From now on, the only person he could trust was himself. It was a hard lesson to learn and it cost an innocent woman her life. A mistake he would not repeat.

The plane touched down in Dallas just as the sun dipped below the horizon. Dodge was still awake. He hadn't slept at all during the flight. His mind was churning through the details he had gathered over the past several days. The realization he had nothing hit him hard. He wished his old partner, Renquest, was there to bounce ideas off of. But the detective he worked so many cases with over the years had left his job for another position in Arlington, Virginia, and the two hadn't spoken much over the past few months.

Dodge reached up to retrieve his bag from the overhead compartment, stopping after remembering his only bag was in the rental car Daughtry stole after bashing Dodge on the head and strangling the life out of Lilly Tremble. The bag contained nothing that couldn't be replaced, but he still hated the idea of someone rifling through his personal stuff. It just wasn't right. As he deboarded the plane, he imagined the rental vehicle was likely no more than a burned-out shell, smoldering in an empty parking lot in Jackson by now. His bag included. Fire is the great equalizer when it comes to trace DNA evidence. Get the fire hot enough and nothing survives.

He hailed a taxi at the airport. There would be no more rental cars for the duration of this trip. The investigation part of this was over. It was all about revenge now. No need to leave a paper trail to make it easier for people to find him, knowing what he had to do next. A fire started to burn in the pit of his stomach as he rubbed his fingers across the scar left from the bullet that tore through his shoulder several months earlier. The area was still tender to the touch. His teeth gritted as he pushed on the spot until pain prevented him from pushing any further.

The taxi driver was reluctant to leave him in the neighborhood Dodge had picked.

"Please, sir, you do not want to stay here. This is bad place," the driver said in a thick foreign accent.

Already out of the car, Dodge waved off the man's concerns and slipped a twenty and two fives through the open window.

"You better get out of here before it turns dark," he told the driver.

The tires on the maroon car with a yellow star on its door kicked up loose gravel as the driver accelerated quickly and drove away. Exhausted from the day's events, his eyes drooping and head starting to pound again, the weary investigator turned to the L-shaped two-story building behind him. The sign on the front read, **Hourly Rates** and proudly proclaimed, **Cash Accepted**. Dodge had hit the ATM before leaving the airport. He took out the maximum he could withdraw, three hundred dollars. It would do for now. Tomorrow he'd find a real bank and have cash wired to him.

The motel was seedy at best. The curtains were all drawn and he didn't notice any prostitutes or drug dealers selling their wares in the parking lot. He had picked the area of West Dallas by conducting an internet search on his phone before leaving the airport. Located across the Trinity River from downtown Dallas, West Dallas was a low-income neighborhood. There were check cashing and liquor store signs on just about every corner. A goodwill store sat right down the street from his motel. He would visit it the next day for some fresh clothes. But those weren't the reasons he chose that particular neighborhood or motel. Something else popped up on his screen during his search for a motel in a neighborhood where no one would think of searching for him. Pawn shops. One in particular, Lucky Lou's Pawn and Gun Store. The website proclaimed they had the best prices in town and were a veteran owned company. They even gave a discount to active-duty personnel and veterans. Sounded like a place Dodge could purchase a gun quiet and cheap.

The manager of the motel was friendly and asked no questions. He simply took the fifty dollars and handed Dodge a key. Dodge had requested a room on the end with a window facing the parking lot. He wanted to be able to see if anyone was coming. The other reason was an end room only shared one wall with another room. Less noise if only one neighboring room was occupied by a working girl. He took the key and made his way to the end of the building.

He slowed and listened at the window of the room next to his. The lights were off and the curtains drawn. The air conditioner was not running. A good sign the room was empty. The air was thick with humidity and he could only imagine if someone were inside, the unit would be running non-stop fighting the oppressive heat. He slipped the key in the door and the latch clicked. A damp smell hit him in the face as the door swung open. The air in his room was off as well. A flick of the light switch brightened the room and the push of a button caused the air conditioner mounted in the wall below the window to roar to life. The old unit was loud, but the cold air instantly began pouring out and the room started to cool. Fatigued and sore, Dodge fell on the bed and was asleep within minutes. There were no dreams. Just deep sleep.

Chapter 13

The morning sun shone through the cheap window coverings, illuminating the room in an almost dusk like glow. Dodge wiped the sleep from his eyes and stretched his aching muscles. The clock on the bedside table didn't appear to be working and a quick glance at the cord revealed it was not plugged into the wall outlet. He grabbed his phone from the table and saw that it was nearly eight in the morning. He had slept for more than ten hours. The rest felt good and he decided he needed to get some fresh clothes and then he would come back and shower. No need in cleaning the grime off just to put dirty underwear back on.

A new-ish t-shirt, pair of jeans, three pairs of underwear and some fresh socks cost him fifty bucks. *Not too bad,* he thought. The wad of money in his pocket was starting to get low. Pulling the thinning stack of bills out of his pocket, he flipped through the edge. There was about one-fifty left. He needed to find a bank and get a wire transfer. He thought about using Western Union, but the fees associated with using one of the oldest money transferring companies in the country were more than he wanted to pay. A commercial bank fit his needs better and was less expensive. If he needed, he could get a cash advance on his credit card, but the high interest rate for that type if transaction made the option a last resort.

He walked to the street, stopping and looking both directions. To the left was Singleton Boulevard. According to the internet maps, it led back into the heart of Downtown Dallas. To the right were fast-food restaurants and a few more motels of the same persuasion he as currently staying in. The streets were busy, but the sidewalks and store fronts were void of people. A stray dog wandered across the street and almost became a victim as it headed in Dodge's direction. It's tail wagging and mouth open, tongue hanging out, the mutt came up to him and sat right at his feet. Its head tilted, looking up at him inquisitively, it let out a muffled bark.

"What's the matter, boy? You hungry?"

The dog barked again and stood, looking up at him with excited eyes.

"I don't have anything for you. Dodge peered down the street to his left and saw a sign for a convenience store. Its red circle with the letter "K" in the middle seemed to be a staple in Dallas. He had seen the sign many times in his travels throughout the city. He looked down at the dog and waved his hand. "Follow me."

The clerk at the store looked at him and smiled as he paid for the items. Two hot dogs and two bottles of water. He asked the man behind the counter if he could have an extra paper tray, the ones the hot dogs were placed in after purchasing. The clerk nodded, reached under the counter and pulled out several of the containers. Dodge slipped the top one off the pile before grabbing his food and drinks and thanking the man. He then went outside to the waiting dog. He placed the empty tray on the ground, filling it with clean water from one of the bottles. Then he unwrapped both hot dogs, put ketchup on one and mustard on the other and handed the mustard hot dog to a now excited new friend.

The dog lay down and ate the food while Dodge scarfed down his own meal. After eating, the dirty white and brown mutt drank all the water, which was promptly refilled and he finished the rest as well.

"Welp, this is where we part ways. Good to meet you," Dodge said as he turned to make his way to the main street headed into downtown. The dog barked again, in a sort of "thanks" and watched for a bit before heading in the opposite direction. A smile stretched across his face as he walked. It felt good to do something nice for someone. Even if it was just a stray dog.

The motel was far from sight before Dodge hailed a taxi. He wanted to make sure no one would be able to trace him back to where he slept. Before leaving that morning, he paid for another night and requested to keep the same room. The woman who had replaced the man from the night before, occupying the desk during the day, shrugged and took his money. No receipt needed.

The ride downtown took less than ten minutes. He asked the driver to drop him off at a bank branch he recognized from back home. The wire transfer took about fifteen minutes to complete and Dodge sat in a nice reception area with a fresh cup of coffee. A television hung on the wall and was playing a show about home improvement. Dodge watched on and off, browsing the news sites from Jackson, Mississippi, looking for any mention of Lilly Tremble's death. He found nothing. However, there was a small story of a burned-out truck being found in an industrial area close to the airport. The police believed it was stolen and set ablaze when no longer needed. Dodge immediately knew the truck was the one Daughtry rented and left in.

If the cops ever found it was a rental, they would be able to track it to the airport and then using the thousands of cameras in the concourses it wouldn't be long before they could pin down him and Daughtry as the ones who rented the vehicle. That wasn't something he could worry about today. He needed to get his cash then cross back over the river into West Dallas and visit Lucky Lou. But first he needed to pay a visit to Detective Alder. Maybe the detective's subpoena opened some doors in regard to Roberts' employment records.

The police station was only a few blocks from the bank. Dodge covered the distance in less than fifteen minutes, stepping through the front doors before the sun managed to drench him in sweat. The receptionist took his name, dialing a number on the phone and announcing to whomever, he assumed it was Alder on the other end, that he was there to see him.

"The detective will be out for you shortly," she said with a kind voice. She then went back to answering phone calls and placing people on hold, all while directing a nonstop parade of citizens with complaints to the appropriate departments.

The woman remained smiling and Dodge couldn't help but think she had the worst job in the damn building. A row of chairs lined the wall behind him and he took a seat. While waiting, the phone in his pocket buzzed. The number had a Virginia area code, but he didn't recognize the rest. He had Patterson's number saved in his contacts, but it could be he was calling and using a different phone. A man in his position probably had several cell phones for different parts of his life. A personal one. A business one. A government one. And finally, a phone he didn't want traced back to him. Used for back room deals and calls to old parole agent friends doing favors for you on the side.

He decided to let the call go to voicemail. With all that had happened the past few days, Daughtry's betrayal and Tremble's murder, he wasn't sure he was ready to talk to his old friend quite yet anyway. Either he was complicit in what Daughtry did, or he allowed a conman to gain his confidence and elevated him to a position enabling him to commit murder. Twice. There was no doubt in his mind now that Daughtry either pulled the trigger for the shot that killed Roberts or he gave the order and knew the person who did. It didn't much matter to Dodge which it was, but he did need to know who was pulling the strings. Someone was paying for all this and he was sure it wasn't a non-commissioned officer who made two thousand a month. The money for a hit like this went much higher to someone with deep pockets. Perhaps a connected defense contractor with a never-ending supply of ex-military operatives looking for work ever since the wars in Iraq and Afghanistan wound to a close.

A door opened next to the reception window and Detective Alder stepped into the lobby.

"Dodge. Come on and follow me back."

The agent stood and Alder held the door as he passed through. The lock clicked behind them. Then he heard a familiar sound. Rattles of chains and the clinking of cold steel. The slip of leather. Before he knew it, Dodge was face first against a wall. His right hand was already locked in a cuff. His left arm being twisted and contorted to make it join the right arm behind his back. The veteran agents first instinct was to fight. Refuse to give his free arm up. He knew how, all he had to do was engage. But his logical brain took over. The numbers were not on his side. One yell and fifty cops come running, batons and tasers in hand. He might get one of them, but he would lose and likely be injured in the process. So, he relaxed and let the detective place him in cuffs.

Alder spun dodge around and used the cuffs chain as leverage. Pulling up and away from the detained agent's body. A move meant to throw the person off balance, making it harder for them to resist.

"Let's go," Alder said, guiding his prisoner down the narrow hallway until they were in front of a room with no windows and a heavy metal door. He pushed Dodge inside and led him to a chair bolted to the floor parked in front of a metal table with a large steel hoop welded to the top.

Once inside, Dodge was securely fastened to the table using an extra pair of handcuffs, Alder disappeared out the door, slamming it behind him. As someone who had been on the other side of this table hundreds, if not thousands, of times, he knew what the score was. He wasn't running the show now. It was time to sit back, shut his mouth and gather information. The sooner he knew what this was all about, the quicker he could prove his innocence and get back to finding justice for Roberts and Tremble. Besides, he knew he hadn't done anything that would get him arrested. Except for being at a murder scene two states away, but he was sure no one noticed him slipping out the back of the complex.

There was a clock on the wall above the door. The hands moved slowly and the internal parts made the tale tell "tick" sound older clocks were known for. Placing the clock in the interview room was an old tactic. When your alone and nervous in a police station waiting to be grilled by detectives, a clock to stare at makes the time seem to drag on forever. Five minutes can seem like an hour when watching the hands of a clock slowly circumvent the numbered face. The constant ticking will keep you focused on the time, not trying to keep your story straight. Sometimes it works. This time it wouldn't.

After a couple of minutes, Detective Alder returned to the room with two cups of coffee. He placed both cups on the table in front of him then reached into his pocket and pulled out a ring of keys.

"If I undo the cuffs, you're not going to give me any problems, are you?"

Dodge shook his head.

"Good then."

The detective flipped through the key ring until he found the handcuff key. He reached across the table and unlocked the cuffs. Dodge rubbed his wrists as the detective placed the restraints in the holders on his belt.

"I'll be more apt to check those things for tightness when I use them from now on," Dodge said.

The detective sat quiet, staring at his prisoner.

Another tactic Dodge had used himself many times. But instead of running his mouth out of nervousness, he calmly asked, "Is that cup of coffee for me?"

Alder slid the cup halfway across the table.

"Why don't you tell me what this is all about?" Dodge said as he grabbed the cup and took a sip. The liquid was hot forcing him to wince as it flowed across the roof of his mouth.

"Blake Williamson is dead."

A wave of panic came over him. Not because he was apparently a suspect, that would be disproven shortly. But because he couldn't imagine any scenario where Daughtry made the trip from Jackson to Dallas in enough time to kill Williamson. The contractor's death meant there was more than one hired gun.

"How?"

The detective leaned forward in the chair. His brow furrowed. "Where have you been? I went to the hotel and they said you checked out."

"When was Williamson killed?"

"His wife found his body this morning in his home. A single gunshot wound to the head. Small caliber, likely a twenty-two with a silencer."

"When did he die?"

"The wife had been out of town on business and returned early today after catching a red eye from San Diego. The coroner places the time of death between noon and three yesterday." Alder leaned back. "So, where were you yesterday between noon and three?"

Dodge took a sip of coffee and placed the cup on the table. "I'm not your guy."

"Why don't you let me decide who is and who isn't a suspect in my murder investigation. This is the last time I am going to ask. Where were you yesterday?"

Dodge reached into his pocket and pulled out a piece of paper. He waved it in the air before sliding it across the table to the awaiting detective. Alder pulled the piece of paper to him and examined its face. Looking over the top of the boarding ticket, he said, "I'll have to verify you were on board before I can let you go."

"Should be easy. I ordered a drink and paid with my credit card. Dodge pulled out his phone and typed something into its face. He then spun the device around so the detective could see what he had done. On the screen was an open banking app with a list of charges. First was the ticket charge on American Airlines. Second was a charge for eight dollars listed as on-board purchases.

The detective waved Dodge's hand away. "What the hell is going on here?"

"Can we move this to your office? I don't like being on this side of the table in one of these rooms." Dodge glanced up at the camera overseeing everything in the room. The detective paused for a moment, then stood and motioned for Dodge to follow him.

The two men sat in the office and, for over an hour, Dodge explained to Alder what he had been investigating and how he came to be involved in the case. He explained about the incident in Afghanistan. How Roberts had been sexually assaulted and how his old boss, her uncle, felt it was all connected to something she knew, something that ended up costing the former soldier her life.

"You came to Dallas to see if her employer was involved in any way," Alder said.

"Yes. Though I'm not sure if his murder makes him complicit in her death or if he found something out after we questioned him," Dodge said. A look of skepticism painted his face.

"Speaking of questioning Williamson, you were with me on that roof top. It was your partner who questioned him. I'll need to talk to him as well."

Dodge shook his head and sighed.

"What aren't you telling me?"

"First, he isn't my partner," Dodge said as he instinctively rubbed the back of his head before continuing. "We were following up a lead in Jackson, another soldier who knew Roberts during her time in Afghanistan. When we found her, she must have recognized Daughtry from somewhere. An earlier encounter in the service—I don't know for sure. We were standing at her door and the next thing I know; it's lights out."

"He knocked you out?" Alder asked. His face contorted in a look of bewilderment.

Dodge nodded. "When I woke up, our witness was dead. Strangled in her own apartment. Daughtry was long gone."

"What did you do?"

"I called the cops and came back here."

Dodge decided to leave out the part about making the call anonymously and not sticking around as a witness to talk to the cops. It sounded bad and he needed the detective's cooperation, not his indignation.

"So where is your partner..." Alder caught himself. "I mean, Daughtry now?"

"Your guess is as good as mine. But I know one thing, he isn't your trigger man for Williamson. No way he made it back here in time to do that job."

"So, we have a killer on the loose."

"Two killers," Dodge reminded him.

"Great. Two killers. So, what's our next move?"

"Our?" Dodge asked, surprised by the offer to help. He had been less than cooperative up to now and wasn't sure why the detective would trust him now. He wouldn't have. That's for damn sure.

"You know more than me about what's going on in this case. Hell, more than anyone. And I'll probably need someone from defense to cut through the inevitable red tape before this is all said and done. Besides, my guess is your old pal, Daughtry, will be coming back for you. I'm not sure why he didn't kill you earlier, but that's where my money is now."

"Cheese in a rat trap."

"It's the best bait."

Dodge's gut tightened at the prospect of getting a chance at Daughtry. He wasn't sure how it would turn out but, more than likely, one of them was going home in a body bag.

Chapter 14

After Dodge left Alder's office, he grabbed a bus schedule off a table in the lobby on the way out. Reading the schedule, he found the nearest stop to his location then scrolled the schedule for a route that would take him back across the river. The jumbled list of bus numbers and times was like reading a crossword puzzle. He gained a new respect for low-income people who rely on public transportation. He was an educated man and he almost couldn't figure out which bus came when and went where but, after concentrating for a moment, a pattern emerged.

The nearest stop to him was a few blocks north. From there, he could catch a bus across the river and into West Dallas. It turned out he was lucky. There was a stop only a few blocks from the pawn shop he planned on visiting. And no transfers in between. The times on the schedule showed the trip would take thirty-five minutes. It was closer to forty-five.

The sun was directly overhead when Dodge stepped off the bus. He was the only person to deboard which meant no one had followed him. At least on the same bus he had been on. He scanned the street for cars that looked out of place. Searching for anyone seemingly over interested in his movements, paying close attention to any vehicles parked along the street. Nothing triggered the hairs on the back of his neck, so he began walking in the direction of Lucky Lou's.

As it turned out, Lucky Lou was a woman. Lou was short for Lucille and Dodge liked her the moment he saw her. She was a short stout woman. Five-four in heels and a personality as loud as her voice. Her interactions with customers were a sight to behold. Most of the men greeted her with skepticism, most likely because of her physical appearance and what he could only assume was a misogynistic, machismo, male dominated culture of a state that prides itself on the image of a lone cowboy riding the range. His trusty gun at his side. Things were bigger in Texas, including the bullshit.

Dodge stood back and mingled in the aisles pretending to look at holsters and other accessories while the last customer finished his business, grabbed his purchases off the counter, nodded as he passed by, and left the store.

"You gonna just linger there in the shadows all day?" a booming voice echoed from behind him.

A little embarrassed his presence appeared so conspicuous, he paused for a moment before looking back at the short robust woman behind the counter. She stared at him, but with a smile. The kind of smile that said, *go ahead and try it. But you won't like how it ends.* Dodge turned on his heels, emerged from between the isles and stepped to the counter.

"So, what can I do for you today?" the woman said.

"I'm looking for a fairly inexpensive handgun. A Glock, forty- or nine-millimeter, if you have one."

Lou looked up at him, the smile still stretched across her face, and said, "Where you from? No way you're a Texas boy."

"Virginia, ma'am. Is that a problem?"

She let out a bellowing laugh. "Not for me! This is Texas, son. You just tell me what you want and after a quick background check, you'll be on your way."

Dodge nodded. "Sounds good to me."

She showed him several models in both calibers. Full sized. Sub-compacts and compacts. Single stack magazines and double stacks. The first thing he noticed was the price difference. The weapons were noticeably cheaper than back home in Virginia. As much as a c-note in some cases. Though anything under five hundred dollars wasn't going to hurt his wallet any. He could sell it right back to Lou when he was done with it, for a discounted price of course.

After some haggling and getting her to throw in an inside the belt holster, Dodge walked away just under five hundred dollars lighter, packing a

Glock 26 9mm. One magazine fully loaded, seated in the weapon, and an extra magazine stuffed in his front pocket. He also bought an extra box of ammunition for good measure.

"You come back and see me, ya hear!" Lou shouted as he left the store.

There was something about having the cold steel of a Glock's frame pressing against his skin that made him feel whole again. He had been wearing a duty weapon for so long, he felt naked without one. Over the years a gun had become an extension of his hand. And he had missed it.

A quick check of the street in both directions eased his mind about anyone following him. Tugging at his shirt to assure the weapon wasn't visible, he faced the direction of the motel and started walking. The sun was hot and his shirt was damp less than five minutes into his trip. *Man, this heat is oppressive*, he thought.

He was almost back to the motel, when he noticed his old friend, laying on the sidewalk in a small patch of shade, provided by an easel sign advertising beer prices outside a liquor store. The dog noticed him and jumped to his feet—his tail wagging and tongue hanging out, he ran to the man who had fed him earlier.

"Hey, boy," Dodge said as he bent down to pet the dog's head. "How ya doing?"

The dog looked up at him and sat.

"You're pretty smart, aren't you?" Dodge stood and looked at the motel just a block or two away. "Let's go and get you some water. What do ya say?"

Dodge opened the motel room door and the dog stopped and watched as he entered. He looked down and patted his hand on his leg and the overheated dog followed him inside. The ice bucket made a good water dish and the thirsty animal lapped cold water until it was empty. A half-eaten sandwich made for a nice dinner and the dog snarfed it down in only a few bites.

"Well, if you are going to stay here, you're in need of a bath."

The dogs head tilted to one side. His ears arched up in an inquisitive look. Dodge opened the bathroom door and the mutt followed him in. He then shut the door behind them.

After his new friend was clean and dry, Dodge let him out to go to the bathroom. He cleaned up the waste and tossed it in the green dumpster parked next to his room at the end of the motel. Then he returned to the room where the freshly cleaned dog hopped up on the chair and curled into its cushion.

"Well, I guess you've made your choice," Dodge said smiling. "I'll be back later. Make sure to keep it down in here cause I don't think they allow dogs. Even ones as cute as you."

The tired animal raised his head, in what seemed to be a nod of approval, and then tucked his nose into his body and closed his eyes. Dodge stepped outside and eased the door shut. The lock clicking behind him. He checked the time on his phone. It read a quarter after four. He wouldn't be back until after dark. A good six to seven hours from now. He hoped, Tobey, that's the name he decided on for his new friend, would be alright for that duration. If Tobey made a mess, he would have to clean it up later. Not a huge deal, as he was sure the carpet had lived through worse than a little animal urine over the years.

It was a short walk from the motel to the main road that ran into downtown. Once at the intersection, he reached into his pocket and pulled out his phone. With a punch of a few buttons, he placed the device up to his ear and waited while it rang. And rang. And rang. Then, on the eighth ring, Alder answered.

"This is Alder."

"It's Dodge."

"I was wondering when you were going to call. Where have you been?"

"I had to run an errand and get a friend cleaned up."

"You're making friends here? I hope you're not planning on sticking around when this is over. I don't need the headaches," the detective said, half laughing but with a hint of seriousness in his voice.

"Don't worry, neither me nor my new friend have any inclination of staying in your city any longer than we have to," Dodge said.

"Good. So, where are you? I'll come pick you up. Then we can plan our next move."

Dodge gave Alder the intersection and within ten minutes a blue unmarked car pulled up next to the curb. The passenger window rolled down and Alder shouted for him to get in. Dodge opened the door and slid in, buckling his seatbelt once the door was closed.

"Where to?" Alder asked, turning the wheel, and pulling out into traffic.

"Let's go to Blake Williamson's house. I want to get a feel for the crime scene." Dodge paused. "Is the wife still in the home?"

"No. We haven't finished the evidence gathering yet. The techs had to leave and work another scene and will be back tomorrow morning."

"Is it secure?"

"Yeah, I have a unit posted outside to make sure no unauthorized personnel gain entry."

Dodge checked his phone. "How far away are we?"

"About half an hour. Depending on traffic."

Alder turned south until hitting the I30 freeway. He then took the on-ramp west. The pair drove for about five miles before exiting onto MacArthur Boulevard and heading north. After crossing the same river that separated Downtown Dallas from West Dallas, Dodge saw a sign for Irving Lake. The closer they got to the lake, the larger the houses became.

"Are we in Irving?"

"Yep. Home of the Cowboys."

"I thought that was in Arlington," Dodge said.

"Don't say that too loud. Kind of a sore spot around here."

Dodge didn't really care about where the football team was located, or whatever local brush-up concerning its placement started an intercity feud, so he changed the subject back to Williamson.

"This is his house?" Dodge asked as Alder pulled into the drive of a modest house for someone with Williamson's means.

The house was a two-story brick home. Built with a mixture of colonial and craftsman styles, the façade of the house was clean and warm. Straight lines intersecting in perfect angles with the trim all painted white. The dark red color of the bricks provided a sense of security, although it was apparently only a sense. The first rooms inside were much the same. Whites and light grays bounded every room, each of which was perfectly square with an exact duplicate on the opposite side of the main entrance. A staircase in the middle led upstairs. Its steps and railing gently curved joining the loft on the left side of the front door. Hardwood floors polished to a high shine spread throughout the main level.

"Upstairs is where they found him," Alder said pointing toward the top of the stairs.

Dodge paused to take one more look at the layout of the first floor, burning it into his memory for recall later. Then he slowly traversed the steps making sure not to touch the railings in case the lab team needed to come back and look for more prints or DNA evidence. The board beneath his feet creaked as his weight shifted and he stepped onto the landing. He moved a few steps ahead, turned and waited for Alder. The floor creaked in the exact same place as the detective placed his weight on the landing.

"That's pretty loud," Alder said looking down at his feet.

"Not sure if you could hear it in the bedroom, but no doubt the shooter wouldn't have avoided hitting that spot," Dodge said.

Eager to see the crime scene, Dodge turned and peered down the hall. "Which is the room he was found in?"

"The master bedroom at the end of the hall." The detective pointed past Dodge to a closed door with a piece of tape stuck to the jamb and door just above the knob.

Dodge sliced the tape with his knife and pushed the door open. A waft of air assaulted his senses. The metallic smell of blood and the aroma of death hung heavy in the closed off room. Dodge stepped into the master suite, followed closely by Alder.

"Man, I never get used to that smell," he said. His nose tucked firmly into his jacket sleeve in the crease of his elbow. "Doesn't it bother you?"

Dodge looked back. "It does. But you get used to it after you've been to a hundred or so murder scenes."

Alder shook his head in disbelief. "I don't think I will ever get used to this smell. For god's sake, I can taste it."

The comment made Dodge snicker as he continued scanning the room for any clues. Everything seemed to be in place and it was obvious Blake Williamson was the target. Nothing was missing and the room had been left undisturbed. The coverings on the bed had been removed by the crime scene team and taken to the lab for analysis and a dried patch of blood shown on the mattress. Dodge guessed the lab would only find hair, fluid and DNA matching Williamson and his wife. This was clearly a professional hit. Just like Shannon Roberts. Not much of a chance they find anything that could lead them to the shooter's identity.

Dodge leaned over the mattress, studying the blood-stained circle. He took his knife out of his pocket and poked at a spot above the center of the dark red spot. As the tip of his knife moved left to right, it got caught on a tear in the fabric. He leaned in closer then shoved his off hand back toward Alder, who had sidled up behind him. Nothing happened and Dodge waited for a moment before glancing back at the detective.

"What?" Alder asked.

"Gloves."

"I don't have any on me."

Dodge stood straight and shook his head, mumbling to himself.

"I didn't think we would need any gloves. The crime scene techs have been through this place twice already. I don't think we are going to find anything that will help," Alder said.

"You said he was shot in the head with a silenced twenty-two?"

'Right."

"Did you recover the bullet?"

"We did. Unfortunately, after bouncing around in his noggin and scrambling his brain like an egg, what was left of the round was unfit for ballistics testing." Alder said.

"Was there an exit wound in the back of his skull?"

"The coroner hasn't put out a report yet. It's only been half a day."

Dodge stared at the detective, saying nothing.

"You want me to call and see if he has finished the preliminary findings?" The detective slid a cell phone out of his jacket pocket.

"Tell him to look for an exit wound. It'll likely be small, but it will be there."

"Not sure it matters. We don't have any part of a bullet to test."

Reaching over and pulling a pen out of the detective's front pocket, Dodge leaned over the mattress and pushed the end into the small hole he had noticed earlier. "He will find an exit wound."

Alder stepped out into the hall and Dodge could hear him grilling the coroner about any findings so far. Then the conversation went quiet. After a few minutes, the detective stepped back into the room, a look of surprise on his face.

"What'd he say?" Dodge asked.

"Well, he wasn't happy as he had already taken the body off the slab. But he pulled the drawer and examined the skull. There was an exit wound. He said he noticed it earlier, but assumed it was formed from one of the impacts of the lead round ricocheting off the bone."

Reaching down and grabbing at the mattress's side, Dodge found a small handle sewn into the edge. He motioned to Alder to help him flip the heavy mattress over and off the bed. Dodge examined the bottom of the mattress and, after a few minutes, noticed a tiny red stain. It was another small hole. The bullet had managed to carry some blood with it through the mattress and transferred it to the back side as it exited.

The bloody mattress sat on a set of box springs. Dodge knew from his experiences moving furniture into his old townhouse, that box springs were light weight and contained very little material other than the wood frame and metal springs used for support and cushion. He reached down and lifted half the box springs off. Then he saw it. Protruding out of the wooden floor was the tail half of a bullet. Small, like a .22 caliber. It appeared to be in good condition. The tip was slightly mushroomed from the impact, but the low caliber round lost a large amount of momentum as it traveled through Williamson's head, then the mattress and the box springs, before coming to rest in the floorboards.

Alder scratched his head. "I can't believe we missed that."

"It happens," Dodge said. "Can you go down to the kitchen and see if you can find a sandwich bag. Preferably one with a zip top. Oh, and check under the sink for a pair of kitchen gloves."

While Dodge waited for Alder to return with a bag to place the expended round in, he decided to use the time to examine the rest of the room. He had already found one huge thing the police missed. There could be others. The closet was closest to him and he figured it was as good a place as any to start. The doors swung open into themselves, folding to the sides and revealing a large walk-in closet. Suits hung on the left side, all arranged by color with their hangers spaced evenly apart. Shirts were next followed by slacks, ties and an assortment of belts in different colors. All separated evenly along the cross bar. His shoes sat side by side, their heels all perfectly lined up and even with the edges of the jackets above them.

The other side was less organized. Dresses hung in no particular order. Slacks and shirts intermixed and comingling with nightwear. Shoes were scattered all along the floor. Some standing up and others laying on their sides. No rhyme or reason to any of it. Dodge wondered how two different people could manage to live together with such differing personalities. The state of both sides of the closet seemed extreme to him. He himself probably fell somewhere in the middle of the two organizational methods.

After finding nothing of interest to the case in the closet, Dodge was walking to the bathroom, when Alder reappeared in the doorway. A plastic bag and one big yellow latex glove. The kind he remembered his mother wore while cleaning the kitchen when he was a small child. He held the two items in front of him, then noticed the closet door was open.

"Find anything in there?"

Dodge shook off the question, then grabbed the bag and glove from the detective and walked back over to the bed. He knelt down, put on the glove and reached over the metal bed frame. Pinching the end of the bullet sticking out from the floor boards, he tried to wiggle the slug loose. It wouldn't budge. Leaning back, he pulled the knife from his pocket, then began to use the pointy tip to try and pry the lead round from its resting place. He moved around the shell, being careful not to let the blade of the knife scratch the stuck round. Any scratches could make ballistics job trying to match the round to rounds used at other crime scenes harder.

The wood around the base of the bullet started to flake away and, using his gloved hand, he began rocking the round back and forth. At first it moved only a small bit, but after a few minutes, the protruding end started to jiggle more and more. After about five minutes, the metal round pulled free from the wooden floor and Dodge carefully placed it in the bag without examining it closer. He sealed the bag and handed it to an awaiting Alder.

"I'll log it in when I get back to the station and send it over to the lab for ballistics comparison," he said while holding the bag up and staring at the tiny lead round. "Looks to be in good shape. Should be able to get some lands and grooves off of it."

As Dodge stood, a pain shot across his back, causing him to pause and grab the bed frame for support to keep from falling forward. He tried to mask the pain, but the expression on his face gave him away. Alder stepped to him and placed a hand under his right arm, lifting him to his feet.

"You okay?" the detective asked, his hand still firmly wedged in Dodge's underarm crease.

"I'm good. Just a little hitch in my back."

"And by hitch, you mean having been shot in the back."

Dodge stared at the detective. But before he could answer Alder spoke.

"Yeah, I looked you up. Always important to do your homework on a suspect."

"It is," Dodge replied, now fully upright as the pain had subsided. "What did you learn about me?"

"Quite a bit. You've been in the Air Force and discharged honorably after tours in Iraq and Afghanistan. You were stabbed once and shot twice. All in the line of duty. The guy who stabbed you, you caught. The guy who shot you is still out there, somewhere." Alder smiled at his accomplishment. "That about sum it up?"

"Yep. The rest is just filler." Dodge chuckled.

"So, are we done here?"

Dodge thought for a moment, his eyes focused on the door to the bathroom. He had been interrupted before getting to take a look at the washroom. Ultimately, he decided, based on what he had seen of the scene thus far, there was no need to spend any more time at the house. The shooter was a professional. The double tap to Williamson's head proved that. Two bullets, same hole. Clearly not a random street thug committing a robbery. The shooter made no attempt to make the scene look like anything other than what it was. A targeted hit. He could think of no reason to waste time trying to find things that weren't going to be there.

"Yeah, we can go now." Dodge gave one last glance at the room before the two men exited and made their way back outside and into the waiting car.

"Where do you want to go now?"

"Back to the motel. I need to check on something."

Alder nodded and started the engine, backed out of the drive and headed back toward I30 and West Dallas. Neither man spoke. Both were thinking about the case and what the professional hit on Williamson meant. Dodge was now sure of Daughtry's involvement, even if he wasn't the shooter. He also now wondered how Williamson's murder was related to Roberts' death. He had a feeling this tracked back far beyond the sexual assault that happened to Roberts in Afghanistan. Something was eating at him but he couldn't place it yet. He needed more information on Williamson and what he was working on. Not to mention his relationship with Roberts, both personally and at work. He just wasn't sure how he was going to get it.

Chapter 15

The car slowed, easing to a stop in front of the motel. Dodge figured it didn't matter if Alder knew where he was staying. He had concluded the detective wasn't one of the bad guys and, while trusting him was hard, it's not as if he had a ton of other options. The pool containing people he could trust had dwindled greatly with the events of the past few days. Betrayal had become a more expected outcome concerning his partners as of late, but he needed someone to watch his back. And Alder didn't make the woo-woo hairs on the back of his neck sprout legs and stand at attention. He would have to do.

"This is where you are staying?" the detective asked, staring at the run down, paint chipped façade of the motel.

"It has a bed."

"So does the Hilton."

"And the Hilton is where someone looking to find me would start their search." Dodge peered over at the motel. "This would be the last place I would look for me. So, it will do fine."

He thanked Alder for the ride and stepped out into the parking lot, watching the cruiser as it pulled out into the street and drove in the direction of downtown Dallas. Dodge stood still until the car made a turn and disappeared behind a row of commercial buildings. He pulled his phone out of his pocket and saw there were no messages or missed phone calls. Then he strode toward his room, past the line of closed doors until he reached the last unit. He inserted his key and pushed the door open. Waiting patiently on the chair tucked into a corner, was the dog.

The old dog's head lifted when Dodge flipped the light switch. His tail wagged, thumping against the arm of the chair as it swung side to side. The thumping increased in volume and veracity as Dodge crossed the room toward the chair. Tobey pushed his head up into Dodge's hand and let out a low bark.

"You got to go take a piss?"

The dog barked again, seeming to understand what his master was saying.

A smile crept across the parole agent's face. Then he scratched behind Tobey's ears before turning back to the door. In one fluid movement Tobey rose and jumped out of the chair following his human to the door. Dodge slid the door open halfway, sticking his head out and checking both direction for the motel manager or cleaning staff. He imagined he could slip the cleaning staff a hundred bucks to ignore his roommate. The manager may not be as easy to bribe. Or as cheap.

After no one caught his eye, he led Tobey around the side to a small grassy patch behind the dumpster and the property adjacent to the motel. Dodge checked the ground to make sure the area wasn't used as a shooting gallery for the motels regular heroin addicted patrons and felt safe to let the dog take care of his business when he saw no discarded needles strewn about. Normally, the rule attentive parole agent would be appalled at the idea of someone not cleaning up after their dog, but it didn't even make the top ten of his things to worry about today. Besides, they were behind a garbage dumpster and he would grab some bags tomorrow for future poop laden adventures with Tobey.

Once back inside, Dodge refilled the ice bucket, placing it in the bathroom so the inevitable water splash when Tobey drank wasn't getting the carpet wet.

"I'll be back in a bit, boy. I need to run down to the corner store and grab some grub for both of us."

As he closed the door behind him, he saw the dog jump up into the chair and curl up. Tobey secured his claim of the tattered chair as his own. Dodge chuckled and closed the door behind him as he walked into the muggy evening air.

He returned a short time later dangling a white plastic sack from his hand. Once inside the room, he opened the bag and removed a can of wet dog food for Tobey, a microwaveable frozen meal with chicken and pasta for him, and the last Bottle of Blanton's Bourbon on the shelf. It was weird to him that a person could purchase hard liquor at any grocery or convenience store they chose to visit. Where Dodge is from in Virginia, the liquor stores are all owned by the State. While beer and wine can be bought anywhere that has a liquor license, hard liquor can only be purchased at a state run ABC store. He preferred the laws governing liquor sales in Texas, but so far it was about the only thing he liked better than Virginia.

Dodge shoved the plastic tray containing his frozen meal into the microwave and set the timer for five minutes. Then he popped the top of the dog food can and used a plastic spoon he took from the coffee station at the corner store to dish out the contents onto the upturned lid from the ice bucket. Tobey waited patiently in the chair; his eyes focused on the makeshift bowl full of food. When Dodge placed the lid on the plastic bag he laid out on the carpet and snapped his fingers, Tobey hopped out of the chair, devouring the food in minutes. Then the dog cleaned his face with his tongue and disappeared into the bathroom for a drink of water.

The alarm on the microwave rang and the now starving agent took the steaming meal with him and sat on the bed and ate. He took swigs from a plastic cup filled with Blantons in between bites. Tobey climbed back into the chair beside him and watched as Dodge finished his meal.

Dodge placed the container his meal came in in the bathroom sink. He washed it, then dried it, placing it on the top of the toilet tank. It would make a better bowl for Tobey's food than the lid of the ice bucket. Besides, now that he had a bottle of bourbon, he would need that lid to help keep the ice he harvested from the machine from melting. And he didn't think Tobey would care all that much.

The water was hot and refreshing as it washed over his tired muscles. He had just finished rinsing the soap out of his hair when he heard a knock at the front door. Turning off the shower and grabbing a towel from the rack, he quickly dried off then wrapped the towel around his waist and stepped out of the bathroom. He glanced over at Tobey, who was sitting up on the chair—alert to the presence of someone outside. *Rap-rap-rap.* Dodge could tell by the sound coming from the metal door, the person outside was hitting the door with the back of their fist. A reverse knock of sorts. Years of pounding on parolee's doors had alerted Dodge to the subtle differences in the way a knock sounds when a hand hits a solid surface in varying ways. It was one of those things he remembered and couldn't forget. Like song lyrics to obscure 1970's Yacht Rock songs, the sound just stuck with him.

He grabbed the now anxious dog off the chair and placed it in the bathroom. Dodge made a shushing sound with his finger to his mouth, then closed the door behind him. His eyes darted to the weapon on the nightstand. With the gun in hand he answered the door, placing his foot parallel to the door, only giving enough room for the door to open about six inches. He peered through the crack as the hinges on the metal door screeched. His hand tightening around the grip of the Glock.

"Well, aren't you going to invite me in?" Detective Alder stood outside his door with a bottle of Tequila raised in his hand.

The door swung open and Dodge stepped back to allow his new partner to enter, taking one last peek outside before shutting the door and turning to the detective.

"This place is even worse on the inside," Alder said as he stared at the dated, smoke-stained paintings on the wall.

The towel laden Dodge brushed past his visitor and opened the door to the bathroom. Jerking his head to the side signaling to Tobey it was safe to come out. The dog ran past him, stopping to sniff Alder's leg, then reacquired his spot on the faded old chair.

"You brought a dog?"

"Of course not," Dodge said from the bathroom while slipping on the pair of jeans and t-shirt he had been wearing earlier in the day.

"I'm confused. You say you didn't bring a dog, yet here I stand staring at a dog in your motel room."

Dodge emerged from the tiny bathroom fully dressed with the Glock stuffed in the back of his waistline. He walked over to the chair and patted

Tobey on the head before parking himself on the edge of the bed next to the dog.

"I didn't bring a dog with me. I don't even own a dog. I found this guy wandering the streets and gave him some food and water."

"Big mistake. If you feed them, they will come back," Alder said begrudgingly.

"I think that's cats."

Alder pointed at the nearly sleeping animal. "Obviously, it refers to dogs too."

Tired of talking about Tobey, Dodge shook his head and asked, "Why are you here?"

"I was headed out to check out the Advanced Systems Technology's facility and thought I would see if you wanted to ride along."

Tapping the LCD screen on his phone, Dodge looked up at the detective. "Pretty sure this is a little past business hours."

Alder nodded. "It is. I checked their website. It seems they run a day shift only. Standard banking hours."

"These types of outfits tend to have a few people working contracts that require overnight coverage. It may be only ten or fifteen people, but my guess is there is someone there all night. Even if it was just a day shift only case, there will be twenty-four-hour security with guards at the gate, a couple rovers and cameras in every nook and corner of the building. Inside and out." Dodge pushed himself off the bed, wincing in pain as he rose. "What is it you're looking to find."

"I don't really know," Alder said. "I was hoping maybe you could help with that."

"Not sure what I can do."

"You know more about this stuff than I do. I'm sure in your time in the military, you dealt with contractors and, well, whatever it is they do."

"Those types of issues were a little above my paygrade."

"What about now?"

"I was out of the air force for more than ten years before I got pulled back in for this mess. And even then, it was more of a personal favor for an old friend. My guess is the Pentagon will shut me down and hand me my walking papers as soon as Williamson's murder pops on their radar. The last thing they want is an outsider snooping around and digging up dirt on someone they were in bed with for millions of dollars."

The detective shook his head. "Fucking brass is gonna brass. Doesn't matter if it's the locals or the Feds."

Dodge nodded.

"So, you want to come or not."

Dodge peered at his phone. He noticed he now had several voice messages from the same number that had called him earlier, after Daughtry killed Tremble and left him with his dick in his hand outside of Jackson, Mississippi. He would need to call Patterson back and fill him in on Daughtry and the whole mess with Tremble and now Williamson. Not to mention, the itch he couldn't scratch. Had his old boss been in on this from the beginning? Did he use Dodge like a bowling pin to get hit by the others and take the fall for everything? And if Patterson wasn't involved, could he now be a target? Would Daughtry make a move on him to tie up loose ends?

The fact was, Dodge had a lot more questions than answers. He needed to be in on every part of the investigation if he had any hope of unraveling this tangled web of murder and deceit.

"I'll go with you. Just give me a second to take the dog out one last time before we go."

Once Tobey was back inside and resting peacefully on his chair, the two men began the long drive across town to the Advanced Systems Technology corporate headquarters to hopefully find some answers.

Chapter 16

Dodge had been right about the security at the federal contracting facility. He had seen hundreds over the years back in Virginia, and geography didn't have an effect on security protocols. The long rectangular building was surrounded by a tall black fence. He had seen the same design many times before at government facilities in Virginia. Cameras kept watch from atop tall posts at regular intervals along the fence's perimeter. Some pointing inward and others pointing outward. The owners weren't just worried about unwanted guests getting in. They wanted to make sure anyone inside wasn't trying to sneak anything out and into the awaiting arms of unauthorized personnel. Inside the fence, the lawn rolled in large mounds. Like waves on the ocean in a design meant to slow any vehicles that managed to breach the fence and make a run at the outside walls of the building. This building's security rivaled that of Fort Knox.

Alder drove past the facility as the two men stared at the black fence as it passed by their windows.

"What do you make of all this?" the detective asked.

Dodge watched in silence as the car turned a corner and they began traveling along the rear of the building.

Alder spoke again. "Seems like a lot of security for office work."

"It does at that," Dodge said, his eyes peeled for anything appearing unusual.

As they approached the next road and the corner of the building, Dodge blurted out, "THERE!"

Alder slowed the vehicle and came to a stop. Out the driver's side window, the two men could see a narrow strip if pavement that had been hidden by the rolling hills built into the landscape. Between two earthen mounds, they could see the road turned back toward the building and disappeared about twenty yards before the edge of the building sprung up from its foundation.

"Where do you suppose that goes?" Alder asked. His eyes squinting, trying to gain a better view.

"I'd say it leads into an underground garage."

"There seemed to be plenty of parking area along the side of the building. I don't know how many people work here but, based on the size of the building, I'd guess maybe a couple hundred. About the same as a Walmart. So, what do they need the underground garage for?"

"For visitors they don't want people to know about."

"Like who?"

"For starters, high ranking Defense Department personnel. Nothing tips off that something secret is going on in a building like a line of military personnel, all in uniform, strolling through the front door." Dodge looked up at the fence and the camera pointing directly toward them. "Better get moving. Don't want to draw any unwanted attention."

Alder accelerated and turned the wheel left at the next intersection. The building was enormous and rested on nearly the entire block. The side of the facility was almost a mirror image of the opposite side. Only positioned squarely in the middle was a set of three loading bays. Two occupied by semi-trucks. Their headlights off, but the lights plastered all over the cab of the truck were glowing red and orange.

"Looks like someone works at night," Alder said.

Dodge nodded. Then he got an idea. "Let's drive back around to the main entrance."

"You want to try and get inside?"

"I want to see how good their security is."

The detective continued, then turned left at the next road and made another left when they reached the end of the building. He approached the entrance slowly and maneuvered the cop car into the drive, which immediately had a switchback so the main gate was parallel with the road.

Dodge knew this would allow for employees to wait in line to be scanned into the facility without blocking traffic on the main road.

The car pulled up to the gate and Alder rolled down his window. An empty guard shack stood in the middle of the entrance and exit lanes. Protruding from a post next to the shack was a silver call box.

"Push the button," Dodge urged his partner.

Alder's finger pressed the round button positioned under a small camera lens. A minute passed before the speaker crackled and a voice came over the box.

"State your business."

Dodge grabbed Alder's arm and leaned in. He whispered, "Show them your badge."

Alder reached into his pocket and retrieved his shield. He held it up to the camera.

Dodge said, "Police. We had a report of someone loitering around the fence earlier. We were wondering if we could come in and get a look at the surveillance tapes from an hour ago."

The box was silent for a moment. Then a different voice came through the static filled speaker.

"Please back out of the facility and come back during business hours. You are trespassing on Department of Defense property. You have no jurisdiction here and we will be forced to remove you if you fail to follow our instructions."

Alder looked over at Dodge sitting next to him. "They seem serious."

"They are."

Dodge waved at the camera and the car slowly backed up until there was enough room to turn around.

"Did you find out what you wanted to know?"

"I did," Dodge said.

"Do you care to share that with me?"

"What do you say we go get a drink?"

"I'm on duty."

Dodge smiled. "Okay. Let's go somewhere and I'll get a drink."

Fifteen minutes later, the two men were saddled up to a long wooden topped bar. The décor was a splash of 1980's beer mirrors and a spattering of spring break get away. Pictures hung on the walls with no discernable order or reason for placement. The one theme they all had in common was they all featured cops. Some from decades long past and others more recent. At the center of it all was a commemorative plaque. Its wooden frame stacked from edge to edge with the badges of fallen officers. Alder saw Dodge staring at the piece.

"There is about fifty in there."

"Are they all from here?" Dodge asked.

"Most of them but, from time to time, an out of towner will come in and place one in the case."

"It's a tough gig," Dodge said turning back to the bartender, who was now standing in front across from them waiting for their order.

"What'll it be, fellas," he said in a low tone, suggesting it was more of a statement than a question. Probably meant to let patrons know if you weren't here to drink, then you could take your ass somewhere else.

Dodge peered over the man's shoulder at the line of brown liquors sitting on a shelf behind him. When he saw the signature round bottle, he ordered a double of Blantons.

"Club soda for me. I'm driving apparently," Alder said, tossing side eye at Dodge.

"Your choice," Dodge responded, picking the glass off the bar and swallowing its contents in one gulp. "Hit me," he said to the short but lean bartender.

The man lifted the bottle and poured another double.

"Sure you don't want one?" Dodge asked the detective sipping his clear fizzy soda water.

"What, you don't like to drink alone?"

Dodge let out a sneer. "Actually, I prefer it."

"You're a strange bird, Agent Dodge."

"I suppose I am," he replied, then finished the drink.

"One more if you will, kind sir."

Alder shook his head and the two men sat in silence for another fifteen minutes before Dodge signaled he was ready to go.

Once back at the motel, a tipsy Dodge stepped out of the car, saying goodnight after telling Alder he would be at the station in the morning, around nine. They could then hash out their next move in the investigation. But he needed to make a call. A call he'd been putting off for a couple days. A call that could change the direction of the entire case.

***

He stepped out into the morning sun after showering and taking Tobey out for a short walk. He had already gotten used to having the little mutt around and had grown quite fond of him. Which only caused more problems. What to do with the dog when it came time to leave. Taking the dog with him meant a long drive in a rental car instead of a short plane ride back home. And that was another thing. He still needed to stop in Indiana before heading back to Virginia. The call from his old boss, Lieutenant Colonel Patterson, had forced him to change his priorities and there was still a lot of work he had to complete before his brother's old place was ready for sale. He currently had a dozen problems and Tobey only added to the list. But all that would have to wait.

He looked up at the blue sky. The sun had peeked over the roofs of the surrounding buildings and he could feel the oppressive heat beginning to set in. Looking at the phone in his hand; he dreaded making the call. Nothing good was going to come from his conversation with Colonel Patterson and a pit in his stomach formed as he dialed the phone. It rang twice before his old mentor answered.

"Dodge. I've been waiting to hear from you. I expected an update much sooner than this, which is why I called you three times."

"I know. I didn't recognize the number at first."

"It's a DOD phone. Where the hell is Daughtry? And why is he not returning my calls?" His voice approached scream level volume as he continued. "Somebody better fill me in on what's going on, right God damned now!"

"Sir, if you'll calm down for a moment, I will tell you what you want to know." *This call was going stellar so far*, he thought.

Colonel Patterson barked into the phone, "Talk now."

Dodge had hoped to calm the old man down a little before breaking the news of Daughtry's betrayal to him but, based on the tone of his voice, that plan was rubbish. Better to rip it off like a band-aid. Get it over with.

"Sir…,"

Colonel Patterson interrupted him. "Cut the sir shit, Dodge. Just get to the damn point."

"Yes, si…, I mean okay."

Dodge told the story from the beginning. The information he and Daughtry gleaned from the recruiter. How that led to the trip to Dallas and Detective Alder. The two men's visit to Florence to try and find Lilly Tremble. Then his voice darkened as he told of Daughtry's treachery and Tremble's murder. The line went quiet. While there was one more piece of bad news he needed to get out into the open, Dodge thought it best to let the old soldier process what he had just heard. It was a lot to take in and was quite a shock to one of his oldest friends, he was sure. But always the investigator, Dodge had ulterior motives. He wanted, no, he needed to see how Patterson responded. The old man's reaction could fill in some of the gaps and help explain if he had any involvement in the last few days' events.

The silence was deafening. Dodge began to wonder if the call had somehow been dropped. As he was about to ask if Patterson was still there, his mentor spoke.

"Is that everything?" His voice was cold and distant. Dodge couldn't tell by the man's tone if he was shocked by what he had heard or if there was something else on his mind.

"No. There *is* one more thing. Blake Williamson's dead."

"Okay. Is that all?"

"That is all, for now," Dodge answered.

The line went quiet again. This time Dodge didn't wait to give his old boss time to think. He needed to speed things up to see where this conversation could go.

"I'm fairly certain there are two shooters now. The person who killed

Shannon Roberts and whomever executed Blake Williamson."

"And you think Airman Daughtry is involved in both of the murders?"

"He killed Tremble and could have killed me," Dodge said.

"Why didn't he?"

"Why didn't he what? Kill me?"

"From what you told me, he could have shot you before, or after, murdering Tremble. So, why didn't he?"

Dodge had been trying not to think about this very thing for a few days now. He had narrowly escaped death less than a year ago. Though it wasn't for the assailant's lack of trying. Dodge had caught one round in the shoulder and one in the back. He spent several weeks recovering in the hospital and months in physical therapy getting his body right after being discharged. The incident was his second brush with death as a parole officer and he wasn't thrilled about another mark in his ledger. As the saying goes, *two is a coincidence and three is a pattern.* Regardless of if there were one, two or ten incidents, the questions were the same. Was it part of the job? Or was it something else? Something about him. Maybe the veteran agent was becoming careless, or complacent? Either way, if he wanted to stay off the coroner's slab, he realized he needed to make some changes.

But this time with Daughtry was different. Dodge was a limp meat sack on the floor. Completely unconscious, he wouldn't have even known it had happened. So, why was he still alive? Why hadn't his traitorous sidekick put a round in the back of his head? Truth was, he didn't have an answer to that question. Yet.

"I don't know why he didn't end me right there on that floor. But I will find out. That I can assure you," Dodge said.

The voice on the other end of the line stuttered. "I'm afraid I have put you at too much risk already and should have never asked you to look into this. I won't have any more deaths on my hands."

Dodge stood silent—the phone pressed up against his ear. Waiting for what he knew was coming.

"I'm pulling the plug," the old man finally said. "When we are done here, I am going to call the Pentagon and get them off your back. Then I'll phone the Governor's office and put in a good word. He's a close friend. You can consider yourself a free man again. I'll make sure the money you are owed is wired into your account and I'll personally reimburse you for expenses. You should have enough in the account by tomorrow morning to cover anything you have incurred and a little extra. Thank you for your dedicated service once again. I also thank you as a friend."

Before Dodge could respond, the line went dead. He stood there for a moment, not sure what had just happened. He had been turned off the investigation, that he knew. He had lost the one thing he needed to find the people responsible for three murders. Access. His sudden call up to active duty had provided him with the means to insert himself into almost any situation with the full force of the US government at his back. Now he was just a citizen. In a state where he had zero jurisdiction and no legal means to gain access to investigative materials anymore. In fact, his continued presence could now put Detective Alder's entire case in jeopardy. He liked the detective and had no intention of hanging him out to dry. Besides he would need the detective's access if he wanted to find Daughtry and figure out what the hell was going on. And that was exactly what he intended to do. Badge or no badge, he would hunt them down and bring them all to justice.

Chapter 17

Alder was in his office when Dodge arrived at the police station. The detective must have left word that he was expecting a visitor, as the receptionist buzzed Dodge in and waved him toward the secure door before he could announce himself at the receptionist's window. He was about a half-hour late because he decided to have one more cup of coffee before leaving the restaurant, after finishing his breakfast. One too many drinks the night before left his head feeling like it had been placed in a vice that morning. The truth was, he hadn't been consuming much alcohol since the shooting. Sure, he had a few glasses of Blantons here and there, but not the usual two to three glasses a night he had become accustomed to over the years. The doctor had asked him to lay off the booze until his wounds healed so, for once, Dodge followed someone else's advice about his drinking and laid off. But that ended last night and he felt a lack of tolerance.

When Dodge stepped into the doorway, Alder was leaning over, staring at a pile of paper scattered across the top of his desk.

"Morning," Dodge said from the open door.

The detective's head raised, and he nodded. "Thanks for not saying *good* morning." He waved his hand, signaling Dodge to come closer. Clearly, he noticed the dark circles under Dodge's eyes, remarking, "You look like you had a rough night."

Dodge rubbed his shoulder. "Been laying off the brown water for while I heal. I guess my body got used to it."

"I got a bottle if you need a little to straighten you up," Alder said, reaching for a drawer in his desk.

His head was starting to pound again. Facilitated by a sharp pain directly behind his right eye. He strongly considered the offer but waved the bottle off and sat in the chair to his left. "I'll be fine," Dodge said. "What ya got?"

Alder slid the bottle back into the drawer and pushed it closed. Then he pulled his chair back and settled in.

"Well, I did some digging into Advanced Systems Technology last night after I dropped you off."

"Find anything interesting?" Dodge asked.

"Honestly, there wasn't a lot out there. According to incorporation records, the company was formed in O-four, after the push into Iraq. It was small with only a handful of employees."

"That story played out over and over from the beginning for the invasion to the pullout in twelve. Everyone who had a ware to sell or a trade to pawn got into the contracting game. There were literally billions of dollars for the taking and everyone got a piece."

Well, after the pullout in Iraq, Williamson expanded his outfit into Afghanistan. After that, trail goes dead," Alder said.

"There was likely a jump in the classification levels of the projects his company was working on when they made the move into the Afghanistan theatre. Pretty common practice. Once the company has shown it has the ability to do the work it was originally contracted to do, it gets a whole lot easier to bid on more sensitive jobs."

"And better paying ones, I assume."

Dodge nodded. "It was likely easier for AST to win the contract, even if it wasn't the highest bidder, because they already had assets in Iraq," Dodge said.

"Quicker to move them from two-thousand miles away than ten thousand," Alder said.

"And cheaper."

Th two men sat quietly for a minute. Then Alder asked the question Dodge knew he was going to ask.

"Do you think this all has something to do with ATS and what they were doing overseas?"

Dodge wasn't ready to answer this question. He didn't have any evidence linking Roberts or Tremble to AST, or Williamson, in Afghanistan. Sure, they were all in the country at the same time, but Afghanistan is a big place and there were tens of thousands of contractors and soldiers on the ground during that time period. Now that he had lost access to the Pentagon, getting information on Williamson and ATS's presence in a war zone would be next to impossible. And that brought up another issue. He wasn't ready to disclose to Alder that he lost all his military connections. He was officially on the outside looking in. No access to personnel files. No access to classified information. He certainly won't be able to push his way into ATS without the use of threats of calls to DC and defense department auditors combing through every financial record the company has ever submitted, searching for overcharges and funny accounting practices. He had lost his edge and things were going to get harder from here on out.

"It may have, but there is no way we will ever have enough time to dig deep enough into that bureaucratic nightmare for answers. The Pentagon is where requests for information go to die."

He watched the detective for a reaction. Finally, Alder leaned back and said, "You're probably right. My guess is they are circling their wagons as we speak. Looks like we are going to have to go at this from the beginning, Shannon Roberts' murder."

A wave of relief swept over him. Alder had taken the bait and bought Dodge some time. Waskom, Texas, 75692. Now he just needed to come up with a plan. It wouldn't be easy. He had no idea if Roberts' shooter was a local or was brought in from back east. He also didn't know where Daughtry was or what his future plans were. But somehow, he knew the two men would cross paths again. Sooner than he imagined.

***

Unbeknownst to Dodge, in a no name motel three hundred miles east, in a little Texas town on the Louisiana border only a few hundred feet from Interstate 20, Airman Daughtry was hunkered down before the final leg of his journey. Normally a four-hour drive, it had taken him more than a day to make his way from Jackson to the Texas border town of Waskom. It had been an arduous trip, one he knew he would have to make the moment Dodge found Lilly Tremble in Florence, MS, and they knocked on her door. He had hoped she wouldn't be home. That she wouldn't answer the door. That he wouldn't have to kill her. But that hope ended the moment she saw his face.

His only mistake was not killing Dodge. He had been under strict orders not to hurt Dodge. It wasn't his job to question his commander's orders, but to follow them. If he was honest with himself, he would have seen those orders were flawed from the beginning. So was the idea to bring an outsider into this. He'd had Roberts dealt with and no one was any the wiser. The local cops had all but given up. Now there were three murders instead of one.

Daughtry never fancied himself an intellectual, but he could do simple math. Three murders were two more than one. Making them much harder to hide and easier to track. He had personally chosen the shooter who eliminated Roberts. A marine he had met in his first tour in Iraq. A sniper. The fact he was able to track him down to a rundown trailer park on the outskirts of Dallas, was like divine intervention. Rarely had a plan come together so easily and the old marine executed the plan flawlessly. Daughtry had paid the shooter twenty thousand for the hit. He also lo-jacked hid his rusted-out Ford pick-up before leaving town in case he needed to locate him again. It turned out he needed him for one more job.

At first, the old marine didn't want to take the contract. He was a sniper and liked to be far away from his targets as their heads exploded. It was easier not to see them as human beings and to construct a backstory in his head to justify the life he was about to take. He had over ten kills in Iraq and every one of them was for the betterment of his country. At least this is what he told himself. But this job would be up close and personal. With a handgun. He would have to look the target in the eyes and squeeze the trigger while trying to block out the whimpering and begging that would surely precede the kill shot. That he didn't know if he could do.

In the end, greed won out. It always did with these guys. Daughtry offered him double his last job and a new truck. The thought of food on the table, booze in the fridge and the nicest truck in the mobile home community was too tempting to pass up and he accepted the contract. Daughtry hadn't known the job had been successful because he had smashed his phone and tossed the remnants over the side of a bridge into an awaiting creek after dumping and torching the rental car.

He had waited to purchase a prepaid cellular from a convenience store when he finally made it to Texas. His first message was to the marine.

Is it done?

The response came almost immediately. *it's done. when do I get my money?*

As soon as I get back to Dallas.

When?

Should be there tomorrow. I'll let you know when I get to town.

kk. don't even think about trying to screw me. i know who you are and who you work for. i'll be waiting.

Daughtry smiled after reading the last message. He doubted the marine knew who he reported to, but it didn't matter. He would tie up that loose end as soon as he got back to Dallas. The marine would never see the money or a new truck. Instead, he would die in a tragic mobile home fire. A lit cigarette falls onto the ratty carpet. Its owner passed out on the couch, drunk. Those old homes are like tinder boxes. The whole thing would be engulfed in flames in a matter of minutes. And the heat from the fire would burn off any signs of the chloroform Daughtry would use to make sure his victim didn't wake up in the middle of the fire. Chances are no one would even care to look for it. Long expensive autopsies were not something usually afforded to poor trailer trash. Someone would have to care, and the airman was sure no one would.

Then his real mission in Dallas would begin. To kill Dodge. Things had changed and he was now an acceptable target. He was going to enjoy wrapping his huge hands around the parole agent's neck and watching as the life drains from his body.

Chapter 18

Alder and Dodge decided to eat lunch at a small diner across the street from the police station. It was close to two in the afternoon and most of the patrons were police officers or administrative staff from the department. Dodge took slow bites from a grilled cheese sandwich, chewing each mouthful completely to extract every drop of grease he craved from his hangover, choosing to wash his meal down with a cup of strong black coffee as his stomach started to settle. Alder ordered a salad with some sort of oil-type dressing on the side. He said he tried to eat a salad at least once a day, per his cardiologist's orders. Each salad could contain three ounces of protein, preferably chicken or turkey. Alder went with chicken and chewed each bite like it was the best meal he had ever eaten. Dodge couldn't help but think he'd rather be dead than eat that way for the next twenty to thirty years. But each to his own.

The two men didn't talk much during the meal and the waitress came and cleared the empty plates from the table after Alder pushed his bowl to the side.

"Anything else I can get you, Officers?"

"I'll take a refill of coffee," Dodge said.

Alder pulled a twenty from his wallet and handed it to the waitress. "Make it to go," he said. "And keep the change."

The server put the bill in her red and white striped pocket sewn to the front of her apron, smiled, then turned and walked away. She returned with a Styrofoam cup filled to the brim and placed a plastic lid over the top of the cup. Placing the drink on the table, she said, "Thank you," and slid over to the next booth to take the order of an elderly couple who had just sat down.

The men exited the diner, Alder tossed a toothpick he finished using to dislodge some food from his teeth, onto the ground.

"Where to now?"

Dodge stopped, his eyes scanned the streets and his surroundings. All he could see was tall buildings. There was no line of sight in any direction for more than a few blocks. He needed to be able to see the entire city. It was just how his mind worked. Getting the lay of the land helped him visualize and process information. It was like looking down on a big jigsaw puzzle, but only the puzzle was in three dimensions.

"Is there a place where I can see the entire city?"

"You mean like a big map?" Alder said.

Dodge shook his head, his index finger pointing at the sky. "No. A place I can see the entire city, from above."

A smile formed on Alder's face. I think I know of a place.

A few minutes later the two men stood at the base of a tall cement structure. Reunion Tower stretched 561' into the Dallas skyline. It stood in three round pillars, all connected to a central column, like a tripod for holding a camera. In this case the camera was a round observation deck enclosed in glass. It wasn't the tallest building downtown. It wasn't even in the top ten, but it's 360° views provided visitors with the best panorama money could buy, with exception of a helicopter ride above the skyline.

The elevator ascension to the top took only a few minutes and, shortly after arriving, the two men were standing next to the crystal-clear glass panels, gazing out over the city. Dodge took a minute to enjoy what lay before him. The building of glass and concrete spaced strategically around the downtown business district was stunning from high above the chaos of the busy streets below. It was like an artist's conception of what a city should look like. Dallas was a perfect mix of modern and contemporary architecture, creating one of the best skyline views anywhere in the world.

After a few minutes, he turned to Alder. "Which direction is the park where Roberts was found?"

Alder turned to his left and walked about a quarter way around the circle shaped observation deck. He then pointed north-east. The tallest building to the left of his gesture, over the historic district. "It's about nine miles that way."

Dodge stepped up to the glass and gazed out over the scene below. His eyes fixated on a point in the distance he couldn't see. But he could visualize it in his head now that he was here. His mind replayed the car ride out to White Rock Lake the first days he was in Dallas, like watching a recorded movie on television. He pictured himself standing on the spot where Roberts was killed, staring across the blue water of White Rock Lake at the hospital where he was sure the deadly shot was fired from. Then he flipped the lake and visualized himself on the roof of the hospital. Rifle in hand. Staring though a scope—the crosshairs resting on Roberts. He squeezed the trigger. His eyes following the projectile as it cut through the heavy air, reaching its target in less than three seconds. Then Roberts collapsed to the ground. The thought sent a shiver down his spine.

Turning east, Dodge stared out into the distance. In the direction of Jackson, Mississippi, and Lily Tremble. He said nothing. Alder wasn't privy to everything that transpired in the little Mississippi town. Dodge wasn't sure how he would take the news or if Alder would call the authorities in Florence, Mississippi, and alert them to his involvement in Tremble's death. If the local police were to find out about Dodge's proximity to the murder, even if just tangent, he would most likely have to return to answer questions. And that was the best-case scenario. The worst-case would be, Alder shackling his hands behind his back and him waiting on the extradition proceedings that would certainly follow. He preferred the ground he was currently navigating. The one where he wasn't arrested and his partner was left in the dark about a small part of the investigation that took happened out of his jurisdiction. It was the only logical choice if he wanted to catch the killer and find Daughtry. He didn't know how many more loose ends might be dangling out there, unaware of a pending expiration date on their existence on this earth. But there was one loose end they might try and tie off. One he could use to bait Daughtry into a trap. Himself.

Next, Dodge circled around to the opposite side of the observation platform. The western side. His eyes once again focused off to a point in the distance. He visualized the front of Williamson's home. The entrance way and portico. His mind focused on the stairs and the bedroom. The spot where they found Williamson, face up on the bed with a hole in his head. Dodge closed his eyes and began trying to fit all the puzzle pieces together. Williamson. Roberts. Tremble. Afghanistan. Daughtry. All these things were connected and Dodge was beginning to believe the attack on Roberts during her tour in Afghanistan had little to do with her death. or the other murders.

Two murders of people who worked together in the same town. A friend and confidant of once of the victims killed before he could speak to her. And now the man who brought him in to find the people who attacked his niece several years ago, has had a sudden change of heart. He has pulled Dodge off the case. Taken away his only tool to find the culprits responsible for the man's niece, his access. At this moment, Dodge was trying to put together a puzzle where all the pieces were white. He could find the edges, but the middle was just a mound of similar shaped, similar colored cutouts. He needed more information before he could draw any conclusions. And now he knew where he needed to begin.

"Find what you were looking for?" Alder asked, stepping up behind Dodge.

Dodge faced the detective. "We need to check out ATS again. Only this time from the inside." Dodge knew what he was suggesting sounded impossible. The last time the two men rolled up to the gate, Alder's badge got them nothing but a trespass warning. He needed to come up with a plan to get him inside. He needed to find out what the company, especially Williamson, was working on. But without his old military connections, he wouldn't be able to bully his way through the front gate. They'd have to try using the badge again. Alder was investigating the murder of the company's owner. He had a legal right to talk to people who knew Williamson and to possibly see the dead man's calendar. It just had to be played the right way. And for that, Dodge needed to be the one going in. Only he wasn't sure he could sell it to Alder.

The idea went over about as well as Dodge had expected. Alder flat out refused letting a civilian use his badge for any reason, let alone one that could provide evidence of the murder of two people in his town.

"How the hell do you expect me to get anything you find in this illegal search past the district attorney? And even if it did, somehow make it to a courtroom and in front of a judge? I wouldn't be able to swear an oath about how the evidence was obtained. I'd lose my professional integrity, not to mention my job and pension."

Dodge could sympathize with Alder. Although he could act with impunity now, he knew what he asked for was a lot. He wasn't sure if the tables were turned if he would be willing to take the risk and sacrifice so much. And after an hour of arguing the ends justifying the means, Alder came up with a solution that might work for both of them. Alder would gain entrance into ATS so that everything was above board. However, he would not be alone. He would have an earpiece, to keep in constant communication with Dodge who would be waiting in a parking lot across the street. And attached to his body, he would sport the latest in digital camera technology. A gift left behind by Homeland Security while providing security for the President of the United States on a recent visit to the city. The wireless camera and microphone had a range of over a half mile. Dodge would easily be able to see and hear what was happening inside. Now they just needed a distraction once Alder made his way into the main offices. One that would buy him enough time to snoop around and look for anything that could be of help in the investigation. Fortunately, Dodge had a plan for that too.

Chapter 19

Everything was going according to plan. They spent most of the evening in Dodge's motel room the night before, double checking the equipment the detective signed out of surveillance inventory. Dodge knew he lied on the requisition form when asked about why he needed it, but he didn't feel the need to rub salt on an open wound. Alder was a by the books guy and it was clear to Dodge, the detective was struggling to justify his deception to himself.

"I don't know about this," Alder said, placing the earpiece into his right ear.

Dodge looked up from his task of hooking up the wireless camera into the folds of the detective's shirt. It was a small box, only a few millimeters thick and stuck to the inside of the shirt with adhesive tape. The case was flexible and worked like a television antenna, only it transmitted a signal instead of receiving one. A brilliant design and Dodge admired the simplicity of it all. The camera lens was built into a tie clip. Innocuous to even the well-trained eye. Dodge bet the gear was probably developed at Langley, then sold to the other agencies when better equipment came along, or the ones they were using had been exposed and no longer of use in the field.

"Push it in a little further," Dodge said, pointing to the earpiece.

The detective wiggled the plastic plug and pushed gently with his index finger until the device was not visible without a good inspection. "There. How's that?"

A quick glance up and Dodge nodded approvingly. Then he finished clipping the camera to the tie and adjusted the height based on the video feed he was receiving on a handheld monitor. He wanted to be sure he could see faces. He could then use the images to mark employees as they exited the facility then learn where they lived. He and Alder could pay them an official visit later for an interview. It all seemed like a good plan. Until it wasn't.

The next morning, everything went to plan. Dodge was waiting for his ride at a little past nine in the morning. He had made sure Tobey was fed and let out to take care of his business. He then patted the dog on his head and closed the door behind him as he left.

Once in the car, the two men went over the details of the plan again. Dodge didn't want to leave anything to chance, including an escape plan. If something went to shit inside, Dodge would create a distraction at the gate to allow Alder time to get out of the building and to his car. Once in his car he could use his phone to call for police assistance if security wouldn't let him leave. It was a numbers game. Dallas PD could bring hundreds of officers and a well-trained S.W.A.T. Team complete with armored vehicles. They would get their man out.

At the gate, Alder used his rank and badge to get past the guards. Dodge sipped coffee and watched from behind the glass of a convenience store across the street. Once inside the main gate Dodge had to switch to the monitor to see what was transpiring.

"I'm in," Alder's voice came over the speaker.

"Roger," Dodge answered. "I have a visual."

All Dodge could see now was the steering wheel and the legs of Alder as he maneuvered the police cruiser through the maze of barricades. Installed to slow traffic and keep threats from advancing closer to the building if they made it past security in a car or truck, giving security enough time to recover and shred the vehicle and its occupants with fire from multiple vantage points.

"I'm at the front. Getting out now and heading in."

"Roger that. I'll be watching," Dodge said. "Don't forget to ask for a cup of coffee once you're in the waiting room."

It was a simple plan. Dodge had been in many of these types of locations over the years. Both civilian and military. Once passed through security, Alder should be taken to the main offices where he will be forced to wait on whomever is in charge now that Williamson is dead. He was counting on a secretary stationed in the waiting room with any visitors and that is where the coffee comes in.

There was a tense moment when security guided Alder toward a metal detector. Dodge wasn't sure of the camera or its black box would set the machine off, but he knew they didn't want the extra scrutiny. Quick thinking by the detective salvaged the moment, as he told the guards he had a pacemaker installed in his chest recently and a magnetometer might set the device off and deliver an unnecessary charge of electricity to his heart and he wasn't a fan of that possible outcome. The guards questioned him about the procedure and Alder even offered to unbutton his shirt to reveal the scar from the procedure. It was a dangerous bluff if it didn't work, but the two men in black uniforms relented and the detective consented to a pat down.

Alder had been on the force long enough to know how to steer a pat-down away from the areas he didn't want the guards to focus on. It was an old trick learned from inmates in county jail. The right reaction, or flinch, as a pat down reaches a benign area, away from where the contraband is hidden, can cause the searcher to waste time searching where the hidden items are not. Then when nothing is found, they may hurriedly finish the search to keep the line moving and the contraband will go unnoticed and into the facility.

The detective had already accomplished this when he mentioned his heart procedure. The mere mention of a pace maker accompanied by a surgical scar made the guard uncomfortable enough to skip the chest area. No one wants to touch someone else's wound. Not for fear of hurting the person, but because somewhere deep in our brain, blood and guts are repulsive. Add in the decades long training history on blood borne pathogens diagraming the spread of infectious diseases, every police and fire and security company mandates employees undergo, and Alder makes it into the facility with his camera.

Once inside the facilities initial security checkpoint, the detective is met by a security escort.

"Good afternoon, sir," Dodge heard the low graveled voice over the speaker.

"Actually, it's Detective," he then heard Alder say.

"Nice touch," Dodge said to no one.

Through the camera embedded in the tie clip Alder wore, he could see the security escort was not impressed with the detective's answer. But Alder grabbed the momentum before the guy could spit out another question. Good move.

"I'm Detective Alder with the Dallas Police Department. I'm here concerning the murder of Blake Williamson, who I believe was the owner of this company."

The security escort stared at the detective and Dodge noticed him sizing up the cop standing in front of him. Never a good sign. He noticed right away the man's posture change. A slight widening of the feet. The dominant foot slid slightly in front of the other. His body turned, angled. The blade, as it is called in self-defense class. He was preparing for a confrontation.

Then he touched his finger to his ear. A moment passed and as quickly as he had shifted into the ready position, he relaxed.

"Follow me please, Detective."

Dodge exhaled. He hadn't even recognized he had been holding his breath for over a minute. He watched as Alder was led through a series of winding hallways and office fronts. The ever diligent agent did his best to try and keep a mental map of the path Alder was taking. He made mental notes of anything that could help him identify the hallways and offices as the escort led Alder deeper into the building. A comic strip on an office window. The placement of an exit sign. Restroom signs and drinking fountains. All were meticulously stored into his biological RAM, to be recalled if and when the time called for it.

After about two minutes, Alder was led into a large room. Its walls decorated with modern paintings and posters of military equipment, ranging from tanks to planes to satellites, plastered on every other available surface.

Alder had made it to the inner sanctum. He was clearly in the place where they brought special guests. The posters being a reminder of what ATS's purpose was. To help the US military achieve victory in the field. The whole scene made Dodge sick to his stomach. It was about money and everyone knew it. That's just the way it was. He optimistically wished everyone would stop with the patriotic theme music and tell it like it was. Pay us and we will do your bidding.

Dodge watched on the small monitor as the guard showed him to a sofa positioned in the middle of the room. He watched as Alder turned, pretending to admire the paintings and posters on the wall. All the while providing Dodge with a layout of the room. Smart man.

Then Dodge noticed something. Something strange. There was no one else in the room. No secretary. No other visitors. The room was void of employees. He also noticed there were no other doors visible. The woo-hoo hairs on the back of his neck stood at attention. The transmitter in his hand raised to his mouth.

"Alder. Don't answer verbally, but I want you to turn to your left if you can hear me."

A few seconds passed and the camera lens swung to the left.

"Good. Now, do you see any additional doors in the room? If you don't see any exits other than the way you came in, focus on a picture on the wall and take two steps toward it."

The camera swung right a hundred and eighty degrees. Then back left and finally left again facing a wall. The picture jostled as he moved closer to the wall.

"Shit," Dodge said, careful not to transmit his concern over the radio. "I need you to focus on the floor." The camera angled down. Dodge had a view of the floor and he didn't like what he saw. The floor was concrete, smooth and shiny. No carpet and not a single rug. "Move the couch forward."

Alder's hands flashed palms up on the screen. As if to say, *What the hell is going on?*

"Just do it," Dodge said impatiently.

Alder looked around the room, then moved over to the couch and pushed the furniture piece about a foot from its original resting spot. Then the camera stopped moving. Its lens focused on one spot on the floor. A small circular metal drain.

Alder broke the silence. "What the hell is going on here, Dodge?"

Dodge was already out the door of the convenience store and sprinting across the parking lot. "It's a clean room!" he shouted. "Get the hell out of there."

Dodge had seen many clean rooms in his career. A small room decorated for whatever purpose the owner needed. But all of them had two features in common. A smooth concrete floor, with a slight canter toward the middle of the room, where all the water and blood could be washed down a central drain and into the sewer system. The rooms were made for interrogating and disposing of bodies once the victim had no more information to provide. Some rooms are empty except for a metal chair placed squarely in the middle, like the ones the CIA and military interrogators used in Afghanistan and Iraq. Civilian ones are more subtle. Retrofitted to look like offices so the victim will willingly enter, their guard down. By the time they figure out something is wrong, it's too late. There is no way out. Luckily for Alder, Dodge figured out what was happening. But he still wasn't sure if he could stop it.

Dodge sprinted across the road, one vehicle, a black truck, nearly careened off the road as its driver slammed on the brakes to avoid slamming into the running agent. Dodge didn't slow, he continued across all four lanes of traffic. A singular focus on his mind. Causing a distraction big enough to allow Alder time to escape.

Once across the traffic lanes, feet firmly on the shoulder, Dodge stopped to have a glance at the monitor. As he stared at the video screen, his heart raced. Not from the track race across the highway, but because of what was staring back at him. It was Daughtry and he was holding the tie clip camera at eye level. A smug smile stretched across his face. The camera then swung around and Dodge could now see Alder on his knees, hands restrained behind his back. A trickle of blood formed a deep red vein that ran from his temple, down his cheek and ended as a stain on his collar. He was out of it, but alive.

The camera swung back to Daughtry.

"As you can see. Your man is still alive," a voice he hadn't heard in several days echoed through the speaker.

Dodge said nothing.

Daughtry continued, "I'm guessing you recognize this room. I am sure you saw many of them during your time in the sandbox."

Dodge remained silent.

"So, you know what we do in rooms like this, Dodge?"

Breaking silence, Dodge simply said, "Yes."

"Good. Now that I have your attention, you are going to do exactly what I say."

"If I don't?" Dodge knew the answer but wanted to keep Daughtry talking.

The camera panned back to the still kneeling Detective. A boot appeared in the frame which then lifted off the ground and slammed into Alder's midsection. The injured detective gasped for air then crumpled face first onto the cold hard floor, wheezing from having the wind knocked out of him.

Dodge's blood began to boil. He could feel the heat radiating upward from his feet, through his torso all the way to his fingertips. His mind cleared and began running scenarios. Best case. Worst case. His fight mechanism had been triggered and his body was preparing for confrontation.

"Lay out your terms," he finally said.

The camera focused back on the enormous man. "I don't want the detective."

"Let me guess, you want me."

"I don't want you either. If it had been up to me, I would have killed you after I finished off that bitch, Tremble."

"But it's not your decision, is it? You simply follow orders."

"That's what good soldiers do. But you wouldn't know anything about that, would you?"

Dodge could hear the anger swell in Daughtry's voice.

"Good soldiers know the difference between a lawful order and one made for self-interest and personal preservation. Face it, you're nothing but a Shammer."

Dodge knew using that term would illicit a strong response from any soldier. Though mostly used in the Army and Marines to describe soldiers who are immoral, unethical and garner no respect from their fellow men, all branches know what the term refers to and no one wants to have that badge bestowed upon them. Especially not one that sees himself as a hero fighting the good cause, like Daughtry.

The camera panned back to Alder, who had managed to right himself, though his chest still heaved trying to regain its breathing rhythm. This time the sole of the boot landed on the right side of the detective's temple. He collapsed to the floor, unconscious. A kick to the ribs followed. Alder couldn't feel anything, well, not at the moment—this was for Dodge's sake. Daughtry knew beating a defenseless man would spur an emotional reaction. It did.

Calmly. Concisely. Dodge spoke six words. "You're going to die for that."

The camera reversed and Daughtry's mug filled the lens. "I'll be in touch." The monitor went black.

Chapter 20

odge stood on the shoulder of the busy road, a look of contemplation on his face as the wind from passing cars hit his face. Some drivers honking as he stared at the now black motionless screen in his hands. For the first time on this case, he wasn't sure what his next move would be. He had underestimated Daughtry. And he had completely misjudged what Blake Williamson and ATS's role in this whole mess was. Williamson and his company were elbow deep in whatever had happened in Afghanistan and what is going on now in Dallas. Whatever it was, it got him killed, along with Shannon Roberts and Lilly Tremble. But what it was, Dodge had no idea. But he needed to find out. Alder's life depended on it.

As a former soldier, his first instinct was to charge headlong at the gate and get his man back, at all costs. But the parole agent part of him, said to take it slow. Devise a plan. Break it down for weaknesses. Have a contingency plan. Break that one down and then create a back-up to the back-up plan. He needed to run scenarios of all options. He already knew the outcome of trying to rush the gate. That only led to one outcome. Him face down in a pool of his own blood. The security guards were most certainly ex-soldiers with combat experience. They would mow him down at the first sight of a weapon. And Alder would certainly die.

As he waited for a cab back across the street in the convenience store parking lot, the normally steady agent was visibly shaken. His hand rubbing the bullet wound scar on his shoulder. He couldn't think straight. He was suddenly flooded with emotions. Anger. Anxiety. Fear. The first two he could handle. He could even use anger to his advantage. Anxiety kept his guard up. Making him uber aware of his surroundings and more alert. But fear, that was the big one. He had known fear in his life. Both on the job and on the battlefield. But it was always for those around him. The soldiers under his command. The victims of heinous crimes, willing to testify against their attackers. That's where his fear had always been placed. But something had changed since that night months ago, when he took two bullets and almost bled out on that cold hardwood floor back in Virginia. For the first time, he feared for himself. For his own mortality. And he didn't care for the change one bit. He would need to find a way around his apprehensive state of mind if he wanted to finish this, because he could very well die trying and he needed to be able to accept that as fact.

Once back at the motel, he slid Tobey out of the chair and sat. The dog hopped into his lap and snuggled in, peering up at him with hopeful eyes.

"Not sure how to play this one, Tobey. I can't call the police. That will surely lead Daughtry to kill him."

Tobey looked away toward the door and then back to Dodge.

"You need to go outside?"

Dodge started to stand and Tobey lept from his lap and ran to the door, stopping and staring back at Dodge as he approached. He turned the handle with his left hand and pulled the door inward. The dog slipped out and around the corner to the small grass patch by the dumpster.

"I'll leave the door open for ya when you are done," Dodge shouted in the direction Tobey ran.

"I need a drink and a shower," he said, after sticking a small stone he found on the sidewalk under the bottom of the door to keep it ajar enough for Tobey to let himself back in, but not let all the cool air rush out.

He poured a glass of Blantons, kicked off his shoes and stripped his shirt, tossing it on the bed on the way to the bathroom. He turned on the water and waited for it to warm up. As he stood on the cold tile, he began to run scenarios in his head. Sipping bourbon in between thoughts. His mind was beginning to clear. He hopped in the shower and the fear he was feeling earlier began to flow down his body. Carried away by the warm water along with the stink of the day. He finished washing, then rinsed off before getting out and patting himself dry with the stiff motel towel.

He peeked his head around the corner and noticed Tobey wasn't curled up in the chair. He pulled on his jeans and briskly walked to the door, which was now closed. He opened the door and scanned the parking lot but saw no signs of the dog. He walked around to the corner of the building and searched the small grassy lot, but still saw no sign of his furry friend. After searching the immediate area for more than fifteen minutes, he decided Tobey must have wanted to return to the freedom of the streets. He had a cool room for a few days and maybe that was enough. Perhaps he was born to be the Tramp.

A wave of sadness rushed over him, but then he returned his thoughts to Alder and the plan he had devised in the shower to get him back safely and put an end to Daughtry and whatever it is ATS was involved in. He just needed to make a call first.

Dodge needed supplies. After his phone call, he located a Walmart nearby and grabbed a change of clothes. New boots, a hat, and cargo pants were needed. It was also time for a fresh set of socks and underwear. He then headed to the sporting goods area and purchased some black under eye makeup, like football players wear during games to keep the sun from reflecting off their cheeks. Lastly, he grabbed a box of 9mm shells and two extra magazines. It was always smart to have extra rounds if one expects a fight, and there was no reason to expect Daughtry to throw up his hands in surrender. He was a killer and would fight to the bitter end.

He paid for the items in cash and tossed the receipt in a trash can located in the parking lot. Good luck to anyone trying to find that four-inch slip of paper in the landfill to tie the purchases back to him. Then he pulled the phone from his pocket to call for a cab but, before he could dial, the phone buzzed. A text message flashed across the screen.

Meet me at the last place SR was. 21:00 don't be late.

It was Daughtry with instructions for a meeting place. SR clearly stood for Shannon Roberts, but why would he want to meet in a public park? Even at that hour of the night, there were bound to be people around. If the park closed at dusk, Dodge was sure the police would cruise through to check for local teens having make out sessions in parked cars or smoking weed in the bathrooms. There was no way Daughtry would try and take him out in front of witnesses. And he would have to be close. At that time of night, there was no way in hell a shooter could fire from the hospital roof and hit a target across the lake. Sure, in the daytime, but not the twilight of early evening. That would be a one in a million shot. Maybe the best shot in the world would have a fifty-fifty chance at hitting the mark. But he decided not to leave anything to chance. He would take the hospital roof out of the equation before the meet up.

Looking at his watch, he had a few hours before he needed to be at the airport. His earlier call had been to Colonel Patterson. He told his old boss it was imperative they meet and Dodge had some information about Roberts and Trembles' murders. The old man pushed back, but Dodge was able to convince him it wasn't safe for him to come back to Virginia as he felt his life was in danger and *he* needed to come to Dallas to meet in person. Dodge didn't provide a location, and instructed Patterson to call when he arrived.

Dodge had already looked up flights out of Richmond. There were two flights from there to Dallas left that day. One flight arriving at four in the afternoon and another at seven that evening. He looked up the flight and checked the seat availability on the first flight. The only thing left were two seats in economy, toward the rear of the plane. Dodge used his credit card to book two tickets. When he didn't show up, the seats would be taken by any stand-by flyers, of which Patterson would not want to wait in the airport for. The later flight was only about half full and had a few seats remaining in first class. Patterson would hopefully book this flight allowing Dodge to know which gate and what time he would arrive. For his plan to work, he needed Patterson. Over the past few days, he had become more and more certain his old boss wasn't being truthful with him at a minimum. But more and more he was starting to get the feeling the man was involved. Patterson would be his leverage.

Dodge had a few hours to kill and decided he should grab some food. He wasn't sure when he would get the chance to eat again before this was all over.

He walked to a fast food restaurant where he ordered two cheeseburgers, some chicken nuggets, a large fry and chose to wash it down with a diet cola. Normally he would've had coffee, but he decided sugar and caffeine would give him a much needed boost of energy to help get him through the rest of the day.

After scarfing down the two sandwiches and chicken nuggets, Dodge took the fries with him and finished them while waiting for a bus to take him to the Airport. He decided to skip the cab and go with a less noticeable form of transportation. He would pile out of the bus at the concourse with a slew of other passengers. Random and unassuming. One person, blending quickly into a crowd of thousands. He would draw no attention to himself that would make anyone watching the monitors think he was there for any reason other than to pick a family member up from the airport. Easy-Peezy nice and easy. He didn't even need to ditch his Glock, as it is legal to carry a weapon into an airport in Texas, as long as you don't attempt to enter through security to gain access to the gates.

Got to love Texas, he thought to himself as he de-boarded the bus outside the main arrival gate. Once inside, he located the electronic board declaring the flights and times of incoming planes and which carousel the luggage would come out on.

"C26," he whispered to himself as he stared at the LCD screen.

He looked left at a sign that read, *Baggage Claim C4*. He was at the opposite end of the terminal and the flight had already landed. Walking briskly, he made his way around the u-shaped terminal. People walked fast, even ran in airports every day, making his hurried pace a common sight and would draw no more than a cursory glance from airport staff or security. As he approached baggage claim C25, he slowed, moving toward the outside wall. The baggage claim sat in the middle with the airline offices lining the opposite wall. The layout forced passengers to stand, waiting for their luggage with their backs to the entrance to the terminal.

The crowd was growing at C26, but he didn't see Patterson. He wondered if he had made a critical error in assuming the Colonel checked bags. He may have packed everything for his trip in a carry-on and bypassed the baggage claim area all together. If the old man was involved and worried about someone following, or watching him, he could have Daughtry or some other contact here in Dallas pick him up in the departure section instead of the arrival section, which would place Dodge in the wrong place to locate him. Then there was the car rental option, though Dodge felt this was the least likely scenario to play out. Patterson was in an unfamiliar city and had become accustomed to having a driver over the past several years. He would use a ride service, Dodge guessed.

Just when he was about to give up on the baggage idea and move to the rental car desks, he spotted his target stepping off the escalator and walking toward the baggage carousel.

Chapter 21

Patterson donned a leather wide brimmed hat that drooped down and covered part of his face. His eyes were obscured with dark sunglasses, but Dodge was sure it was him. Dodge watched the old man from a distance, trying to ensure he wasn't seen. He also was keeping a keen eye out for anyone else who may be waiting for the Colonels arrival. Namely, Daughtry. He watched and moved along the outside wall every few seconds. If his old boss thought he caught a glimpse of him, he didn't want to be standing in the same place if the old man tried to get a second look.

But the man didn't move from the baggage claim area. Nor did he appear to be looking for anyone. This reassured Dodge it had been a solo flight and no one was waiting to meet Patterson. Once the luggage began spilling out on the conveyor, the Colonel moved closer. Then he did something strange. He took his carry on and tossed it onto the moving belt with the luggage from the plane. Dodge watched as Patterson turned and walked away from the carousel and went into a nearby restroom.The move caught him off guard. He watched the restroom entrance while glancing at the carousel to see if anyone removed the small suitcase.

After a few minutes, Dodge made his move. He hustled to the conveyer just as the suitcase appeared from around the opposite side. He maintained visual contact with the opening to the restroom as he grabbed the bag off the carousel and set it on the ground. It was light. Too light. The hairs on his neck began to tingle. He didn't like the way this was playing out. Something was wrong. Was the old man a step ahead of him? Had the hunter become the prey?

He unzipped the top of the bag and peered inside. Nothing. The bag was empty. He looked at the handle on top. The airline baggage tracker sticker was missing and there was no name tag or any identifying information attached anywhere. Another glance at the bathroom door, then he flipped the bag on its back and finished unzipping it. The only thing inside was two small moisture absorbing silicone packets.

"God damnit," he said. "It's fucking brand new."

Dodge zipped up the bag and placed it back on the conveyor. He then turned his attention to the restroom. His eyes scanned the crowd. Searching for a familiar face or anyone paying too close attention to him. Nothing. Now just a few feet from the entrance to the restroom, the nervous agent took one more look around, then stepped in.

A man brushed past him as he turned the corner which opened into two halves with a center dividing wall placed down the center. Both sides of the center wall were lined with sinks and electric air dryers for washing up. To the right was a row of urinals. To the left side of the room were toilet stalls. Not seeing Patterson at the urinal, Dodge turned to his left and pretended to wash his hands where he could see all the stalls in the mirror. Only three were occupied. He leaned over the sink to splash water on his face, which allowed him to look back under the doors without drawing attention to himself. He hoped he might see something with the shoes or pants that would indicate Patterson was one of the men using a stall. But he hadn't paid that much attention to what the old man had been wearing. The suitcase distraction had worked. He had hyper focused on that, paying less attention to the target. A rookie mistake he now had to deal with.

After two stalls were empty and only one person remained on that side, Dodge stepped over to the entrance. Attached to the wall on the inside of the opening was a retractable yellow nylon strip that could be clipped to the opposite wall, declaring the restroom closed for maintenance. Dodge pulled the strip across and waved away a man in his thirties, who cursed at him for the inconvenience. He then went back inside and waited for the last two people at the urinals to finish, wash their hands and leave.

Once the restroom was clear, he made his way back to the only stall still occupied. Stepping up to the door he stood for a moment, then knocked. Hard. The thin metal door bounced under the pressure from his knuckles. He waited, but there was no response. His knuckles rapped against the grey door again. Still no response. The sinking feeling he experienced earlier upon finding the luggage empty, returned. Something was amiss and he was starting to believe he was *on the wrong end of the shit stick*, as Chief Johnson would say when things collapsed around a parole officer under his watch.

"Patterson? It's Dodge," he said softly.

He saw no sense continuing the charade any longer. If he was in there, he knew Dodge was the one on the outside. If Patterson was not the person in the stall, then the tables had been turned against him and that meant his old boss was on to him. Dodge pushed against the door. Soft at first, then harder. He pressed his shoulder against the gap in between the door and the privacy slab and immediately regretted his choice as pain radiated down his arm landing in his fingertips. He winced and pulled away. *Don't use the wounded arm, jack ass.*

After shaking off the ill effects, he finally used his foot and kicked in the door. Which swung in, slamming against the side of the stall. Dodge moved in before the door kicked back closed. He looked at the man propped on the toilet. Pants pushed down around his ankles. His head tilted back and mouth agape. A trickle of blood ran from under his hat down his face. Dodge reached out and removed the sunglasses revealing his eyes wide open and cloudy. He was dead. But it wasn't Colonel Patterson's eyes staring back at him. Dodge reached down and felt the man's pants pockets for a wallet. They were empty. No ID. Nothing to identify him.

"This can't get much worse," he said to no one, before placing the man's sunglasses back on and pulling the door closed behind him as he backed out of the stall.

Dodge washed his hands and used a paper towel to wipe the door handle, sink and the retractable maintenance sign, which he left strewn across the doorway to give him time to get the hell out of the airport and regroup. Patterson had tossed chum in the water and Dodge went for it like a bull shark in a feeding frenzy. He didn't know where his target was or who he was with. The only thing he did know, is old man was neck deep in whatever was going on with ATS. Which meant if Roberts was killed for knowledge she had about ATS's business practices, then he was an accomplice to her murder as well. The Colonel had betrayed his oath to his country. Put himself above others for selfish reasons. Darker than that, he betrayed the trust between family members. A blood betrayal. A more reprehensive form of treachery didn't exist in his mind.

He exited the airport and hailed a taxi. The bus would be a safer bet as no one cared who got on and off where, but he wanted to put as much distance between himself and the dead guy in the airport as quickly as possible. Luckily, a line of cabs was always waiting for fares and he was inside a dirty red and white hybrid model, headed away from the airport in a matter of minutes. Pulling his phone from his pocket, he checked the time. 8:00 pm the digital numbers flashed. He told the driver to head for White Rock Lake Park, which prompted a look in the rearview mirror from the driver.

"I know it closes at dusk," Dodge said, ignoring the curious eyes in the rearview. "There's an extra twenty in it for you if you can make it in half an hour."

Dodge slipped the twenty through the slot in the plastic divider installed behind the driver's seats. The man behind the wheel reached back, snatched the bill, then pressed the accelerator. They made the trip in twenty-five minutes.

The cabbie pulled over at the entrance to the park, which was now blocked by two single armed gates chained together in the middle. Dodge handed the man another twenty-five dollars but pinched the bills between his fingers as the cabbie grabbed the bills.

"Forget I was here," Dodge said.

The man nodded. Then he drove away.

Dodge checked the time on his phone. He was about a half-hour early. The sun was setting, casting eerie shadows across the hot pavement of the parking lot. The hospital was across the lake and Dodge watched as reflections from the red and blue emergency lights flickered off the waves and the wails of sirens echoed across the lake. No one was going to be taking a shot from the roof of the hospital tonight. One phone call, placed during his taxi ride, making reference to a possible suicide attempt from the roof of the hospital, brought the entire Dallas Fire and Rescue squad along with a smattering of police cruisers. It wouldn't take officials long to figure out the call was a hoax, but the roof would be clear.

He watched for a few minutes longer, then turned and began the walk through the parking lot to the trail head. His steps were slow and deliberate. One foot in front of the other. Not too fast. Not too slow. He needed to be sharp. The sun had dropped below the horizon, causing the trail lights to switch on. The lights were dim and their poles placed far enough apart to create shadow gaps on the trail beyond the lamps reaches. Add in the lingering twilight effect and his eyes were having trouble adjusting to his surroundings.

He squinted as he approached the hill behind the spot where Shannon Roberts had been murdered. He left the trail and began walking up the small mound toward the buildings housing the restrooms. The buildings were a possible attack point for anyone lying in wait for him. Sliding the Glock out from his waistline, he approached the small outbuilding. His eyes moving from side to side. Searching for anything out of place. A door held ajar by a rock. A silhouette peeking out from behind a tree. A car that shouldn't be there. He saw nothing.

The sirens at the hospital had gone quiet and most of the emergency vehicles had left. Only one fire truck and a police car remained and, once they extinguished their emergency lights, the vehicles faded into the darkness and out of sight. He turned his attention back to the building. Both restrooms were clear. Assured no one was going to appear from the building and attack, he then headed down the hill toward the lake and the kill spot.

He stood still. Listening. Waiting. It was quiet. Only the hum of car tires passing over a nearby road filled in the thick air. As he reached into his pocket to check the time on his phone, the device buzzed. He stared at the screen, noting the time was 9:00 pm. The message was from an unknown number. Daughtry had smartly switched to a burner phone.

Walk 200 yards north up the trail. Have a seat on the bench and await further instructions.

Further up the trail meant more isolation. It placed more distance between him and the parking lot—the only place police will likely check for nighttime trespassers. Daughtry was luring him to a spot where no one would find him until morning. As he walked, he contemplated if he would even make it to the bench. Each step forward brought the feeling of impending doom. But he had to keep moving. Alder's life depended on it.

The further the trail wound away from the parking lot, the less lighting there was. This caused Dodge to almost walk past the bench. The four foot, steel framed, wood slatted bench sat about twenty feet off the trail at the water's edge. Its placement meant to provide relaxing views of the lake. The nervous agent's mind wandered to old people sitting at the lake's edge, feeding the local wildlife and shutterbugs trying to get the perfect shot of a sunrise shimmering over the calm water. The perfect shot. Words that snapped Dodge out of his temporary trance, forcing his thoughts back to the current predicament.

A small strip of worn grass led from the trail down to the bench. Many people had made the short journey. As far as he knew, all of them had left the bench alive. He wondered if he would be the last to sit there as he followed the thin dirt line to the shoreline. He stood at the water's edge. He decided if there was going to be a kill shot, he might as well let them have a clean line of sight. The seconds ticked on. Each one felt like a minute. But nothing happened. His head swung from left to right and when he was sure he wasn't going to die on that strip of sandy beach, he turned and sat on the bench. As he settled onto the contoured painted boards, his phone vibrated.

He looked at the time. It was Daughtry. Dodge had to admit, the airman was punctual.

Police storming the hospital was a nice touch.

His adversary was watching him. Dodge tapped a message on the screen's small keyboard.

Had to be sure.

I guessed you would have a plan for the rooftop. So, I planned a little something different.

Dodge didn't like where the conversation was going. He concluded; he was not going to die sitting there on that bench. Daughtry had plenty of chances to take him out. From the time he entered the park to when he provided himself up as a target standing at the lake's shore. No, this was about sending a message. Sometimes the best way to get a point across is to not do something expected, but to do the unexpected. So, he decided to play along.

What do you have in mind? If you come on out into the open, we can settle this her and now.

Staring at his phone, Dodge waited for a response. No more messages appeared. At least not on his phone.

Chapter 22

An unusually cool breeze came off the lake and washed over Dodge. A chill wrapped his spine, causing him to shiver. The sun had completely set and while the temperature had cooled down some, his phone told him it was still in the mid-80s. He leaned forward on the bench, contemplating if he should get up and leave or stay to see if he could find out what Daughtry had meant when he said 'he was trying something different.' The words sounded ominous. It meant the experienced investigator was behind the eight ball and was forced into a reactionary response. He preferred to be on the offensive in these situations. Maybe leaving would swing the pendulum in the opposite direction, putting him in the driver's seat, enabling him to be the one to call the shots.

As he sat there playing out possible outcomes to both choices, a familiar scent wafted past his nostrils, but he couldn't quite place it. He stood and raised his nose into the air and took a deep breath in. Then turned away from the water and drew in another. The smell was less potent facing away from the water. He spun back and faced the lake. Now the odor was more pungent. Almost an assault on his senses as a breeze from across the lake drifted past him. Then it hit him. He knew what the smell was.

Jet fuel had a particularly strong odor to it. Jet-A and Jet-A1 fuels are made by running kerosene through a more rigorous refining process. Other additives are mixed in, such as sulfur and cetane, which result in a more combustible fuel mixture. Carrier air hangers reeked of it. As did the area around refueling trucks that littered the airfields of Afghanistan and Iraq. The aircraft fuel was so volatile, the trucks were stored far from any structure and never parked near base housing units. However, jet fuel had one more use. And it was this use that sparked the recognition in Dodge's subconscious.

For over 20 years the US military had a strong presence in Afghanistan. A direct response to the deadly attacks of September 11, 2001, on the World Trade Center complex and the Pentagon. Within days of the attack, CIA operatives were flown into the country controlled by religious zealots known as the Taliban. The Taliban were strict Islamic fundamentalist who ruled with an iron fist and regularly subjected its citizenry to beatings and even mass killings. All of that was bad, but what brought them to the attention of the US Intelligence apparatus was their monetary agreement to provide sanctuary for the most wanted man in the world, Usama Bin Laden. The architect of 9/11.

Much of the US strategy in Afghanistan was adopted from its experience in Vietnam, where the military built forward operating bases across the country where troops could be housed and aircraft could bring replacements and supplies. Patrols would be launched from the bases and, because of the large military presence, the bases drew a great deal of attention from the Taliban and Al-Qaeda and often came under enemy mortar fire. One of the bases, Bagram Airfield north of Kabul, covered over thirty square miles of Afghan real estate. The base housed over 10,000 troops and contractors. It even contained Subway and Pizza Hut restaurants as dining options.

A base this large produces a lot of garbage, not to mention the other waste created by war, including human excrement, body parts of dead insurgent fighters and ordinance. All of which was placed into a huge pit built near the base, doused with jet fuel, and lit ablaze. This was what triggered the memory for Dodge. The glow from the fires burning night and day. Never stopping.

Staring across the lake, he noticed a shape in the distance. Fuzzy and distorted from the rippling of the water's surface at first, slowly coming into focus as it neared shore. He squinted, trying to make out the object approaching his location. The odor from the fuel grew as the object drifted ever closer. Dodge stepped closer. He felt the water soak through his shoes.

He focused hard on the object, which he now recognized as an old wooden rowboat. The kind park departments all over the country have tied up to piers for hourly rent by tourists and couples wanting a romantic paddle across the pond.

But this boat wasn't empty. There was somebody sitting upright in the middle. Dodge couldn't make out who it was, but feared it was Alder. He ventured further out—the water now up to his knees. The boat, and the man in it, was only twenty-five to thirty yards from his position. He strained his eyes. The boat drew closer and then he saw who was occupying its middle seat. The man was Colonel Patterson. His arms were bound. Tape wrapped his head and covered his mouth. There was a dark spot on his forehead, which Dodge discerned as blood.

Dodge pushed against the weight of the water. The bottom had shifted from sand to mud. His feet sank deeper into the murky soil. With each step closer to the boat, his journey became more of a struggle. The mud acted as a suction cup around his boots each time he tried to raise his legs. Holding them in place and threatening to keep his footwear in its grip. He pushed forward, the water nearing his chest. It had taken him close to five minutes to get within fifteen feet of the boat and his old boss. Then things went from bad to worse.

The brilliant flash of light and blast of hot air forced him to dive under the water. The water was dark and murky. Once he had his bearings he peered up at the surface. Flames danced above his head. His lungs began to burn. He hadn't had time to take in a big gulp of air before submerging to avoid the flames. He needed to surface for a breath. His head swung and he began to swim underwater toward what he hoped was shore. He kept one eye on the surface, searching for a break in the flames. He used the mud to pull himself forward until he felt the bottom change back to sand. He hoped he had gone far enough because he needed to surface or he was going to drown if he didn't surface for air in the next few seconds.

His head burst through to the open air, mouth agape as his lungs took in life affirming oxygen. With his feet firmly on the sandy bottom he stood and wiped the water from his face. He was facing the shore but could see the glow from the boat on fire glimmering on the water's surface. He spun and caught the last glimpse of the charred vessel as it sank below the waves. Shortly after the last of the jet fuel burned away and extinguished, pitching the lake back into darkness.

Dodge stood there. Staring at the open water. The whole place reeked of charred wood, burnt flesh and sulfur. The same smell he remembered from the burn pits all those years ago in Afghanistan. The thick odor attacked his senses, forcing his stomach to convulse. He lurched over and vomited. His thoughts were overloaded with bad memories and images of his dead friend. Burned alive. He could still see the fear pasted on Patterson's face just before the boat burst into flames. Dodge could not think of a worse way to go.

Water dripped from his soaked shirt as he waded back to shore. He could feel the greasy skim from the kerosene residue on his skin and his clothes stunk of expended fuel. No way a cab driver was going to let him into their car smelling like the fuel man in a pit crew team. He needed to get cleaned up. As he walked down the shoreline back toward the building on the hill with the restrooms, he began to worry someone may have spotted the fire on the lake and called the police. It would be tough trying to explain to the Dallas PD why he was coated in fuel and why there was a dead man tied to the remains of a sunken boat at the bottom of the lake, burned to a crisp. Not a good look.

Dodge stopped, stepping away from the trail and waited to see if any emergency personnel showed up to investigate. After five minutes and no sirens or red flashing lights lit up the parking lot, he hurried to the white outbuilding housing the restrooms. A solid kick above the handle busted the frame and the door swung open. A loud crashing noise ensued as the inside metal handle slammed against the cement wall. Dodge stepped in and closed the door behind him.

The lights were motion activated, turning on as soon as the door opened. He quickly found the control and doused the lights. After a second to readjust to the change in brightness, he was able to see enough to find his way to the sink, where he stripped off all his clothes and began scrubbing them to try and get the stench of fuel oil out. He also washed his body from head to toe, using all the paper towels to dry off. Once he was convinced his clothes no longer carried the foul odor, he twisted his shirt, pants, and underwear between his fists to wring out as much water from the fabric as possible. Then, using the powerful hand dryer, he was able to get his shirt and undergarment dry. His pants were still damp, and he tossed his socks in the trash as his boots were still wet.

Once he was redressed, he checked his pockets. One wallet and one room key. But his phone was gone.

"Shit," he mumbled.

Had it slipped from his pocket when he was in the lake? Not that it mattered, once he was waist deep, the water would have flowed into every crevasse and ruined the device. That phone was the only connection between him and Daughtry. And via the transient property, to Alder. He needed to see if he could find it.

After getting dressed, he cracked the bathroom door and, when he saw no one lurking in the parking lot, slipped out, doing his best to close the broken door behind him, and hurried back to the bench where he waited for Daughtry to contact him earlier. As he gazed out over the water, there seemed to be no traces of what had happened earlier. The smell of fuel had dissipated and was barely noticeable. In another hour, the odor would be gone completely. Everything swallowed up by the lake and dragged to the bottom, hidden from view.

Dodge remembered he had had his phone out waiting for a message from Daughtry when he spotted the boat out in the lake. He turned and faced the bench. There, on the ground in front of the bench, he saw a flash of green light. Moving closer, he saw the rectangular outline of a cell phone. He reached down and picked up the device. As he bent over, he heard the ping of metal on metal. The loud clank caught him off guard. Then there was an impact next to his left leg. Dirt kicked up, splashing across his face and left arm. Someone was shooting at him, and they were getting close. He needed to find cover.

He jumped up and dove over the bench, crashing into the ground on the other side and landing on his bad shoulder. He let out a grunt as he flattened himself out on the ground trying to make himself a smaller target. He could see the lake from under the bench and he knew this meant a round could be ricocheted off the ground, under the bench and hit him. Or the shooter could simply wait him out until he exposed his head and then it would be lights out. He needed to think fast. Unlike the fire on the lake, the sounds of gunshots would most certainly bring the police racing in, guns drawn. He would avoid being shot by the good guys if he was lucky. Nope. Sticking around wasn't an option.

Chest flat on the ground, he sucked in a massive gulp of air and shot to his feet. Sprinting as hard and fast as his tired legs would carry him. First, he ran right, parallel to the lake shore for five seconds. Then he cut hard to his left. His boots digging deep into the hard soil, almost losing one as he spun and picked up speed again. His chest heaved. First in, then out as his legs covered large swaths of ground with each step. Another five seconds and he threw his right arm out, like he was preparing to head in that direction, but then stuck his heel and juked right. He ran at an angle back toward the parking lot, which put him closer to some cover and more distance between him and the shooter.

His pace slowed as he neared the parking lot and the restrooms he had washed up in earlier. Lungs burning, spit coming from his mouth with every breath, Dodge careened his head to the left and squinted to see the lake. Clouds had rolled in and shielded the moon's glow. He could barely make out where the dry land ended and the water's edge began. He slowed even more. A brisk walk. He watched the part of the sky above the lake. If he was lucky, he might see the muzzle flash and be able to hit the ground and avoid taking a round to the head. It was all he could do. But nothing came.

Dodge decided not to test fate and he quickly made his way through the parking lot and back to the front gate, where he slid under the chained bars and walked down the road until he felt he was safely out of range. Pulling the phone from his pocket, he opened the car ride app and, within five minutes, he was tucked away in the back seat of a small SUV and headed toward his motel.

He had the driver drop him a block from the motel. If Daughtry had found where he was staying, he didn't want to roll up with a huge target painted across his chest. Instead, he would use the alleys and side streets to approach from the backside of the motel, utilizing the dumpster as cover for his approach. As he knelt behind the steel blue box, the smell of decomposing food lofting from its guts, he peered past the corner at the long row of doors lining the motel parking lot. There were three cars, all unoccupied, sitting out front their owners' respective rooms. No one was milling about. It was dead quiet. The same way it had been most nights. But when your senses are on alert and someone is gunning for you, silence can be the loudest sound in the universe.

The time ticked by. Each minute passing as hours in his head. After what seemed like the better part of a day, he slid out from behind the dumpster and slowly walked to the door of his room. The blackout curtains were pulled. Unable to see inside through the window, he positioned himself with his back pinned to the wall and used his left hand to knock. He listened. Nothing. Pulling the Glock from his waistband, he pressed the electronic key onto the pad. A green light flashed and he heard a click. He took a deep breath and exhaled. Then he pushed the handle and shoved the door aside, stepping in, the white dot at the end of the barrel flashing across the room from left to right. *Front sight in a fight*, he used to tell his students at the academy. The saying meant, when in a close quarters, fight, the shooter only needs to worry about placing the front sight on the target. No need to line up between the posts of the rear sight. If the target is close enough, and the front sight is on the target, the round will find its mark.

But this time there was no need for gunplay. He was the only one in the room. Using his foot, he closed the door behind him and slid the chain lock across. Then he sat on the bed and laid back. The adrenaline dump had worn off and every muscle in his body ached. His head was beginning to throb. His whole being felt like a can of smashed ass. He was exhausted.

As he lay there, his mind wandered. He was finding it difficult to focus on any one thing. Thoughts raced through his head like cars speeding through an intersection. Colonel Patterson. Detective Alder. Daughtry.

Tobey. Everything had gone to shit. His assumption was that Patterson was somehow wrapped up in all this. Maybe he had Shannon Roberts killed because she found out something. Something that could have had him put in a cell for years. Maybe he got her this great job out in Dallas after she left the Army. It would be simple for someone with his pull. A simple phone call to an old friend would provide a cushy job in a nice metropolitan city. A place where she could thrive or blend into the masses. It all made sense. Until about two hours ago that was. The moment his old boss was set ablaze right in front of him. It was a development he hadn't anticipated upending everything he thought he knew. Which, if he were to be honest with himself, wasn't much to begin with.

His play with Patterson had been a colossal failure. A plan derived to put him on the offensive had backfired and had placed him squarely behind the Eightball. A corner pocket shot from being eliminated from the game. And to make things worse, he had gained no useful intelligence from the risk. A total mission failure.

Chapter 23

nts had begun to pilfer the coagulating blood pooled around the man's head. His lifeless body limply spread across six feet of hard Texas soil. A product of his own making. Daughtry stood over the ex-marine sniper, emotionless, staring at the man he had once trusted on the battlefield with his life. The man he had just killed.

"How did you let it come to this?" he asked the motionless corpse, reaching down to lift the high-precision weapon from the man's grip. "At least you'll get a full military burial, which is more than you deserve." Then he tossed a used needle and plastic baggie containing heroin on the ground next to the dead shooter. Cops would assume he was killed in a fight over drugs. In a way that wasn't a lie. Drugs put the man in this position. Had he stayed clean he would have been retained in the service and wouldn't have been a gun for hire. It also would have meant Daughtry would have been able to trust his old friend to keep his mouth shut. Addiction changed that. Addicts couldn't be trusted. So, this is where the friendship had to end.

With the rifle in hand, he glanced once more across the lake. Dodge was still alive. He had hoped to take care of two problems at once, but it hadn't worked out that way. Now he had no idea where the pesky agent was staying and no real way to find him. The Detective had been of no help. He was loyal to the end. Never once giving his partner up. Not even as the knife blade slid across his belly and Daughtry removed the cavity contents one by one, splaying each out on the table in front of the horrified detective. Then in a rather undramatic last gasp of air, the cop's heart gave out and his body went limp.

The routine had worked for interrogators in Afghanistan. But the key was the person being gutted wasn't the one with the desired information. It was the person tied up, their eyelids stuck open with surgical glue, forced to watch a friend or family member being disemboweled that would eventually tell the interrogator everything they knew. Troop locations. Weapons stash. Hell, they would give up their God if asked. Anything to be able to shut their eyes to the horror happening in front of them. He had even heard tell, this was how the CIA found Bin Laden's secret compound, though he didn't put much stock into the rumor.

His initial foray into the torture arena had produced no results. Except a dead cop, for which he was forced to dispose of the body in a chemical barrel at ATS. In three days, the barrel and its contents would be covered in a hundred feet of New Mexico earth capped with foot-thick concrete lid. No one would ever find the detective's body. The acid would take care of any lingering DNA.

Daughtry did worry about Colonel Patterson. His body would certainly float to the top of the lake and be spotted by some jogger bobbing on the waves. Or more likely, it washes ashore to the horrified stares of an older couple up early to watch the sun rise over the urban lake. Which is why he chose the jet fuel mixture. The gel like liquid burns hotter than the surface of the sun, incinerating all skin and hair and leaving only lumps of charred muscle and bone. Sooner or later the cops would be able to put the pieces together. The open-ended trip from Virginia to Dallas. His relationship to Shannon Roberts. The personal ties to ATS and Blake Williamson. It would all be exposed one day. But that day wasn't going to be today. He still had one more loose end to tie up. Dodge.

He wished he would have killed him at Lily Tremble's house in Mississippi. He had been following the news out of Jackson and he had heard nothing more about her death. He was in the clear. Just another tragic story of a woman found dead in a failed break-in or domestic violence incident. But he had been under orders not to harm Dodge. He had found Tremble and those in charge felt the agent could be of more use. Ultimately, used as the fall guy for a couple of murders. He, too, would then be killed in a horrible accident.

Burnt to death in a motel fire. That was Daughtry's plan. He would find the place where Dodge chose to stay. Most likely a wooden framed building cheap motel. Baked in the Texas sun for twenty-five years. The place would burn like a tinderbox. He wouldn't even need any accelerant. Just a match and some trash piled in the right spot. Some construction adhesive applied to the jamb to make sure the door can't be opened from the inside and the last loose end is tied off.

It wasn't the way he hoped to be able to do it. Arson seemed cowardly. Not a soldier's way of doing things. He wanted his final battle with Dodge to be up close and personal. Snapping his neck with his bare hands. He wanted to feel the life drain from his body. For Daughtry, it had become personal and soldiers handled personal matters a different way.

He took one more look back at the dead man on the ground. He counted the expended brass in his hand to be sure he had policed all the used casings from around the body. He had heard only three shots. He shoved the casings into his pocket and disappeared into the busy city streets.

***

He yawned, stretching his arms out over his head. The light escaping from the slit between the heavy curtains pierced the center of the room. Wiping his eyes, he could see dust particles dancing through the beam. He reached for his phone on the bedside table—the charger cord catching for a moment before releasing and falling to the faded red carpet, then he saw the time. It was after eight in the morning. He had crashed not long after his head hit the pillow the night before and managed to get an entire night of uninterrupted sleep.

He knew he was tired. His mind and body had been racing non-stop for several days. Each day punctuated by an adrenaline dump with very little time to recover. It had all finally caught up with him. He would have liked to use some of the time during the night to plan his next move, but he knew his body was telling him it was time for rest. He needed the break. But it was now time to end this. Fully rested and, once he got some coffee in his system and food in his gullet, he would work on a plan to take down Daughtry and whoever was pulling his strings.

After a quick shower, he picked up the clothes he had been wearing the night before off the chipped and faded yellow tile covering the bathroom floor. The unmistakable odor of petroleum still clinging to the tightly woven fabric. He needed some new clothes. He was beginning to think not packing a bag for this trip was a huge mistake. He pulled the shirt over his head and stretched it down over his chest. Then he slipped on his pants, he left his underwear off, deciding instead to dispose of them in the trash can tucked under the bathroom sink. He wasn't a fan of the feel of rough cloth against his private areas, but he also had zero desire for petroleum residue tightly pressed against such sensitive body parts. It was going to be hot out there again. Sweat and gasoline do not mix.

After a quick stop at the local clothing store to replace his old clothes, Dodge decided to head back in the direction of the motel. A rumbling in his gut reminded him he hadn't had any food since the day before. So, he darted into the nearest convenience store where he purchased two premade breakfast sandwiches and a large cup of coffee. He stood outside the doors and watched traffic pass on the street out front as he scarfed down both biscuit sandwiches, before going back in and topping off his coffee.

A push on the lid to secure the hot beverage in the cup, then he stepped out the doors and began walking toward the motel. As he turned the corner and entered the far side of the parking lot, he noticed a police car sitting outside the manager's office, causing Dodge to freeze in his tracks. The engine was running but the emergency lights were not flashing and the cruiser was empty. He stood still for a moment, then a uniformed officer appeared from the office. His partner trailed close behind. Dodge bent down to one knee, placing his coffee on the ground next to him. Then he pretended to tie his boot. He could see the patrol officers through the tops of his eyes while keeping his face pointed at the ground. He watched as the two officers made their way down the sidewalk leading to his room. The men stopped at the door to his room and knocked.

Both officers seemed to be in a relaxed stance. Neither had a hand anywhere near their weapons, which made him think while the two officers were looking for him, they weren't expecting any trouble. He rose to his feet and jogged over to within ten feet of the men. Stopping short as neither officer had seen him approach and he didn't want to spook them.

"Excuse me," he said calmly and flat toned. "Are you looking for me?"

Both officers spun around and gave him the once over. Which made him realize he had tucked his Glock into the back waistband of his jeans. Not a good thing. He would prefer it if the police didn't know he had a weapon.

"Are you Paul Dodge?" the tall blonde haired one on the right said.

Dodge nodded. "Can I help you officers with something?"

"We are investigating the disappearance of one of our detectives. His name is Alder and we know you have been down to the station and spoken with him on several occasions."

"I have. Did I hear you right? Did you said he was missing?"

"The officers shared a glance. Then the short one sporting a thin mustache said, "Missing? We didn't say he was missing." He looked at the blonde officer, who shook his head.

Dodge knew the game the two beat cops were running. But luckily for him they were terrible. It's not a good idea to use the term disappearance then deny someone has, in fact, disappeared. These two had a lot to learn, but it wasn't Dodge's job to train the two in the art of investigations and witness interviews. For that is what he figured he was. The police knew he had been in contact with Alder. They also likely knew he and the detective met the day of his disappearance. His guess was Alder kept meticulous notes on the cases he worked.

Dodge wondered if he would gain any inside knowledge from getting a look at the detective's case files. After pondering the thought for a second, he truly believed Detective Alder had been honest with him and hadn't been holding anything back. He also decided he needed to stay out of the police department's interview room. He wasn't interested in wasting any time answering questions on the record or possibly talking himself into a corner and winding up with a murder rap tied around his neck. No, he needed to end this thing with Daughtry and, once he had everyone involved in whatever was going on, he would let the police know and they could take over. His interest in justice began and ended with Daughtry.

The officer's stared at him waiting for a response. Dodge decided it was best to tell the truth. Well, parts of it anyway.

"Oh, I thought you said one of your detectives had disappeared? Maybe I misunderstood. Anyway, I met with Detective Alder yesterday." He used his title to make it appear their relationship was strictly professional with no personal entanglements. This would hopefully cause the officers to believe he had nothing to hide. "We met at the office to discuss a matter I was in town to deal with. He felt the issue I was working on and his own case could be connected. After we talked through our two separate cases, the detective brought me back to the motel. That was the last I saw him."

"Did he say where he was going or who he planned to talk to?" the officer with the mustache asked, writing down what Dodge had said into his field notebook.

"I'm afraid not. I was going to be leaving town in a few days and I had planned to buy him lunch before I left for all his help in my matter."

The tall blonde officer asked, "And what is it you are working on here in Dallas?"

"It was a Department of Defense personnel matter. I'm not allowed to share specifics. You know, privacy rights and all."

Mustache cop's brow furrowed. "If you can't talk about it, how was Detective Alder going to help you with your case?"

Dodge needed this conversation to be over. He had to answer too many questions, which could lead to a more complicated story. The more details he spouted, the more he would have to remember at a later date if detectives working on Alder's disappearance brought him in for an interview. As a cop, the best thing you can do for your case is catch someone in a lie. An untruthful witness can supercharge a case and refocus all attention toward the witness, or now the main suspect.

Dodge needed to keep police attention off of him as much as possible if he wanted to find Daughtry and end his reign of terror. The fact patrol officers were even talking to him meant, at minimum, he was a person of interest. A title that came with fun things like having your motel room watched all day and night and having a tail car follow your every move. He would have to take extra precautions each time he left the motel to make sure he wasn't being followed. Not an ideal situation.

Thinking on his feet, Dodge realized if he was a suspect, this conversation would be taking place in a small room at the station with a detective grilling him for answers. Patrol officers are sent to retrieve suspects of crime, not interrogate them. So, he decided to take the fight to them, so to speak. "Look, I've said all I can say. If you have any more questions, you can call the Pentagon's public relations line and see if they are willing to provide you with any information. Or you can stick me in the back of your cruiser and take me downtown. But I would appreciate it if you would make a decision, because I have a few loose ends to tie up before I head back to Virginia."

Both men stared at him for a minute, then the tall officer gestured to his partner it was time to go.

"We will be in touch," mustache cop said.

"Thank you, and feel free to stop by anytime."

Dodge watched as the men pulled away, waving by pointing his finger in their direction when they passed him. It had been a dick move. He was sure he was being cursed at that very moment, but now that they were gone, he needed to move this show forward and get the hell out of town as quickly as possible.

Once in his room he sat at the small table, his Glock resting in front of him. He removed the magazine and ejected the round from the chamber. Getting Daughtry to come out into the open was going to be hard. With Patterson dead and Alder more than likely wrapped in plastic in a shallow grave somewhere outside of town, Dodge had no bargaining chip or anyone to trade himself for. Waiting around to be clunked in the head in a dark alley or taking a bullet to the face as he entered his motel room was not high on his list of ways to die. He had never been one to wait for things to happen. If forced into a situation, a subtle amount of pressure in the right areas to spurn things along was his chosen path when things got tough. But he had a problem. He had no earthly clue where Daughtry was. But he was sure Daughtry knew, or at least would very soon find out, where he was staying.

Chapter 24

Dodge slid five twenty-dollar bills across the counter. Prepaying for the room for three more nights, before heading out in search of a new place to stay. His idea being, if Daughtry was looking for him, might as well give him a place to focus his attention. A place where he wasn't. He folded the remainder of his cash and shoved the wad into his front pocket and stepped back out into the heat of the Texas day. The sun was directly overhead now, catching the windshields of the few cars lining the motel parking lot. He squinted past the glare back toward his now empty room, secretly hoping Tobey would trot around the corner of the building, excited to see him again. But the only thing that moved down the row of doors was the constant drip of condensation from the air conditioners mounted under the front windows. After staring down the walkway for a few more seconds, he turned on his heels and walked away for the last time.

By the time he made it to the intersection of North Westmoreland and Singleton, his back was already wet with sweat. He needed to catch a bus or a cab before he melted in his new clothes and they smelt no different than the ones he had tossed a few hours earlier. Shoving his arm out into the flow of traffic, he hailed an approaching taxi, jerking his arm back at the exact moment a small box truck swerved from the far lane, its tires climbing the curb as it came to a rest a few feet from where Dodge stood. Stunned by the act of nearly being struck by a two-ton vehicle, Dodge froze. At that moment, the rear door to the truck slid up and two men, dressed all in black and wearing Gator type face masks, leaped from the box.

The men in black had a hold of Dodge, one under each arm, the one on the left reaching behind and sliding the Glock out of his waistband. Shocked by the speed and strength of the men dragging him toward the truck, Dodge decided fighting back at that time would lead to a serious injury, or possibly him being tossed out into oncoming traffic and killed by a passing motorist. Better he waits and bides his time. If Daughtry wanted him dead, the driver of the box truck would have plowed over him and sped away as his body lay broken on the sidewalk. No, they were told to bring him in alive. Which bought him some time.

The cuffs were cold and overly tight. He never liked the feel of steel against his skin. Handcuff training was his least favorite part of teaching at the academy. He had a system where the new recruits practiced applying cuffs and uncuffing using him as a test dummy. This allowed him to get a feel for what recruits were doing wrong and provide immediate feedback and improve their techniques. It was something you couldn't do by watching someone else being shackled and he really felt it added something extra to the training routine.

He moved his hands back and forth, twisting his wrists in the vice-like grip of the handcuffs, hoping to hit that sweet spot where the steel wasn't pressing directly on the nerve bundle or vein, keeping his hands from going numb so he could maybe use them when the time came. If the time came. He was positioned sitting against the box truck's drivers side wall. One of the guards who grabbed him sat across from him with the barrel of a .45 caliber Colt 1911 pistol pointed at his chest. The other man sat against the cab of the truck. There were no windows in the box, but the top was made of a light-colored plastic that allowed some light to penetrate what would normally be darkness. At the top of the box, on the front and back was a metal grate that allowed air to flow through the space, presumably to cool it down for the two men stuck back there guarding the prisoner.

The one thing Dodge was sure of was his comfort was not a factor for the person who designed the mobile kidnapping room on wheels. The last twenty minutes had been like riding on a sheet of plywood with metal wheels. Every bump and jostle of the vehicle he could feel in his soul. His hands were going numb and his tailbone throbbed. As much as he dreaded the moment the vehicle would come to a stop, he also needed to get the blood flowing in his extremities again if he stood any chance of surviving this encounter.

As he sat on the dusty floor, his knees now pulled up to his chest, to take some pressure off his aching tailbone, he felt a lump in his back pocket. He hadn't noticed it before, mainly because he had been so focused on the tightness of the handcuffs causing shooting pain to radiate through his hands to his fingertips. But now that he had switched seating positions, he felt sharp metal object poking his left butt cheek. The object was short, hard and had what felt like a knot on one end. It was his keychain!

Upon leaving the motel room, Dodge had collected all of his belongings and, since he didn't have a backpack or suitcase, he had to shove everything he owned into his pockets. His phone went into his front right pocket. Wallet in his right rear. The room key and toothbrush in his front left, along with the extra magazine for the Glock. The abduction had gone so smoothly, so quickly, after the men relieved Dodge of his weapon and placed the cuffs on him, they didn't complete the search. In their defense, he carried no bags and donned only a t-shirt and jeans. Once he was secured in the back of the box truck, he posed little threat to the two men riding with him.

What the two men didn't take into consideration, or possibly didn't know, was a part of Dodge's job as a parole agent was to arrest parolees who had been found to violate the terms of their supervised release. Meaning he had to secure the prisoner with handcuffs before placing them in the back of the transport vehicle. The thing about handcuffs is, if you put them on, you must be able to remove them. And this takes a key. A key is what was stabbing Dodge in the ass at that very moment.

The guard to his left only took an occasional break from scrolling on his phone to look up and give Dodge a grimacing glare, before returning his attention to his phone. Which was important, as he was the only one of the two guards who had a view of Dodge's arms and hands. The guard training the .45 colt at Dodge's torso could only see the front of his captor. His focus only briefly distracted, when his partner snickered at something playing on his phone then, after a few seconds, his attention would return to Dodge.

But this was enough time for Dodge to use his fingers to fetch the key from his back pocket.

Using the tip of his finger, he located the ring the key was attached to. Unfortunately, there were several keys locked into place on the ring, so pulling the whole thing out quietly as possible without alerting either guard of his actions was going to be difficult. Time also became a factor, as Dodge didn't know where they were or where they were going. The truck could slow to a stop at any time and he needed to be free of his bindings if there was even a slight chance at escaping when the back door rolled up once they reached their destination. That moment was his only chance at a clean escape.

His middle finger slid around until it found the small circular metal ring holding the three keys together. Once inserted into the hole, he contorted his wrists up and away from his body. The cuffs tightened against his tendons and the tiny bones that ran along the sides of his wrists. His fingers snapped free of his pocket and made a slight thump as they contacted the wall behind him. Neither guard seemed to notice his gaffe as the road noise coming from the large tires rolling over the rough pavement and the sound of passing cars outside the thinly insulated box drowned out anything inside. After securing the key ring in his palm, he found the only round key of the three. His fingers turning, positioning the shaft over the area of the handcuff where the small keyhole is located. He had cuffed and uncuffed enough people in his career to know exactly where the key needed to be. It was muscle memory for him.

But this time the task was made harder, as he needed to bend his wrists in a way that extended the chain between the cuffs to its limit, while still maintaining enough dexterity in his hand to push the key in the hole and twist it using only his fingers to unlock the cuff. The end of the key bounced around the smooth stainless-steel surface of the face of the cuff. Each bump in the road dislodging the end of the key from the tiny hole, until he was finally able to secure it in the locking mechanism. He took a deep breath and slowly turned the key until he felt a slight click. Then he rolled his wrist outward enough to loosen the cuff and slide his hand free. He immediately felt the tingle caused by the free flow of blood into his fingers.

After a minute, full feeling had returned to his hand. He inserted the key into the other cuff, but only loosened it so he could move more freely. He wanted to be able to use the cuff as a weapon against the two guards. After the cuff was loosened, he found the tiny button on the blade edge of the frame and spun the key around. The top of the key had a point that was made to push the button which locked the cuff's rachet mechanism, keeping the device from tightening any further. He felt the click of the lock and returned the key to his pocket.

Dodge was pondering the best time to make his move when the truck made a hard right turn. Both guards were thrown off balance and the one sitting across from him, leveling the pistol at him, was forced to place his right hand, the one holding the gun, onto the floor to maintain his balance. The newly freed agent pulled his hand from behind his back. Then in one fluid motion he extended his right arm, the unfilled cuff dangling from the end of his hand, and threw a haymaker right at the gun guy's head. The man saw it coming and pulled his head back slightly. Dodge had been counting on this and never planned to hit the man with his fist. That is what the steel cuff trailing his hand through the air was for. The hardened steel of the restraint device landed right on gun guy's temple. His head snapped to the side and the .45 Colt dropped to the floor. His eyes rolled back and all Dodge could see was white. He was out cold.

His partner had been caught off guard by both the sharp turn and Dodge's newly found freedom. But he was in no position to grab the gun from the ground or defend himself against the attack that was coming. In an effort to save his phone from being broken from his loss of balance during the turn, he failed to catch himself and tumbled onto his side, clutching his phone in both hands. Dodge used his momentum from the haymaker and carried it though until the steel of the cuff landed on the side of phone guy's neck. He shrieked in pain, dropping his precious phone to the floor as he lifted his hands to protect himself from another massive blow to the head.

But it was too late. Dodge was already on top of the guy, delivering body blows to his exposed kidney area. With each punch, Dodge could feel the tension in his body release a little. He could also feel phone guys ribs crack. It was as if the parole agent was releasing all his pent-up anger over Alder, Shannon Roberts, Lily Tremble and Colonel Patterson, even though he had been the first one to betray him by bringing him into this mess. Dodge's final blow, a hard right using the cuff like a pair of brass knuckles, to the temple finished the man off. Blood gushed from the gash in his head, but then slowed to a trickle. Dodge felt his neck for a pulse. He was dead.

The exhausted agent turned to the other guard, lying on the floor. He was still out cold. Dodge grabbed the pistol off the floor, then racked the slide to make sure there was a round in the chamber. He searched the dead guy for his weapon, also finding an extra magazine along with the Glock taken from his waist band during his abduction. In the dead guy's front pocket was a knife which Dodge used to cut one of the man's pant legs off. He wrapped the cloth tight around the ejection port and circled the end of the barrel several times. Forming a makeshift silencer. He then shot the unconscious guard in the head.

The homemade silencer caused the weapon to jam in what is adequately named a stovepipe. This is where the last fired bullet's empty casing gets lodged in the ejection port. Sometimes smoke from the bullet's explosion seeps from the open end of the casing, looking like a stovepipe sticking out the top of a house. After clearing the Colt's jam, Dodge stuck both .45s into his waistline and inspected his Glock. A quick rack of the slide ensured the weapon was chambered with a live round and the weapon was functioning. Then he leaned back against the side of the box and waited until the truck slowly rolled to a stop.

Chapter 25

The backup alarm echoed inside the metal box, causing Dodge to wince each time the sound hit his ears. The driver had stopped once and he could hear two men talking, but was unable to make out what the two men said. After some back and forth, the truck began moving again. Dodge could feel his body get heavy on the left side as he leaned against the slow turn to the right the truck made before stopping and then reversing. The whole truck jarred as the back of the truck came to rest against something. Dodge had seen enough delivery trucks over the years to know the driver had backed into a loading dock—the contact was from the back of the truck coming to rest against the massive rubber stoppers attached to the edge of the dock to prevent damage to the truck and the receiving bay.

The cab door opened and closed. He could hear the driver's footsteps as he walked past the back of the truck. The sound of a metal door opening and closing. Then silence. He wasn't sure what was going to happen next. His initial plan had been simple. Wait for the door to open and shoot anyone standing on the other side. Once the threats were all down, he could figure out where he was and get the hell out of there.

As the minutes ticked away, he began to wonder if his plan was the best idea. *Think through the plan*, he thought. Run scenarios and find the flaws. His mind worked like a movie camera. He began seeing himself in different situations, each with a slightly different outcome. In most of those he either took a bullet or was killed. That wouldn't work. Looking around the back of the truck, he saw the only things he could use. The two dead men.

The metal latch clanked and the hinges and springs moaned as the door rolled up. Two men stood outside the box truck, semi-auto pistols at the ready. Each one stared into the blackness of the metal box. After a few minutes, one of the men pulled a flashlight from his belt and clicked it on. The beam bounced around the walls and ceiling before coming to rest on the two guards. The dead men were propped up against the cab wall, arm to arm.

"What the hell?" one of the men outside the truck shouted.

"Get up in there and check on them," the other man said. His weapon and flashlight still trained on the two dead guards.

The second man, tall and fully bearded, holstered his weapon and climbed into the back of the truck. Once inside, tall bearded guard took the flashlight from the other guard, whose face was also covered completely in hair but was shorter and a little robust in the mid-section, and slowly made his way back to the two bodies.

"You better get up here," he shouted to the fat one.

The remaining guard climbed into the truck and joined his partner standing over their two compadres.

"Are they dead?" the tall bearded one asked.

"Jesus Christ, man. Bob has a hole in his forehead. Of course, they are dead."

"Where is he?"

Both men looked around the empty cargo area.

"He must have jumped out somewhere along the way," the robust guard said.

"The fucking door was secured with a padlock. How the hell did he get out?"

"I don't know…"

The short guard didn't finish his sentence. He was interrupted by two gunshots and both men fell to the floor. Dead.

Dodge used his off arm to roll the first two guards to the side and off him, his Glock still pointed at the men he just shot laying on the floor. He stood, using his arm, he wiped some blood that had smeared on his face from one of the men he used as a distraction and cover. He nudged the third and then the fourth guard with his foot. They were dead for sure. Each with a hole in the center of their chest.

There was no longer an element of surprise. It was likely the shots could be heard both inside and outside the building. He didn't know where he was and had no idea how many more armed guards were waiting for him. Plus, looking at the last two men he killed, based on the full beards and combat clothing, he assumed were ex-soldiers, or contractors, who spent the last two decades doing wet work for the agency. After the withdrawal from Afghanistan, the only work they were able to find was as mercenaries to the highest bidder. He hated people who chose such a path. Killing as a soldier was an unfortunate part of the job. But killing for money, that was dishonorable. A betrayal of their oath.

Dodge knew he may not have much time before the loading dock area was full of armed guards and murder for hire thugs. He needed to get out and figure out where the hell he was. He stripped the two freshly killed men of any ammunition, including the magazines from the Glock nine-millimeters they were carrying, then hopped down from the edge of the truck, where he stared into an empty room. He grabbed a prybar, used for opening crates he imagined, and smashed the only camera mounted on the wall above the loading dock. He then used the hardened steel bar and smacked the doorknob to the outside, making sure to damage the inside mechanism so the door would be inoperable.

After tossing the crow bar to the ground he turned all the lights off and made his way to the only other door in the room. Peeking through the edge of the glass, he noticed the door opened into a hallway lined with offices. All the office lights had been turned out and he saw no outside windows. The only light was from the overhead set into the ceiling. There was a steel door at the other end with a small rectangular window about three-quarters of the way from the floor. He could see nothing else.

A loud banging came from behind him, and he realized the guards outside were trying to get in. The door was holding, but he had no idea if the driver to the truck had left the keys in the ignition. If he had, the guards could move the box truck and get in behind him. If he was stuck in that hallway, anyone approaching from the door at the other end would place him right in the meat grinder. He would get chewed to pieces from the crossfire. He needed to get the hell out of there.

He opened the door and raised his weapon. He quickly maneuvered past the first set of offices. No one was there. For the sake of expediency, made the tactical decision that, if the lights were turned off in the remaining offices, they would be empty. It was a risk, but so was getting caught against opposing forces in that hallway, so he picked up the pace, ignoring the remaining offices, and covered the distance to the door in a matter of seconds. Once positioned at the door, he peeked through the window. There was nothing on the other side. Just a wide-open room. No desks. No office equipment. No people. The room was fifty yards across and twenty-five yards deep and appeared to have never been used for anything.

Dodge checked the handle and it turned. He opened the door and slid though. Using his foot, he leaned back and kicked the door handle sideways. He checked the handle and it still turned. He took a step back and with all his weight, he slammed the sole of his boot into the side of the knob. This time he heard metal crack and bend. Again, he tried twisting to see if the door knob would turn. It wiggled slightly, but the door remained shut. Confident the jammed door would buy him precious time, he turned and hurried across the open expanse of the deserted room. He had made it almost half way, when a set of speakers in the ceiling cracked and a familiar voice filled the room.

"Major Dodge. How good to see you could make it."

Dodge froze in his tracks. His eyes tracking every wall, scanning for windows and doors. There were only two. The one came from and the one he had been trying to reach. The voice spoke again.

"Where do you think you are going? There are only two doors to that room. You know what is behind one of them. And I can assure you, you won't like what is waiting for you behind the other. Give yourself up and I will make sure you die a quick death."

Dodge looked up at the ceiling. Above his head was a fisheye camera. It hung from a pole and was able to move 360° to have a view of the entire room. Dodge stared at the camera for a minute. Then he pulled out his Glock and fired two rounds into the device. Its cover shattered into a dozen pieces. Sparks and smoke flew from the camera as it spun an entire circle before coming to rest, its lens pointing straight at the floor. He put one more round into the lens for good measure before sprinting to the door at the other end.

"I see you have made your choice," the voice from above said. "Fine. Have it your way." The speaker clicked and silence followed.

"What an asshole," Dodge said to no one as he reached the door on the far side of the room.

The door was the same as the one he jammed at the opposite end. He stood with his back against the wall. His weapon at the ready position. He took one quick peek through the glass. Two sets of eyes stared back at him. Things had gone about as badly as they could have. He was trapped in an empty room. Two exits. Both were covered by bad guys with guns. How did he allow himself to be taken so easily? He should have fought back on that street corner. At least he would have died on his terms. Whatever that was worth.

"Shit," he screamed into the void. The word echoed throughout the cavernous room. Then he took a deep breath and exhaled. Again, he took a breath. Exhaling in a long slow breath, he felt his heart rate slow. His hands stopped shaking. He felt calm. It was decision time. Fight or flight. Since there were only two doors and he had enough ammunition, the choice was simple. Fight.

Without hesitation, he pulled his Glock up to his chest, closed his eyes, pictured his target where he last remembered it, then spun and fired one shot through the glass. He didn't need to visually check to see if his round had found its target. The sound of a dead weight crashing to the floor on the other side of the door assured him the bullet had found its mark. Dodge lowered himself as close to the floor as he could get without laying down. The large room filled with a low thumping sound as the guard still standing fired multiple rounds into the steel door. A few bullets made their way through the now busted window, but the rest lodged harmlessly into the thick insulation packed tightly between the outer door skins meant to help dampen the noise from the warehouse area from seeping into the offices on the other side.

Dodge had now removed three guards from the playing field but, without knowing how many more lay in wait, the information was useless. He needed to get out. Then the speaker in the ceiling crackled again.

"That is three of my men you have killed. But don't worry, there are more where they came from."

Dodge didn't know if the speaker also contained a microphone allowing communication between the two rooms, but he answered anyway.

"That's fine with me," he yelled while doing a tactical magazine change to top off the Glock.

"You can't possibly think you will win. You are outnumbered and out gunned," Daughtry said.

He could hear Dodge. At least he could mess with Daughtry's head a little before he died. Which is exactly where this was headed. "There are only two doors leading into this room. It will be like shooting ducks in a row."

"You can't shoot them all."

"I don't have to. After the first two fall in the doorway, anyone else will have to climb over the bodies of their dead comrades. And that takes time. Time is not your friend when breaching a door." Dodge decided to push a little harder now. It was time to put up or shut up. "Had you actually been on a field OP in the sandbox, instead of stroking off some general back behind the wall, you would have known this. The truth is you are just a hired killer. You have no honor."

The silence spoke volumes. He struck a chord and a smile stretched across his face. But the feeling of accomplishment was temporary. Either Daughtry was going to make a move and try to breach the room or wait it out. His men could take turns resting and manning the doors. Dodge needed to remain vigilant. Alert. Dozing off for even a second would provide the men on the other side of those doors time to burst through, then it would all be over.

He pulled the Colts from his waist band and placed them on the cement floor. Then he removed the extra magazines from his pockets and lined them up next to the pistols. Three for each Colt and each one held eight rounds. So, with the two in the chambers, he had fifty .45 caliber rounds. The Glock had a full fifteen rounds, plus one on the pipe and an extra mag three rounds short of capacity. Around seventy-five total shots. Not ideal, but it could be worse. It was time to wait to see who flinches first.

Five minutes had passed and no one had attempted to breach the doors. In fact, it was quiet. Too quiet. Thoughts started trickling into his brain. What was Daughtry up to? Why hadn't he been talking? It was the silent times that caused your mind to wander and impatience began to creep in. Dodge fought the urge to check the door. After ten minutes, he decided it was time to make a move. Sitting here kept him alive for now. But it wasn't a solution. He needed a plan. Unfortunately, the sudden crash of steel on steel from the door he had disabled earlier, meant he didn't get to choose the plan. He would have to think on his feet.

The banging continued to echo throughout the empty room. Dodge grabbed all the weapons off the floor and jammed the extra magazines into his pockets, then he stood up. Why wasn't anyone lobbying shots across the room at him from the window in the other door? His shot earlier proved the windows aren't bulletproof. He slid over, his back to the wall and one eye on the door on the other side of the room. He listened. Nothing. In one quick motion he poked his head over and glanced out the shattered window. Again nothing. No one was there. A smeared trail of blood on the ground led down the hall, ending at an elevator about thirty feet away.

Dodge stood, back against the wall, Glock at the ready. What the hell was Daughtry trying to accomplish? The banging on the door at the other end continued to echo in his ears. He was finding it hard to think. His head was beginning to pound along with the beat. Then it hit him. At the next bang on the door, he began counting. One, two, three…BANG! Four, five, six…BANG! Seven, eight, nine…another bang. The attack on the door had a rhythm to it. Three seconds and the men slammed something into the door. They waited three more seconds and then repeated the maneuver. The guards weren't trying to break the door down. They didn't want in the room with him.

Dodge took another glance through the broken window. The hall was still empty. He tried the door handle. It turned. He leaned back against the wall. He remembered when he and his brother used to go rabbit hunting as kids. When the two boys would find a brush patch with signs of rabbit occupation, his brother would circle around the patch and take up a position on the opposite side. Dodge would step into the tangle of brush, thorns and sticker bushes barking like a dog as he went. Pretty soon the game would become nervous and try to flee the predator, running in the opposite direction of where the threat was coming from. Right into the path of his brother who was waiting with his 4-10 shotgun pulled tight against his shoulder. The furry little white rabbit never stood a chance.

He looked back at the door across the room. Then at the door beside him. They were trying to drive the game to the hunter. It was a trap. And playing along appeared to be the only option. Dodge ran his index finger down the slide of his Glock, the tip finding the little tab protruding from just behind the ejection port, providing confirmation the weapon was hot and ready to fire. He unholstered his weapon and grabbed the doorknob with his off hand. Taking a deep breath, he pushed the door open and stepped into the blood-stained hallway. Instantly, his nose filled with the metallic smell of blood. Just inside the door was a pool of coagulating blood. Bits of hair and bone stuck to the cement and a trail of smeared blood led away from him. Dodge stepped over the puddle, then turned and closed the door behind him. The handle on the inside had a deadlock built in. He knew from earlier there was no key fixture on the outside of the door. He secured the lock and realized someone could just reach in through the broken window and disengage the locking mechanism. Dodge tucked his weapon into his front waistband, grabbed the handle of the lock and twisted clockwise with all the force he could muster. Using all the leverage his two hundred plus pound frame provided, he grunted as he pushed up off his toes and down on the lever. The metal began to fatigue under the pressure, bending past its designed limits. Dodge gave one more powerful wrench and the handle sheared off. Leaving only a sharp twisted nub of aluminum for someone to try and grab ahold of. He dropped the broken piece of metal on the floor, readied his sidearm and began making his way toward the gray elevator doors at the end of the hall.

Chapter 26

Daughtry watched his prey from the moment he entered the hallway outside the warehouse room. He had had one of his men slap a small wireless camera to the wall directly above the elevator doors. He wanted to know the minute Dodge stepped into the elevator, which was controlled from a switch panel in a sealed off room behind a locked door. Once he stepped foot inside, his men would take control of the lift, stopping it on a predetermined floor. One that he had specially chosen, in the parking garage two floors beneath their feet.

The camera's picture was grainy but he could make out Dodge at the other end of the hallway messing with the door. His view of the door was blocked by Dodge's tall frame so there was no way to see what he was trying to accomplish. Daughtry guessed it was an attempt to slow down anyone who tried to enter the room from the warehouse side. He had disabled the door to the loading dock, and the one at the opposite side of the room, by destroying the doorknobs functionality with a few well-placed kicks with his boot. It didn't matter in the end. The parole agent's actions were in vain. No one was going to enter through that door. The mouse was trapped in the maze now. Ending up in the place Daughtry preplanned for him was the only outcome.

The picture flickered in a flash of light and went black. Daughtry glared at the man sitting in the chair monitoring the elevator controls. The seated man twisted knobs and pushed buttons, frantically trying to get the fisheye camera back online.

"Must be a break in the wireless signal, sir," the man said, refusing to look up and make eye contact with his boss.

"Get it back," Daughtry responded.

The man continued to press buttons, finally turning to his boss standing over him. "I'm going to try and reboot it."

"How long will that take?"

"Maybe a minute."

Daughtry gazed at the screen, still black with the intermittent flashes of bright light. "Do it. But first shut the power off to the elevator. We don't want to let our rat out of the trap."

With the push of a red backlit button, the elevator was dead. Even if Dodge was inside, he couldn't make it move. Daughtry impatiently waited for the camera to reset, his eyes never leaving the screen.

"Just about there, sir. Ten more seconds."

The screen went full dark then the feed came back up. The camera took a few seconds to focus before the door came into view. But the door was the only thing in the picture. Dodge was nowhere to be seen.

"Where is he?" Daughtry's tone reflected the anger churning in his gut.

"I don't know, sir," the man at the console said nervously.

"Is he in the elevator?"

"The elevator is shut down. But even if you hadn't told me to disable it, there isn't a camera inside."

Daughtry, still staring at the monitor, paused to think. What was Dodge up to? Had he found a way to disable the camera from all the way across the room? That was it. The son of a bitch messed with the camera somehow.

"Do you have a recording of the moment before the camera went black?" Daughtry asked.

"Yes, sir. It recorded everything up until it malfunctioned."

"It didn't malfunction." Daughtry stepped closer and bent over to get a better look at the screen. "Go back to where Dodge was fucking with the door."

The man in the chair reversed the footage.

"Stop. Right there. Play it from here."

The two men watched again as Dodge stood with his back to them, disabling the door lock. At one point he turned slightly to his right, blading his body toward the camera. They could make out his face. But only one hand was visible.

"Stop it," Daughtry said loudly.

The other man paused the playback.

"Now back the feed up a few seconds, then play it at half speed."

The man did as he was instructed. Once he found a point a few seconds back, with Dodge's back facing them, he hit play and reduced the playback to half-speed. The video clicked by frame by frame, until Daughtry placed a hand on his shoulder and told him to stop.

Both men leaned closer.

"I don't see anything, sir."

"Where is his other hand?" Daughtry asked.

The man at the console shrugged. "I dunno. Maybe at his side."

"No," Daughtry said pointing to a place on the screen showing Dodge's waistline. "Move the video ahead two frames."

Again, the man did as he was instructed and slowly inched the playback forward.

"Stop! Right there," Daughtry's finger tapped the screen. "You see that?"

"What?" the seated man asked.

"Right there. That little speck of light by his beltline."

"I guess," the man said. "It's probably a reflection of some sort."

Daughtry shook his head. "No, it is not. Let me see your weapon."

The man in the chair leaned to one side and pulled his firearm out of its holster. He reversed it, so he was holding the barrel with the butt facing Daughtry, who didn't need to take the weapon to see what he suspected.

"Send the team from the other side in," he said frantically.

"What is it, sir?"

"Your damn weapon has a laser sight."

"Yeah, we all have them. So?"

Daughtry turned toward the door. "The camera never stopped working. Dodge just made us think it did."

The man at the console spun around in his chair. "Why would he do that?"

Daughtry opened the door and stopped before exiting. "So, we would reset the camera."

A blank face stared back at Daughtry.

"To buy time to get out," Daughtry said as he shut the door behind him and ran to the elevator. Grabbing a small radio from his back pocket, he clicked it on and said, "Reengage the elevator."

After a moment, a voice came over the radio.

"I turned it on, but it isn't responding, sir."

"Shit," Daughtry said to no one. He turned to look back down the hall. He needed something strong enough to pry the doors open with.

He ran back to the control room. He pushed through the door, his eyes searching for anything he could use, finally landing on a steel wire mesh cage housing a set of servers for the building's computer system. He stepped over and gripped a piece of flat iron that secured the door. With a powerful grunt, his massive arms flexed and the piece tore loose from the thinner metal of the cages frame. He then motioned for the other man to follow him and they both ran back to the elevator doors.

Daughtry pointed at the door, instructing his backup to be ready. He jammed the piece of flat iron into the crease between the doors. He tensed his massive arms and applied pressure to the bar. A crack appeared. He pushed harder, widening the crack until he could turn the bar sideways and lodge it between the doors. Then he slipped both his hands in the space. Placing one on each door and grunting as he pulled the doors apart and the bar fell to the floor. He used his foot to slide the bar along the bottom of the door track, blocking them from closing.

The other man moved in, pointing his weapon into the dark void of the elevator shaft. Nothing. By the time the guards from the other side of the warehouse were able to break through both doors and reach the elevator, the only thing they found was an empty hallway and an empty elevator whose doors had been jammed open using a .45 colt, with laser sights, taken off one of their dead comrades. Their prey was nowhere to be found.

***

Dodge wiped the grease from his hands onto his jeans. He looked back up at the elevator sitting motionless above his head. He could hear footsteps and the voices of the men above searching the elevator, looking for him, forcing a smile.

He noticed the wireless camera mounted on the wall above the elevator doors when he first entered the hallway. It was a tactile decision to ignore the device to make anyone watching, namely Daughtry, believe they were one step ahead of him. If they could see him and he didn't know he was being watched, they could take more time to plan an assault on the hallway and elevator. Time is what he needed.

Dodge decided to continue to follow the same script he had been using up to that point. He disabled the lock on the door to buy more time for when the guards came through the warehouse to drive him into the elevator. He guessed the elevator would be controlled by Daughtry's men and, when he stepped on it, they would take him to a designated floor and that would be the end. He would end up pushed into a hole out in the Texas prairie. Covered with dirt and forgotten about. That wasn't going to happen.

Shooting had always come natural to him. He had a talent for it. His favorite part of the academy was firearms. Specifically, hip shooting. Hip shooting is when the weapon is drawn from the holster quickly and is never raised to chest level. Instead, the weapon is fired from the hip. The technique is meant to train officers how to draw and shoot in a scenario where the threat is three feet or closer and it isn't practical to raise the weapon to chest height and punch out toward the target before firing. It is meant to be a *save your life* type of shot. But Dodge turned out to be quite accurate when shooting from his hip. He would practice every time he went to the range. Increasing the distance between himself and the target after every few shots. Until he got to a point where he could hit center mass at up to thirty feet.

To be able to accomplish this shooters feat, a person needs to be good at judging distances and line of sight. Meaning, knowing where the barrel of the weapon is pointed without raising it to eye level and staring down the slide. Dodge had become very adept at this and had trained with a laser sight system at the department's firing range to help his accuracy on quick draws.

He hadn't paid too much attention to the laser sights mounted on the Colts he had taken off the dead guards. The Department of Corrections didn't allow aftermarket products to be installed on department issued weapons, so he didn't own one personally. But he knew how it could be of use to him.

Using the breaking of the door's lock as a distraction, Dodge slipped one of the Colts from his waistband and as he turned sideways to the camera, he slid the colt against his belly, pointing the barrel at the camera mounted on the opposite wall. Once he was sure his aim was close, he turned on the laser. He only had a few seconds to spot the red dot and adjust his aim so the laser was pointed directly at the camera's lens. He knew from a case out of the prison system, laser pointers could be used to disable cameras. An inmate once stole a laser pointer from a teacher's desk and tried to use it to beat the cameras and break out. His attempt ultimately failed, as cameras are only one part of a prison's security and, unfortunately for him, he had no way of opening locked security doors. The guards simply waited until he was in a man trap, two doors on either side of an enclosed space meant to keep inmates from gaining access to other areas of the prison by allowing only one door to open and close at a time. But the laser idea had worked.

He located the red dot and quickly moved it until it disappeared into the camera's lens. Then he slowly walked toward the elevator, his weapon now raised to his chest for stability in keeping the laser on the target. He continued walking until he stood only a few feet in front of the elevator doors. He could now make out the dim red led light on the camera, indicating the device was on. It was now a waiting game. He guessed whomever was monitoring the camera would reset the device, thinking it was malfunctioning, and that would buy him time to jam the doors open and disable the elevator's control panel with a few hard smacks from the butt of the Colt.

Dodge then opened the access panel located in the ceiling, stretched his arms high and jumped, pulling himself up through the hole and onto the roof of the elevator. Once on the roof, Dodge stood, dusted off his pants and looked up. He quickly realized the elevator was on the top floor of the building. Since he hadn't gone up any stairs as he made his way through the warehouse from the loading docks, it meant he was on the ground floor. Which meant the elevator only traveled one way, down. And as far as he knew, elevators didn't have escape hatches built into their floors. He was going to have to find another way down.

The walls of the elevator shaft were constructed of poured concrete. Electrical conduit and other pipes ran down the wall to his left. The buildings designers probably thought it was the most convenient way to get the electrical, phone lines and internet delivered to each of the building's floors. Dodge stepped over and peered down. The space between the elevator's wall and the shaft wall was tight. Too tight for a man of his size. He then looked up again. His eyes focusing on the wall opposite the one too narrow to climb down. He saw L-shaped pegs sticking out of the wall's smooth surface. Every foot or so, there was another peg. They alternated left and right. He stepped closer, making sure to avoid the trap door in the ceiling as he approached the edge. Looking down he could see the pegs extended down the wall. He looked back up and could see the pegs were installed all the way to the ceiling of the shaft. The pegs were some kind of built in ladder for scaling the elevator shaft. Likely for maintenance or rescue teams if the lift were to break.

Dodge reached out and grabbed one of the iron pegs. He tried to shake it to test its stability. The rung didn't budge. It was a solid footing. Then he stepped onto the ladder and slowly climbed down. Once at the bottom, he located an access tunnel that had more electrical conduit and a large bundle of wires all tied together into a nice tight cable leading into it. Dodge examined the wires and realized they were computer cables for carrying data. The group of wires was at least two inches in diameter, sparking memories of one of his deployments before leaving for Afghanistan.

He was stationed in Germany for three months. A pre-deployment station located at an airbase in the middle of Germany. The station was used for shipping goods and services to the sandbox, including computers and servers. The station had anything a military unit would need to get a communication post up and running once in country. While providing security for the freight packing and shipment process, he noticed a large container containing rings of bound wire. Similar to what he was staring at now. He remembered the label on the box said, *server data harness*. He considered it was an odd name but walked away never giving it much more thought. Until now. There was a server room somewhere at the other end of this wire bundle. If he could locate that room, he may be able to cause enough chaos for a distraction. A distraction that could lure Daughtry out into the open.

Chapter 27

The small access tunnel was cramped, dark and damp. Crawling on his hands and knees was the only way to maneuver the space. More than once his back scraped against the pipes and wires running the length of the ceiling as he slowly made his way through the tunnel. Surprisingly, the space was well lit. The builders must have guessed it would be easier for maintenance to find and make repairs if the space provided adequate light. The architects and electricians probably hadn't planned on their access tunnel being used as a covert means to sabotage the servers it fed so he could kill a guy, but people can't be expected to foresee everything. Their loss was Dodge's gain.

After a few minutes of crawling, he noticed some of the computer cables turned upward. He slowed and listened. Straining, he could hear what sounded like two voices coming from up ahead. They were muffled and Dodge was not able to make out what the two people were saying. But there was something about one of the voices. It sounded familiar. The tone had a military cadence to it. It was Daughtry. He was sure of it.

As he crawled closer to the source of the voices, he freed the Glock from his waistband, holding it tight in his right hand, while creeping forward. His eyes turned up to an access panel above his head. The panel was square in shape covering an opening large enough for an average sized man to fit through. It was solid built in as part of the floor, so he couldn't see into the room above, but he could hear Daughtry's voice clearly now. The airman was yelling at the other person in the room about the camera back at the elevator. The first part of his plan had worked. In an attempt to bring the camera back on-line, Daughtry had ordered the camera reset. Now to wait for the second part of his plan.

As he lay on the cold cement floor, listening to Daughtry shout about how Dodge had disabled the camera with the laser sight on the guard's colt, his mind once again flooded with thoughts of Shannon Roberts. He still didn't know how she fit in to all of this. She obviously knew something about Advanced Systems Technology. Something that got her killed. But he simply couldn't put his finger on what that was, or what the company was doing that would be worth killing four people to cover up.

His thoughts were interrupted by Daughtry and the other man in the room above stomping to the door and closing it behind them. Dodge waited and counted to ten before sliding into place directly below the access panel and pushing up on one corner. As the edge of the door broke free, light from the room rushed in followed by a blast of cold air. Air that cold meant one thing. He was below the server room. Servers put out an extreme amount of heat and require a large amount of power to keep the room cool to prevent overheating and malfunction.

When he was sure no one else was left behind in the room, Dodge pushed the trap door up, sliding it to one side. Then he pulled himself up into the cold room, putting the door back in place once he was safely inside. Next, Dodge located the server array. It was tucked away in a corner of the room, in a steel cage. The cage was open. Its front tore open, like it had been chained to a truck bumper and ripped open with the press of a gas pedal. He surveyed the room for anything he could use to malfunction the servers with. He moved to the desk and stared at the monitor. On it he could see Daughtry and the other guard.

Daughtry was prying on the door with some sort of steel bar. Dodge looked back over at the server cage, then back to the monitor. He shook his head and mumbled, "Damn, that guy is strong."

He watched for a few more seconds as the elevator door was forced open. He needed to hurry. It wouldn't be long before the Airman figured out Dodge had disabled the elevator and only had one way out of the shaft. He grabbed a cup of coffee, one of the men had left on the desk and ran over to the server cage. He then pulled the mangled door open and poured the liquid right into the cooling vents of several of the electronic boxes. Sparks flew and the room filled with a loud hum before the lights on the units all blinked several times, finally turning black. Electronics have a natural aversion to liquids and whatever they were saving and sharing, it was now gone forever.

Dodge hopped back over to the monitor and watched as the men stared into the empty elevator shaft, before turning and running back in the direction of the server room.

"Come on back, shithead. I'm ready for you."

With a quick step around the desk, Dodge pulled the trap door ajar, leaving it partially open which had a direct line of sight from the main door to the room. Then he circled back around the desk over to the main door. Making sure he was on the side the door opened into, he slid as tight against the wall as he could, placing his right foot out in front of his body a few inches to make sure the door wouldn't smash him in the face when it flung open as the two men returned.

He assumed the guard would enter first as he was furthest from the elevator when the men figured out where Dodge was. Plus, he guessed Daughtry would see the man as expendable and let him enter the room first. Protecting himself from the first shot. Not a bad strategy, but quite cowardly of him. So, Dodge would have to wait before taking out the guard until Daughtry was in view.

He could feel his hands shake as he waited for the two men to return. His hands wet with anticipation, he tightened his grip on the Glock in his left hand, pulling it up to his chest, the muzzle aimed at the door in case he had to react quickly. Then he heard footsteps outside, getting louder until they stopped just outside the room. He took a deep breath and exhaled. An electronic beep sounded and the door slowly opened. Dodge watched as a weapon appeared. Followed by an arm. Then he heard a voice.

"Sir, the floor!"

It was the guard, who bounded into the room, pointing his Colt at the trap door ajar on the floor. Dodge pointed his weapon at the guard who remained fixated on the access door and waited a second more. Then another arm appeared. The flat piece of steel absorbed by the massive hand gripping it. It was Daughtry. Dodge didn't know anyone else with forearms the size of normal people's legs.

With one fluid move, Dodge used all his weight to slam into the steel framed door. Its weight coming to rest on the arm protruding past it, pinning it momentarily to the jamb. Dodge heard the crunch of bone and Daughtry let out a scream. The guard, now alert something was wrong, spun to face Dodge, raising his Colt as he turned. Dodge slid to the right and used a hip thrust to the rear to pinch the now broken forearm once more for good measure. He then fired a single shot into the guard's leg. The man fell to the floor, dropping his gun as he grabbed his leg, squeezing the wound in pain.

With the guard occupied, Dodge kicked the weapon into the access tunnel and turned his attention to Daughtry who was now picking himself up off the floor. His eyes were filled with rage. His right arm limp at his side. Dodge could see a slight cut in his forearm and a little piece of bone protruding out from the wound. A compound fracture. That was going to hurt for a while. But even with only one good arm, Daughtry was a formidable foe. Dodge took aim and placed a round into the top of the gigantic man's right foot. He fell like a giant redwood to the floor.

"You son of a bitch," he screamed. "You broke my arm and shot me in the foot."

Dodge looked down at the man squirming on the floor. "I figured I'd make it fair."

"How the fuck is this fair?"

"You're bigger than me."

Dodge turned to glance at the guard still lying on the floor behind him. "You better keep pressure on that wound. I think I might have nicked the femoral artery. The way your heart is racing, I'll give you ten minutes if you let go." Dodge pointed his Glock at the man. "I'd use both hands if I were you."

Then he turned back to Daughtry. "Get in here." His weapon now aimed firmly at the airman's head.

"I can't walk, asshole."

"Slide on your fat ass then," Dodge said. "But if you don't get in here, I'll take no issue with splattering your brains over that white floor behind you."

Daughtry started to spin around on his hind quarters. Dodge tapped him on the head with the muzzle of the gun.

"Uh-uh. Face first."

"How the hell am I supposed to do that? You shot me in the damn foot."

"Those big strong hands and arms are good for more than strangling innocent women. Use 'em."

Daughtry struggled at first, but after a few feet he was able to pick his whole body off the ground with just his one arm and move forward a foot at a time. Dodge watched, from a safe distance, and was amazed at the feat of strength and pure determination a career in the military provided the airman. All at taxpayer expense. Even with his service and the show he was putting on there on that floor, Dodge wasn't sure it was worth the money. He had turned his back on his country while using the blood of innocence to enrich his pockets. His ledger was red and the ex-Air Force Major wasn't sure there was anything Daughtry could do to even it out. Moreover, he didn't plan on giving him the time.

The door closed and the two men lay bleeding on the floor. Dodge used some zip ties meant for bundling cable to keep it tidy, and restrained the wounded man's feet and hands. He bound the guard's hands in front so he could keep applying pressure to his leg wound. He then turned to Daughtry. Zip ties were hardly enough to hold a man of his strength. So, Dodge improvised. He zipped his hands behind his back palms facing out with the back of his hands touching. This position would take some of his strength away by making it harder to stretch his arms and pull through the zip ties. After securing Daughtry's wrists, the next thing he did was use the zip ties to bind his index fingers together. Then his middle fingers. Lastly, his ring fingers. He would have to break his fingers, practically tear them off, if he wanted to be free. He was strong, but that was next level crazy.

Once finished, Dodge took the microphone from the desk. He looked at the guard, who was beginning to turn a pale gray color. "Is this on?" he asked.

The man nodded.

Dodge pulled the mic close to his mouth and depressed the button on the base of the microphone stand. He spoke firmly and matter-of-factly into the mic.

"This is Paul Dodge and I have Daughtry in my custody. The police are on their way so, unless you want to go to prison in Texas for the rest of your lives, I suggest you lay your weapons on the ground and get the hell out as quickly as possible. I have not seen any of your faces, so I have no way of describing you to the local authorities. The server has been destroyed along with all the surveillance footage from today. If you leave now, I won't hunt you down. You can return home and forget about me and this place. You have ten seconds to comply."

Placing the mic back on the desk, Dodge watched the monitor covering the loading docks. One man exited. Then another. Finally, a total of six men had taken him up on his offer and decided to save their own asses. He didn't know if that was all of them, but he could deal with any stragglers he stumbled across as he left. Wounding a few more traitors wouldn't cause him any sleep loss.

Now he turned his attention to Daughtry.

"You and I need to talk."

Chapter 28

He turned his eye to the room as he passed through the doorway, closing the door behind him. His hands shook. The anger inside him built up until all he felt was raw emotion. And he had acted on it. He wasn't proud of his loss of control, but he also couldn't change the past. All he could do was move forward and try to forget. But he knew, deep down, forgetting wasn't a likely outcome. That is what the Blantons was for.

Cracking Daughtry took less time than Dodge imagined. Apparently, large muscles don't translate into mental toughness. He would be lying to himself if he said he wasn't a little disappointed in the airman's lack of tolerance for pain. Making the murderer squirm was something he had looked forward to.

The toe of Dodge's boot was dark. Like leather when it gets wet in the rain. But water wasn't what had soaked into the ends of his boots. It was blood.

"Let's start from the beginning, shall we?" Dodge said, standing over Daughtry. His boot pressed into the top of the airman's foot. Blood oozed out from around the tongue and shoestrings, enough to form a small puddle on the floor. "What did Shannon Roberts learn about in Afghanistan that got her killed?" He eased up on the wound so Daughtry could answer more clearly.

"I'm not telling you shit," Daughtry said defiantly.

Dodge shook his head. "This is going to hurt me more than you." Then he pressed the heel of his boot directly at the entry point to the wound. Daughtry let out an ear-piercing scream. "Yeah, no. Apparently this does hurt you more."

Sweat rolled down the airman's face as he tried to regain his composure. "I don't know anything. I was just the cleanup guy. Patterson was the one in charge. I was only following orders."

"That dog ain't gonna hunt," Dodge said as he began searching the room for anything he could use to extract more information from the wounded man. After a few minutes of opening drawers and cabinets, he returned to Daughtry holding a piece of internet cable he ripped from the server array.

"What the hell is that for?"

Dodge kicked Daughtry in the chest, forcing him to fall back. Then he knelt at the man's feet.

"I'm going to take this piece of wire," he held it up so Daughtry could see it, "and feed it into your bullet wound from the bottom of your foot. I'm sure the frayed copper wires will cause significant pain as they scratch their way through the twisted meat and nerves inside your foot. Once I can see the end from the wound entry point in the top of your foot, I'll grab both ends and drag your fat ass around this room like a kid pulling a sled. Eventually, you will tell me what I want to know, or the wire will tear through the parts holding your foot together. You'll likely pass out from immense pain. But I'll make sure you wake up as I put a hole in your other foot and repeat the procedure."

Then Dodge reached down and snatched his feet off the ground, lifting them high to keep his captive off balance and flat on his back where he had an almost zero percent chance of being able to get up and cause trouble. Holding the computer cable in one hand, the other hand gripping the man's ankle, he held the frayed end up so Daughtry could get a clear look at it.

"Last chance."

The big man drew in a breath and spat. The saliva hit Dodge in the arm, but instead of wiping it off, he bent a two-inch section of the computer cable onto itself and shoved the broad end into the hole in the sole of the airman's shoe. The two men's eyes never breaking contact. When Dodge felt resistance, he pulled back just a bit to let blood from the wound work as a natural lubricant. Then he pushed harder until his actions elicited screams for him to stop. Dodge obliged but left the wire in to ensure his captive remained focused on what could happen if he lied or gave the wrong answer.

"Ok, talk," Dodge said still holding the man's legs in the air. A quick glance at the guard with the leg wound, then back before continuing, "I don't know how much longer your boy over there can hold on. He looks quite pale. So, if you want both of you to live, tell me what I want to know, now."

Daughtry's face glistened with sweat, despite the cold temperature of the server room. He laid his head back on the floor and moaned.

"Okay, just leave my god damned foot alone."

"Talk, or things are about to get messy in here," Dodge said.

"Colonel Patterson was in on it from the start," Daughtry said. "He was the one who first approached me and the others."

"Approached you about what?"

"He knew his career was over and he had an idea on how we could make a lot of money after the withdrawal from Afghanistan."

"How and what?" Dodge asked.

"It all started after his retirement. The Colonel moved back to Virginia and bought that horse ranch. Apparently, he hadn't done his research because horses are fucking expensive. Too expensive for a Colonel's retirement salary. The whole place was bleeding money."

"So, he needed money to keep his ranch going. Why didn't he simply go into contracting? He still had the clearances and a lifetime of defense connections."

"He couldn't go back."

"Why?"

"Because the Pentagon had discovered what he had done," Daughtry said.

"Done? What are you talking about?"

"What he had done to Roberts."

"What the hell are you talking about?" Dodge said, his impatience growing by the minute.

"Apparently he liked little girls."

A sinking feeling came over Dodge. His stomach clinched as the acid raced to his throat, burning as it rose into his esophagus and leaving the taste of bile in his mouth. Daughtry must have noticed the look of surprise on his face because he busted out laughing.

"You didn't know the Colonel was a pervert. How do you feel about your hero now?"

Dodge swallowed hard attempting to regain his composure. The news hit him like a gut punch, but he needed to keep probing. The revelation about his old boss was simply one piece in the puzzle.

"So, people higher up in the Pentagon knew about his past. But how does that play into Shannon Roberts' murder?" Dodge asked.

"You don't get it. Roberts was in on it since the beginning."

"In on what? What is it they were doing?"

"You spent time in the sandbox. There is only one thing Afghanistan has that people want," Daughtry said.

Without hesitation, Dodge answered, "Heroin."

Daughtry nodded. "And since the DEA left the country several years back, there is an overabundance of the stuff again."

"Ok. Fine. The drugs I get. But why kill Roberts? And how does the attack on her during her service play into all of this?"

"That whole mess almost blew the entire mission. Those dumb ass soldiers and contractors had no idea the kind of shit storm their joyride with Roberts might bring down on us. Once they attacked, Roberts wanted to report the men to base Security, but we couldn't have that. If it came out that she had been raped, the Pentagon would have shipped her home and we would have been left with no contact in country."

"But she did report the attack," Dodge said.

"Yeah, the dumb bitch went to see a shrink on base. He is the one who reported the attack. She said she didn't know it would cause a problem, but that was a lie."

"And the Army sent her home and discharged her with a medical."

Daughtry nodded. "And then we were forced to find someone to replace her and figure out what to do with her once she returned stateside."

"That's where Lilly Tremble came in," Dodge said.

"Uh-huh. She was an easy mark. A single parent soon to be discharged and returned to nowhere Mississippi. She had nothing to look forward to, so we gave her the assignment while she still had time in country. By the time the formal withdrawal began, we were established and lines of communications were open."

Dodge thought about what Daughtry had told him so far. Drugs were big business. But it was also a risky business. Getting drugs into the US was harder than it used to be. Technology had increased and the DEA was surely paying attention to what was coming from Afghanistan.

Daughtry continued, "Once Roberts was back in the states, the Colonel got Williamson to give her a job here at ATS."

Dodge's suspicion about where he had been brought in the back of the box truck was confirmed. But he didn't know what role ATS played in the drug smuggling operation. The warehouse was empty.

"And Shannon Roberts was killed because she had become a threat to your operation?" Dodge asked.

"Our partners, they had concerns about her keeping her mouth shut. Patterson had called in a favor and had the Pentagon's investigation shut down."

"That's a hell of a favor."

"It cost him a lot of money. But once the withdrawal went sideways and American soldiers were killed by that suicide bomber, everyone's attention refocused. Her case was filed away and forgotten about."

Daughtry went on to detail how the drugs were shipped through several countries before ending up in Russia. Once in Russia, the Russian Mafia moved the heroin and turned the profits into crypto currencies and that money was used to purchase weapons from the black market and the Dark Web. You could buy anything on the hidden internet. Drugs, passports, guns and even hit men. It was the digital world's wild west.

Once the weapons were obtained, they were shipped to ATS and modified with accessories, before being sold to drug cartels in Mexico and dictators in Central and South America. It was a good plan and, according to Daughtry, the group was making a million dollars a month. Each participant would decide when to cash in their share of the profits, or purchase anything they wanted using internet buyer's markets. Dodge's knowledge of crypto currency was limited, but he knew criminal organizations all around the world had been running the scam successfully for decades, because it worked.

His focus turned back to Roberts.

"If the Colonel had the investigation into Roberts' attack effectively ended, why kill her?"

"She wouldn't let it go. She wanted us to deal with the men who attacked her."

"She wanted them killed."

Daughtry nodded. "It was over and if those guys started turning up dead, it wouldn't be long before it was tied back to her. To us."

"And Lily Tremble?"

"Once Roberts was out of the picture, killing her was the next logical step. We needed to cut off any loose ends before we shut it all down."

"And Blake Williamson? Was he a loose end?"

"He was a greedy piece of shit. We found out he had been skimming from the profits. A little here and a little there. But sooner or later it added up to enough that someone noticed. When I went to see him that day you and the detective were at the hospital, he had no idea who I was.

"After I left, the dumb bastard made the call that sealed his fate."

The whole thing came down to what it always did. Money. It isn't about the drugs and guns. It wasn't about betrayal or unit discipline. In the end it was pure greed. But there were still a couple of things he didn't understand. The first being why Patterson brought him into this whole mess.

"Okay. I only have two more questions. First, why me?"

Daughtry closed his eyes then shook his head. "I tried to talk him out of that. But he had to know."

"Know what?" Dodge asked.

"About what he had done to Roberts."

"Why not send you to find out who else knew and have you eliminate the threats to your operation?"

"I never understood his obsession with you. I always thought you were an asshole. But he insisted on getting you reinstated. He knew what your job was and figured you wouldn't turn down an old friend and the chance to lock up a few rapists."

As Daughtry continued to spill his guts, Dodge understood more and more the plan had been to kill him in the end. Once he had outlived his usefulness, they would have killed him. Probably buried him next to Detective Adler somewhere out in the Texas prairie. It was time for his final question.

"Who is the big player in all of this? Who calls the shots? Because I know for damn sure it isn't you," Dodge said.

"I told Patterson you weren't as good as he thought you were. You really have no idea, do you?"

Dodge felt the emptiness return to his stomach. He had been in this room interrogating Daughtry for over half an hour. The whole time his captive told him everything he wanted to hear. It had been too easy. He knew deep down things had gone entirely too smoothly. The guards in the truck. The warehouse and the elevator. It was as if everything had led him to this exact moment. But why?

Just then, the door to the room swung open. Dodge spun on his heels and stood face to face with a ghost.

Chapter 29

Dodge stood motionless. The muzzle of his Glock leveled at center mass on the figure standing in the doorway. The look in his eyes must have been one of bewilderment, because Corporal Shannon Roberts simply smiled at him.

"By the expression on your face, I assume you are surprised to see me, Mr. Dodge."

Dodge tried to shake off his confusion. Roberts was alive and talking to him. He composed himself as best he could. "I gotta say, I didn't see this one coming."

"That was the whole idea," Roberts said, entering the room. A Berretta 9mm pistol dangling from her arm. "Until my stupid Uncle went and mucked the whole thing up by getting you involved."

Dodge, remembering he had tucked his weapon in his waist band, let Daughtry's legs fall to the blood-soaked floor. He then turned slightly in Robert's direction and took a small step back to maintain a view of all three of his opponents when he spoke to any one of them.

Roberts eyes focused on Daughtry, who was attempting to sit up.

"I thought you said you could handle this?"

The wounded airman's head fell to avert eye contact with the person who had been pulling his strings over the past several years.

"I'm sorry, ma'am. Things got a little out of control." He gazed back up at Roberts. Straight into the barrel of her Berretta. The sound echoed as the bullet tore through Daughtry's chest and slammed into the floor behind him. The airman collapsed backward, an expression of surprise on his face as his body went limp. Shot through the heart, he was dead before his head hit the tiled floor.

Roberts turned the weapon in the direction of the other wounded guard. His face was grey and beads of sweat rolled down his forehead and across his cheeks. He started to raise his hands, a last-ditch effort to shield himself from a speeding bullet but clamped back down on his wounded leg fearing death from bleeding out more than getting shot. Dodge, currently helpless to prevent the coming violence, watched as Roberts squeezed the trigger and the man's head split open and brain matter splattered the floor behind him. Dodge couldn't see the look on his face because his face was gone, now just a pile of blood covered flesh and goo.

Dodge turned his eyes to Roberts who was now pointing her weapon at him.

"I just took care of both of our problems. Now maybe we can come to an arrangement. I can always use a friend on the other side of the law. You know, to help smooth things over."

Dodge stared back at the woman he had been told was dead. "How did you do it?"

"Do it?" she asked. "Oh, you mean make everyone believe I was dead. That was easy. There is very little money won't buy. In this case, a lot of money was needed, but we have made plenty."

Dodge shook his head. "You needed cops, medical examiners and paramedics at a minimum to make this all go smoothly."

Roberts laughed. "You think this is going smoothly? We paid off the coroner and the Paramedic unit that showed to the scene ahead of time. It took some convincing to get them to play along, but everyone has a price. The paramedic was easy, he was a veteran and brought back a little heroin problem from Afghanistan. Unfortunately, he passed quietly in his sleep a few nights ago."

"Let me guess. Overdose," Dodge said.

"Barely made the papers," she said smiling.

"The coroner?"

"He was a little tougher. He took the money, but we needed to be sure he wouldn't turn on us later."

"You threatened his family."

"Family? We're not monsters, Agent Dodge. The good doc raised show dogs. Pomeranians to be exact. Yippy little things. They bark at everything. I'm more of a cat person myself."

"So, you threatened to kill his dogs if he didn't go along with your plan," Dodge said.

"Yes. I mean, we had to let him know we were serious. Sacrifice one for the good of the many. You were a soldier, so you understand."

Dodge thought about Tobey and immediately felt the lump in his throat return. "You killed one of his dogs?"

Roberts looked at him as if she couldn't understand why he was surprised. "Not the mother. We made him pick one of the pups."

"You made him pick? What the fuck is wrong with you people?"

Roberts' expression suddenly changed. Her lips turned down. Her eyes squinted. She was getting tired of all the questions and soon would decide his fate. His delaying tactics were drawing to an end. But he needed to know one more thing.

"What did you do with Detective Adler?"

Roberts mulled over the idea of revealing anymore to her captive. Then she pressed her lips together and nodded.

"Adler got the same offer as everyone else. He was just late to the game. Things were going fine and no one was the wiser. Then you showed up and got his inquisitive blood flowing again. The case was all but forgotten about." Her almost black eyes stared through him. "His death is on you."

Dodge knew this was it. He just needed a few more seconds. "So, if I take the deal, how does it work? Is it all in cash, or do you also pay in crypto currency?"

The serious and determined expression returned to her face. Then he thought he saw a slight smile curl on her lips.

"I'm afraid that time has passed." She motioned at the guard lying dead on the floor. "Push him into the maintenance tunnel."

Dodge glanced at the opening and then back at her.

"And you can leave your weapon on the ground right here." Roberts leveled her Beretta at his head.

Dodge pulled the Glock from his beltline, slowly and deliberately placing it on the ground at his feet. He then turned toward the lifeless body, grabbed the man's feet, and used his legs to spin him toward the square opening in the floor. After his legs dangled over the hole, Dodge reversed his position, reaching under his shoulders and slid the body into the crawlspace. He repeated the maneuver with Daughtry, though the sheer size of the man made it difficult for him to move his massive frame alone.

"This would go a lot quicker if you helped," he said, looking over his shoulder at Roberts.

"You're going to have to just try harder. Use that Air Force work ethic my uncle used to talk so fondly about."

"Unlike the grunts in the Army, we chose to work smarter, not harder."

Feeling a little better after the inter-service dig, Dodge bent at the knees and using all the power from his legs, pushed the airman closer to the hole. It took two more attempts to maneuver the body to the edge of the service entrance. Then, using all the strength he could muster, Dodge pushed the man until the weight of his frame carried him forward and his limp body tumbled into the hole. A thud echoed up from the tunnel as he crashed on top of the other body to the floor below.

Dodge stood and peered down into the service tunnel. Daughtry's body lay twisted at the bottom. His head faced down, but his torso was twisted and dodge could see his belt buckle gleaning up at him. He could also see something else. The outline of a black pistol grip on the cement floor beside his outstretched arm. This was his chance. He could leap into the tunnel, grab the gun and make his way back up the elevator shaft to the warehouse and out into the open air. Roberts had no other men with her in the room and Dodge assumed that was because all her henchmen had, in fact, left the building when he made his offer over the intercom system before she showed up.

"Now, turn and face me and step away from the hole," Roberts said. The gun in her hand was still pointing at him.

Dodge spun on his heels until he was face to face with her. He was trying to keep the backs of his feet as close to the edge as possible to make the movement back into the hole as quickly as he could manage without hitting any part of his body on the lip of the opening as he lept in. He also needed to worry about his landing. He was going to fall right on top of Daughtry. Who was softer than the cement floor, but he also risked a broken ankle for a bad landing on that deflated meat sack.

"Mr. Dodge, I would like to say it has been a pleasure, but you have been a pain in my ass for long enough." Roberts raised the Berretta, pointing the dangerous end directly at Dodge's head.

This was just one of several mistakes the former Corporal made, tactically speaking, since entering the room. Her first mistake was revealing herself to him, alive. He hadn't even suspected she was still up and about, walking and talking. Let alone being the shot caller for a multimillion-dollar drugs to weapons smuggling ring. She was holding four aces and laid her cards on the table before the other players were even able to place a bet. Amateur hour. Her second mistake was not checking everyone else in the room for weapons. She could have completed the task herself, by ordering Dodge on the floor and having him and her two employees place their weapons out in the open where she could have removed them from the playing field. It is never a bad thing when you control all the firepower in a fight. Her third mistake was letting Dodge get anywhere near a possible escape route. Having him push the bodies into the maintenance tunnel seemed to be overkill. The two men were already dead and now he knew she had the same fate in mind for him. Why not just shoot him, leave all three of them in the room and set the building on fire. A little accelerant and a match are all it would take. The elevator shaft was essentially a chimney, providing air flow from the rest of the building and fueling the flames below. The bodies would be ash before fire personnel were able to quell the flames enough to venture that deep into the building. No one would likely be able to identify the remains. A clean get away.

Her last and fatal mistake was about to unfold. With the gun leveled at his head, Roberts had taken the largest target out of play. Dodge's center mass.

He always taught recruits at the academy to aim for the largest available target. Depending on the circumstances, that target could be a chest, leg or even a head in some cases. But if the torso is right there, all of its vital organ contents staring at you, that is what you aim for. Better chance of hitting something and causing a wound that stops the threat immediately. But she had chosen the head. Like some John Woo movie.

Dodge simply stepped back. He heard the shot as his head passed the floor line and he crumpled onto Daughtry. She had missed high. He felt the concussion from the round as it passed above him. She had been closer than he would have liked. His arms and legs went in opposite directions as he tried to keep some sense of balance as he rolled off the dead guy and onto the floor. His hands immediately started reaching around the body, slapping the concrete trying to locate the gun. His eyes staring up at the hole waiting for Roberts to peek down and see him alive and start shooting again.

He saw the barrel of her Beretta first. Its unmistakable muzzle design sliding into view above him. Then the rest of the gun, followed by her hand, wrist and arm. All the while his own hands searching feverishly for the Colt he knew was down there. He took his eyes off Roberts to orient himself. He then realized he was on the wrong side of the body. As his eyes turned up toward the light from the room above, he saw Roberts' head begin to appear. Her bangs had fallen over her face and were dangling in front. Then they made eye contact.

Dodge reacted quickly, diving over Daughtry and the other guard and taking him out of her line of sight for a split second. It was enough. By the time Roberts repositioned her head to get a bead on him, she was looking down into the barrel of the Colt .45 Semi-auto pistol. Her final mistake. Dodge saw her eyes widen as she realized the error she had made. He watched as the whole scenario ran through her mind. It was the eyes that gave her intentions away in the end. It was always the eyes that betrayed you.

It was quick. Barely discernable for most people. A twitch of the hand. A dart of the eye. A clenching of the jaw. But Dodge saw the tells. Her mind was made up. It was going to be her or him. One on one. Only one of them was going to walk away. Dodge chose himself.

The stunned look on Roberts' face as the round penetrated her skull, above the right eye, remained as she rocked forward, the gun still clenched in her hand and tumbled headfirst into the maintenance tunnel. Her limp body crashing on top of her dead colleagues with a quiet thud. Dodge moved in, the Colt still aimed at the pile of flesh and bone before him. Her head faced away from him, showing the damage a .45 caliber round does when exiting a person's skull. A large part of the back of Roberts' head was missing. Probably scattered across the floor and walls of the security room above. A small chunk of bone, with blood-soaked hair still attached, had gotten tangled in her ponytail. It dangled over the edge of the bodies, swinging like a pendulum, drops of blood falling like sand from an hourglass onto the floor. He was sure it was some kind of metaphor, but couldn't, or didn't want to, waste any time on it. It was time to leave.

He found an extra magazine on Daughtry and reloaded the Colt. He didn't think any of Roberts' henchmen had stuck around, but he hadn't lived this long because he made a lot of weak assumptions. He pulled himself up through the hole in the floor, sliding the cover back over once he was clear. The bodies disappeared from sight as the door fell into place. It reminded him of a documentary he once watched about mummies in Egypt. The natural light being blocked out as the lid to the stone sarcophagus was slowly slid into place. It was poetic in this case. He stood and looked around the room and saw his Glock on the floor where he had placed it only a few moments before. Reaching down, he picked up the gun, checked it for damage, ran his finger down the slide and felt the little tab that indicated there was a round in the chamber. Satisfied the weapon was ready and functionable, he shoved it in the front of his waist band. He then made his way down the hall to the elevator, which was still not working because of his jamming the doors open on the floor above. There appeared to be no stairs or other rooms. The security office must have been built on the bottom floor and they meant it to be more like a vault with limited access and tight security. He would have to get out the same way he got in.

Dodge used his pants legs to wipe the dust and grease from his hands. He removed the Colt, which had been holding the elevator door open, then wiped it clean and tossed it on the floor of the elevator, reached inside and pushed the button for the bottom floor. The doors closed and he heard the hiss of the pullies and cables begin moving the elevator car down. He stepped over the bodies of the two henchmen he had dispatched earlier. The doors he had intentionally damaged to buy himself some time, were both open. The areas around the door handles were dented and scratched on the opposite side. The guards must have used a battering ram or other heavy object to bust the locking mechanisms and force the doors open. His plan had worked.

As he passed the offices down the long lean and narrow hallway toward the loading dock area, he caught a whiff of cigarette smoke. The smell got stronger the closer he got to the door leading into the dock area. Dodge stopped and pulled the Glock from his waistband, then slowly moved toward the door. The odor was strong as he stepped into the cavernous room. His eyes darted, first to his right, then left, finally settling on the glow from the end of a lit cigarette and the silhouette of a man standing in the back of the box truck that had been used to abduct him and bring him to the warehouse.

Dodge raised his weapon. Pointing the muzzle directly at the shadowy figure. He took three steps forward and stopped.

"Come on out," Dodge said. "Slowly, and with your hands in front where I can see them."

The cherry on the end of the cigarette glowed red and then it fell to the floor. Sparks danced across the floor of the truck before being extinguished under the man's shoe.

Chapter 30

The man stepped forward, his face appeared as he exited the dark box of the truck and into the light of the warehouse loading dock. He wore a black suit. His jacket covered a red shirt. Not bright red, but more of a maroon deep red. No tie, so his top button was, allowing a little tuft of hair to peek out the V-shaped gap. What he wore on his upper body suggested a man of means. Even his hat looked Italian made. But his shoes betrayed him. Black leather, scuffed at the toes. Rubber soles, not leather. Which meant he was mobile. Walking a lot on different surfaces. Probably sometimes on wet concrete or pavement, where leather soles slip and slide. Especially after they have been broken in. No. He was a working man. Not from the Pentagon either. Dodge expected a DoD employee to be wearing a uniform. Maybe even a name tag. A ribbon or two on the left breast pocket. Things that told everyone who he was. That was important in the military. Separating yourself from the pack is how you got promoted. Dodge guessed the man was from one of the alphabet soups back in Washington DC. Defense Intelligence, maybe. Or NSA.

"Mr. Dodge. I wish we could be meeting under different circumstances, but time being what it is, here we are."

Dodge kept his Glock pointed at the man's chest. He wouldn't make the same mistake as Roberts, less than a half-hour earlier. "I'm tired and sore. Do you mind getting to the part where you tell me who you are and what you want?" Dodge made a quick scan of the room again. He saw no one else. No hired guns. No bag men. Nothing. He stared back at the man. "If your one of these assholes, I'll put you in the ground next to your buddies."

The man bellowed a laugh. "Mr. Dodge, if I was one of them, you'd be dead already."

"That's what they thought," Dodge said as he took a step closer.

The man's scuffed rubber soled shoes didn't move. "I assure you, Mr. Dodge," the man paused before continuing, "may I call you Paul?"

"Most call me Dodge. What do I call you?"

He hesitated, then said, "You can call me Barton."

Barton, Dodge thought. It sounded normal. Too normal to be a cover name. It was likely his real name or a close variation of it. Maybe an earlier version of a family surname. Possibly from when his family first came to the country. A lot of Irish and Germans changed their names over the years, wanting to fit into new communities a little better. There used to be a lot of prejudices for a lot of different ethnic groups. Some have always been there. Others have come and gone.

"Well, Mr. Barton. I suggest you tell me what the hell you want, or you get out of my way. Or you can do both. But either way, I'm going to walk out that door. How you decide to leave will be based solely on the decision you make right now."

The man still didn't move. The two men stood, silent, like in a western movie. Waiting for the other to twitch or show a tell before drawing. Barton twitched first.

"Why don't we both get out of here and find a place where we can sit and talk for a bit. I know a place nearby where we can have a drink. I believe you fancy Blantons?" He said it while whisking his arm toward the door. "I assure you; you will want to hear what I have to say."

Dodge stared into the man's eyes. They were dark and emotionless. He had seen those eyes sitting across the table from him in an interview room more times than he cared to remember. Soulless and calculating. His normal reaction would have been to follow one of his earliest rules. When in doubt run or shoot. Doesn't matter which, but under no circumstances do you willingly get in the stranger's van. But he wasn't sure he had a choice this time. The cops would come sooner or later and, when they did, he would be the first one they came looking for. He lowered his Glock but chose to keep a firm grip on it in the event things went south.

"The police will show up here eventually. A homeless man or a group of teens looking for a place to party will get brave and find a way in. They will find the bodies, and even if they don't call the cops, they are teens. And teens talk. Someone will overhear, a teacher or parent, and the police will be alerted. The bodies will be found."

"Let me deal with that. I assure you no one will miss them. And no one will find their bodies." He swept his arm once again in the direction of the door. "Now, I really do think we should leave and let my team do what they do. Don't you?"

Dodge hesitated for a second and then tucked his weapon back into his waistline and followed Barton out the door and into an awaiting vehicle. It was not a white van, but a black Mercedes EQS SUV. The windows were tinted and Dodge got a look at the license plate attached to the rear bumper as he stepped around the rear of the vehicle on his way to the driver's side rear door. Government issued. A man exited out the driver's door and opened the rear door for Dodge. Dodge nodded and slid into the soft leather interior. The door emitted a cushioned thud as it closed behind him. Barton slid in next to him and the driver, now back in the front seat, hit the gas. Tires squawked as the vehicle lurched forward, pushing Dodge back into cool leather. In a matter of seconds, they were out the front gate and the ATS was a fading sight in the rear window.

The two men rode in silence as the driver maneuvered the Mercedes through traffic and it wasn't long before Dodge realized they were headed on a direct route for the airport. Not Dallas Fort Worth International, but Love Field. The original airport served the Dallas Metro region until 1974, when Dallas Fort Worth International was opened. Love field also happens to have a long military history, dating back to World War one. Dodge suddenly regretted getting into the van.

As the Mercedes continued to weave in and out of traffic, Dodge looked over at Barton. He was tapping the screen of his cell phone. Stopping only for a moment before beginning tapping again. He glanced across the cabin at Dodge.

"We will be there shortly."

"I didn't think the airport would have Blantons," Dodge said.

Barton turned his attention back to his phone. "I told him you were coming."

"Him?"

Barton didn't answer, but the smile quietly lingered on his face.

Dodge could now see the airport through the windshield. He watched as the driver turned into the main gate entrance and then immediately turned again and began driving down a narrow road that skirted the outside of the airport fence. The Mercedes shook as a passenger jet passed overhead, its engines pushing full power trying to keep the massive airliner in flight. Dodge watched as it continued its journey, until banking hard and disappearing out of his view. The road continued, making a wide arching curve as it bounded the end of the runways. Up ahead he could see three hangers. They sat far from the passenger terminals on the opposite side of the airport where no one could see who, or what, was coming in and or leaving.

The black Mercedes pulled up to a gate and a woman dressed in a blue security uniform pushed a button and the gate slid open. She nodded at the driver as he passed and he nodded back before continuing across the tarmac toward the three hangers. They passed the first hanger, then the driver slowed and turned sharply. He maneuvered the vehicle though the doors of the second hanger, which were only open wide enough for a car or truck to slip between. Inside the hanger, lights were on and it was spacious and empty, except for a private jet sitting dead center at an angle to the enormous sliding doors they had just driven through. The driver kept clear of the aircraft's wings, circling wide around behind and coming to rest about ten yards from the cabin door, which was open. Boarding stairs butted up against the fuselage under the door.

Dodge strained his neck trying to look past Barton to get a better view of the jet and who might be waiting inside. Without leaning clear over onto his carmates lap, he couldn't get a good view of much more than the bottom half of the plane's fuselage. Barton's phone buzzed in his hands and he stared at the screen for a second before turning to Dodge and saying, "He's ready to see you."

As he reached for the door handle, Dodge took one last look at Barton who was, once again, concentrating on whatever was on the screen of his cell phone and no longer speaking. He opened the door and stepped out into the hanger, closing the door behind him. His eyes watched the door of the plane as he made his way past the front of the Mercedes and toward the boarding stairs. He took one last look back at the SUV. Cigarette smoke wafted out of a gap in the rear passenger doors window, then the engine revved and the SUV pulled away. Dodge watched as the taillights slipped through the hanger doors, turned left, and ventured out of sight. He then faced the stairs and slowly climbed, not knowing who or what awaited him at the top.

As Dodge stepped into the aircraft he looked to his left and saw two seats. One for the pilot and one for a co-pilot. None of the little lights and switches that you would expect to be lit with little red lights during flight were on. The plane was shut down. Except for the main cabin. Two rows of overhead lights, one row on each side, shone brightly down the outside walls, illuminating a set of chairs facing each other on the starboard side. The chairs were larger than an office chair, but smaller than standard living room furniture. They were covered in brown leather and one of them was turned open to the isle, meaning they were mounted on a swivel base, allowing the user to spin 360° and face anyone in the plane without getting up. A small dark wood table rested between the pair of leather chairs. The port side had three chairs all facing the front of the plane, which appeared to be of the same design as the other two. No tables. Just ample leg room for stretching out and enjoying the flight.

At the rear of the cabin, on the port side, was a small opening large enough to fit one person. There was a bar with various kinds of liquor and glasses all tucked away in high lipped shelves built into the walls. Each glass rested upside down by what appeared to be a foam or rubber nub that the glass was pushed down over and held securely into place during take-offs, landings, and turbulence during flight. Ingenious he thought. The last thing you wanted were glass pieces flying all around the cabin every time it hit a rough patch in the air. On a small counter, next to a tiny sink, sat a bottle of Blantons and two empty glasses.

On the right, or starboard side, was a door. It was closed and a little red sign above the handle read, **OCCUPIED**. Dodge stood in the center of the aisle not sure what his next move was. He waited. Then waited some more. After about five minutes, he heard a loud whooshing sound. The sound of an airline toilet flushing. Then a pump kicked on. He imagined it provided water to the sink. After a few seconds the door opened and a man stepped out. Dodge smiled. He immediately recognized the face staring back at him.

Chapter 31

It had been over a year since Dodge was living on a boat in the waters off St. Thomas. He was on extended leave and found his way to the island on a sailboat he bought with money given to him by a good friend who passed. After stops in Key west and Puerto Rico, he found a little spot of water in the bay off the shore of Charlotte Amalie to lay anchor. He had hoped his vacation could turn permanent. A life of sun and seafood. A little rum here and there wouldn't hurt either. Unfortunately for him, a hurricane hit the island, which started a chain of events that led him down a dark path and introduced him to the man standing in the lavatory door, Mr. Brown.

"Dodge," he said reaching out a hand. "Want a drink?"

Dodge shook his hand and the man pointed at one of the two chairs with the table between them.

"I thought you'd never ask."

Brown stepped over to the small bar area and put a double shot of Blantons into each glass and made his way back over, sitting in the chair opposite Dodge. They each took a swallow, Brown about half and Dodge the entire glass.

"I see you still drink too much," Brown said.

"It's been a long day."

Brown refilled the glass. This time, Dodge sipped the brown liquid and stared at his friend. Though friend might be a strong word for someone who puts your life in danger, then uses you for their own purposes. He felt the label co-worker more appropriate. But he liked the man and, most of all, he trusted him. The pair had developed a mutual respect that only those who've been in combat can appreciate.

Brown nodded and took another pull from his glass. "What exactly is going on down here?"

Dodge's mind wandered a bit. He thought about his first encounter with Daughtry and the subsequent meeting with Colonel Patterson, his friend of so many years. He wondered if he really knew the man at all. He had placed him so high on a pedestal for so many years, he was having trouble dealing with what he now knew to be true about his mentor and how his betrayal of oath led to his untimely death. To be clear, Dodge wasn't saying Patterson didn't get his just deserts. We all make decisions and those decisions often come full circle. More poetically said, we reap what we sow. Patterson had hooked his wagon to a tornado—one that left a trail of death and destruction in its wake. In the end it cost him his life.

Dodge spent the next half hour rehashing all the events of the past week. Brown listened with the enthusiasm of a stump. Probably because he already knew everything. He just wanted to hear it from the horse's mouth. Dodge would have done the same thing if the tables were reversed. One last chance to catch any discrepancies before moving on and briefing the brass. When he finished, Dodge swallowed the last of his bourbon and let his body relax into the soft leather of the chair. He looked out the window at the empty space of the hanger outside.

"But I suppose you knew all of that already," he said.

"I did."

"So, why am I here?" Dodge asked, still peering out the window thinking of Tobey. Wondering if he was okay.

"You're here because I need to make sure you know the whole thing," Brown said.

His eyes turned to Brown. "And to know if I can keep a secret."

"That too."

"You know I can," Dodge said sharply.

Brown said nothing. He simply stared back at Dodge.

Then Dodge figured it out. "This isn't for you, is it?"

Brown shook his head.

"This is for management. They sent you here to check me out. Make sure I could tow the line. Keep my mouth shut."

A slight smile curled up on Brown's lips.

"What the fuck are you smiling about?"

Brown leaned forward in his chair. Placed his hands on the table and said, "They also sent me here to see if you could handle it."

Dodge straightened up and the leather swished as his pants slid across the chair's surface. "You've been here the whole time."

Brown nodded.

"How long?"

"Where's Tobey?" Brown asked.

Dodge's head dropped and he blurted out, "Asshole."

"Understand, I was under orders not to interfere. I was to let you either succeed or watch you fail. We have no charter inside the borders of the US."

"They tried to kill me. Twice!" Dodge exclaimed.

"Three times, to be exact."

"Three?" Dodge ran the events of the past week in his head. The park and the warehouse. Those were the places his life had been most in danger. Where Roberts' henchmen had taken shots at him. "Where was the third?"

"The motel," Brown said.

Dodge couldn't remember anything happening at the motel where he felt his life had been in peril. In fact, right up until the police showed up and questioned him about Adler's disappearance, he believed no one even knew he was holed up there.

Brown must have seen the wheels turning in his head, because he spoke up before Dodge could ask.

"We noticed a guy hanging around the back of the motel early one morning. He was carrying a small red plastic can."

"Dodge thought for second, then said, "gas?"

Brown nodded.

"They were going to burn me out. Man, what is it with those guys and burning people."

"DNA and fire don't mix."

Staring at Brown, Dodge said, "But I'm still here?"

"Just didn't seem fair to me. Besides there were other people in that motel. Couldn't let any innocents get hurt."

Now, it was Dodge's turn to smile. "I thought you couldn't interfere. Orders and charters and all."

"I might have left that little nugget out of my report. Besides, you hadn't finished your work yet."

"Well, I appreciate the help." Dodge swiveled the chair toward the aisle and stood.

"Where are you going?"

"I assume our work here is done. Besides, I need a shower and clean change of clothes."

"I was told you didn't have a suitcase."

"I packed light. My thought was, either I would find the answers I was looking for quickly, or I would get shut down before I even got started out here. I had enough room in my backpack for both of those scenarios. In hindsight, I broke one of my rules."

"Which one was that."

"Always be prepared."

"Well, have a seat. I've been ordered to give you a ride back."

Dodge looked around the cabin. Then over at the mini bar. "Could be worse ways to get home I suppose." He eased back into the chair. "When do we take off?"

Brown looked across the aisle and out the window. "Just waiting on one more passenger. Besides we have a lot to talk about."

"I was hoping to get a little nap in."

"You'll get all the sleep you need when you're dead."

Just then Dodge heard the whine of an engine. He leaned over and peered out the window. He watched as a black SUV circled the plane, the same as the one he had been brought in had done. He followed the vehicle until it disappeared behind the plane, before catching view of it again as it pulled to a stop on the other side. He looked back at Brown who was smiling again.

Dodge watched as two men exited the vehicle on the driver's side. He could only see their heads behind the black SUV, then they walked out of sight around the front of the vehicle. He listened to the footsteps coming up the boarding stairs. But the sound was off. It was heavy and light. Two people but something else. He turned in his chair and faced the door. The first man entered the cabin. The man looked back at the opening and then down.

Tobey popped around the corner unsure of his surroundings. Then he saw Dodge. His tail wagged, he let out a high-pitched bark and ran directly to him. Dodge knelt and patted his friend's head. As quickly as he ran over, Tobey turned and hopped onto one of the empty chairs across the aisle, curled up into a ball and laid his head down. Dodge sat down and simply watched Tobey. He said nothing and neither did Brown. He then turned to face Brown and said he was now ready to go.

Brown nodded to one of the men who had accompanied Tobey onto the plane. The first man said something to the second guy, then entered the cockpit. The boarding door swung closed with a thud and the second man pulled the latch, locking the door for flight. The engines roared to life and, within ten minutes, the jet was in the air. Dodge watched out the window as the ground below him faded further away before disappearing underneath a layer of clouds.

"How long before we get to Richmond?" he asked, tipping his empty glass in Brown's direction. *There is always time for one more drink.* Another rule he planned to start paying more attention to.

A ting filled the air as the neck of the bottle tapped the rim of his glass and the brown liquid splashed in. Once the glass was about half full, Brown sat the bottle on the table. He then leaned back into his chair and folded his hands over his lap.

"Yeah, about that..." he said as the plane banked to the south.

Dodge relaxed into the cushioned leather chair. For the first time in a long time, he didn't worry about where he was headed. He figured he would just enjoy the ride.